My name is Barry Allen, and I'm the fastest man alive. A particle accelerator explosion sent a bolt of lightning into my lab one night, shattering a shelf of containers and dousing me in electricity and chemicals. When I woke up from a coma nine months later, I found I was gifted with superspeed.

Since then, I've worked to keep Central City and its people safe from those with evil intent. With the help of my friends Caitlin and Cisco at STAR Labs; my girlfriend, Iris; her brother, Wally; and my adoptive father, Joe, I've battled time travelers, mutated freaks, and metahumans of every stripe.

I've tried to reconcile my past, learned some tough lessons, and—most important of all—never, ever stopped moving forward.

I am . . .

THE FL

BY BARRY LYGA

ASH™

HOCUS POCUS

AMULET BOOKS
NEW YORK

For my father, who bought me my first comic book.
And my second.
And my third.
And . . .

PUBLISHER'S NOTE: This is a work of fiction. Names, characters, places, and incidents are either the product of the author's imagination or used fictitiously, and any resemblance to actual persons, living or dead, business establishments, events, or locales is entirely coincidental.

Cataloging-in-Publication Data has been applied for and may be obtained from the Library of Congress.

ISBN 978-1-4197-2815-0

Cover illustration by César Moreno
Book design by Chad W. Beckerman

Printed and bound in USA
10 9 8 7 6 5 4 3 2 1

ABRAMS The Art of Books
195 Broadway, New York, NY 10007
abramsbooks.com

ZOOM WAS DEFEATED . . .

They'd watched the Time Wraiths wither his body and carry him, screaming and terrified, into the Speed Force, to suffer whatever torments were reserved for those who would attempt to destroy the Multiverse.

Now they had gathered at Joe West's house—Joe, Cisco, Wally, Caitlin, Iris, and Barry—to celebrate their victory. Their teamwork. Their lives.

But Barry didn't feel like celebrating. Yes, he had outwitted and outrun Zoom. He'd saved not just his friends but also the untold quintillions of lives across the Multiverse. He should have been ecstatic.

Instead, Barry could think only of his father, murdered before his very eyes by Zoom. The Reverse-Flash had killed Barry's mother, and now Zoom had taken Henry Allen. Two evil speedsters. Two parents gone.

He stepped outside, to be alone. To think. But Iris knew him so well. She noticed and she joined him, sitting on the stoop. He'd loved her his whole life, and now she finally reciprocated. And yet . . .

"We just won," he told her. "We just beat Zoom. Why does it feel like I just lost?"

"Because you've lost a lot in your life, Barry. More than

most." She leaned toward him. "But maybe you and me, seeing where this thing goes . . . Maybe that can give you something for a change."

"That's all I've ever wanted to hear you say," he told her, struggling for the words. "I wish I was in a place where I could try that with you. But I feel so hollowed out inside right now. I feel more broken than I've ever felt in my life. If I'm ever going to be worth anything to you, I need to fix what's wrong with me. I need to find some . . . some peace."

Iris swallowed hard, then gazed directly into his eyes. "Barry, listen to me. You waited for me for years. You let me get to a place where this was possible. So I am telling you: I am going to do the same thing for you. Wherever you need to go, whatever you need to do: Do it. And when you get back, I'll be here."

Choking back tears, he said only, "OK."

"I love you, Barry," Iris said.

With almost infinite slowness, they leaned in to each other and kissed. It was the kiss Barry had spent his life waiting for, and in the warm moment of that kiss, he decided: He was going to go back in time. He was going to change history, the way he had when he made Pied Piper a good guy, the way he had when they fought Vandal Savage, the way he had when he saved the city from a tidal wave.

He would rescue his mother, preventing her death at the hands of the Reverse-Flash.

One small change to the universe. One thread tugged in the vast tapestry of reality. The universe wouldn't even notice, but for Barry . . . for Barry the change would be monumental. If his mother never died, his father wouldn't go to jail. The Reverse-Flash wouldn't sabotage the particle accelerator. No Reverse-Flash, no singularity. No breach to Earth 2. No Zoom. His father would live. Caitlin's fiancé would live. It was all upside. Everyone would win; no one would lose.

"I love you, too," he told her. "And I always will."

Iris touched his hand, then went back into the house. Barry watched through the window as she rejoined their friends.

Now. He would go right now. To the past. He would fix everything and paper over the hole in his heart.

As he turned to go, though, he heard the door open behind him. It was Iris, standing there, framed by the light of the house behind her.

"You're in pain," she said slowly. "I get that. So if you're not ready, you don't have to be with me. But you can't be alone. Not now. Not tonight."

So he went inside with her, into the embrace of the family he'd cobbled together out of friends and coworkers and people he loved. And in the morning, things seemed different and not so bleak, as things in the morning so often do.

He did not go back in time.

Instead, he went forward. One healing step at a time.

MONTHS LATER . . .

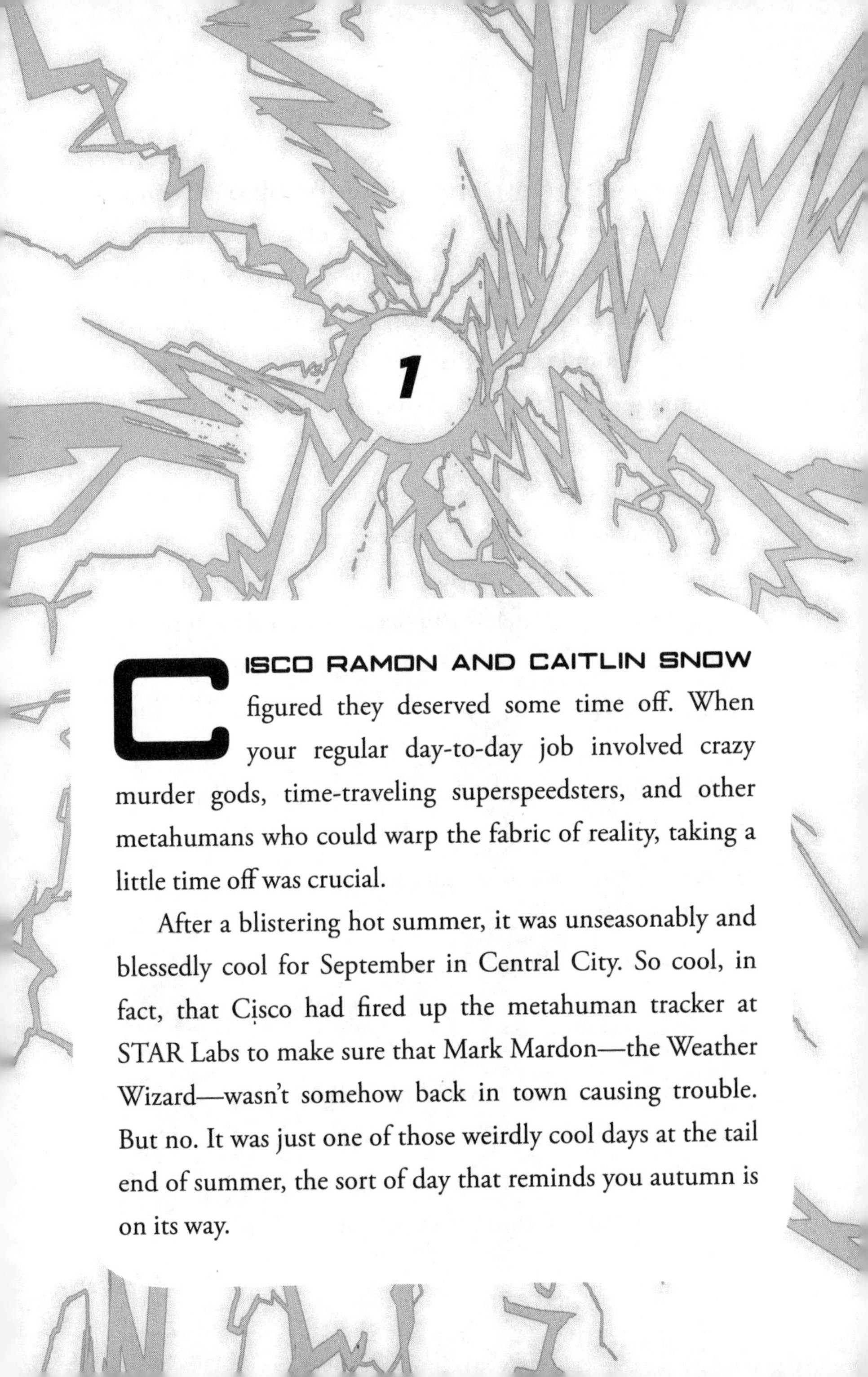

1

CISCO RAMON AND CAITLIN SNOW figured they deserved some time off. When your regular day-to-day job involved crazy murder gods, time-traveling superspeedsters, and other metahumans who could warp the fabric of reality, taking a little time off was crucial.

After a blistering hot summer, it was unseasonably and blessedly cool for September in Central City. So cool, in fact, that Cisco had fired up the metahuman tracker at STAR Labs to make sure that Mark Mardon—the Weather Wizard—wasn't somehow back in town causing trouble. But no. It was just one of those weirdly cool days at the tail end of summer, the sort of day that reminds you autumn is on its way.

Since it was so nice out, they decided to take a little break and head to the Central City Pier. Central City was landlocked, but the nearby Gardner River gave it the illusion of being a beach town. The pier was a boardwalk stretching close to a mile along the coast of the river, with jetties extending out over the water so that fishermen could cast their lines and waste the day away.

"I could totally be the world's greatest fisherman," Cisco pointed out as they walked past an older man slumped in a beach chair, his hat over his eyes. He was napping as his fishing line dangled lifelessly in the water. "Fish are tuned to sound, right? I could channel my Vibe powers into the water along a fiber-optic cable that looks like a normal fishing line. And then—"

"Can we just enjoy the day?" Caitlin teased. "The sun's in the sky, the temperature is actually below the boiling point, we have the world's most amazing kettle corn, and there hasn't been a meta attack in three whole days." Central City tended to get attacked by someone with superpowers—a metahuman—at least once a week. Usually on Tuesdays, for some reason.

Cisco grinned and lowered his sunglasses. "I can't help it, Caitlin. I see the world as it should be, not as it is." Cisco himself was a metahuman, with the ability to "vibe." He could see possible futures, peer into alternate realities, and even open breaches into the Multiverse if he tried hard enough. He was even learning how to produce and project his own vibrations, though that was coming along a little more slowly.

"Such a burden, I'm sure." She stuffed a handful of kettle corn into his mouth. "That should shut you up."

Cisco tried to talk around the kettle corn, but all that came out was muffled nonsense. With a happy shrug, he chowed down instead.

They strolled past an old Ferris wheel, then past the entrance to the House of Mirrors. The rides and attractions had already closed down for the season, but some of the food stalls were still open, and the fine weather had enticed a multitude of Central Citizens to come out. They gathered here and there in clusters of families and friends, enjoying a rare day without killer man-sharks or giant sentient gorillas.

"Maybe we should head back," Caitlin said, gazing at a group of people lounging along the balustrade of the pier.

"But we just got here!" Cisco whined.

"It's just . . . Seeing all these people, so happy and safe . . . It reminds me that this is why we do what we do. We should be back at STAR Labs."

"Not enough danger around here for you?" he joked.

"It's not that . . ."

"Then what would we do back at the lab?"

She shrugged. "Get ready for the next time the city needs to be saved?" She didn't sound entirely convinced, and Cisco knew it.

"Twenty more minutes," he told her. "I want to get funnel cakes at the Broome Street kiosk, OK?"

Caitlin pretended to consider it, then nodded enthusiastically. "Funnel cakes. You know I can't resist."

"My true superpower," he said modestly, and then tossed a kernel of kettle corn into his mouth.

They walked farther up the pier, chatting, when Caitlin broke off and pointed. She tugged Cisco's arm, stopping him in his tracks. "Look! A magician!"

"I almost dropped the kettle corn!" he complained. "And aren't you the one in a hurry to get back to work?"

"I love magic!" she exclaimed, grabbing Cisco by the elbow. "C'mon!"

She dragged him away from the river, closer to the attractions and buildings. A group of about fifteen people gathered around a man standing atop a park bench. He was tall and rangy, his limbs loose. He wore a white tuxedo with a matching high-collared cape, blindingly bright in the sunshine, as well as an impeccably knotted black string tie. His black hair was slicked back so efficiently that it looked like a molded plastic widow's peak had been glued to his skull.

"PREPARE! TO BE! AMAZED!" he cried, gesticulating wildly for dramatic effect.

"This dude is *way* overdressed," Cisco grumbled. But he joined Caitlin in the small group of onlookers nonetheless.

"I! WILL! SHOW YOU! TRUE!" The man paused his grandstanding for a moment and grinned broadly. He had a hooked nose sharp enough to qualify as a weapon and a mustache and tiny goatee, both waxed to pointed perfection. They twitched when he smiled. "MAGIC!"

The magician finished and paused again, clearly waiting for applause. When none came, he shrugged his bony shoulders and gestured, producing a slender wand as though from thin air.

"Whoopee," Cisco muttered, rolling his eyes. "The old wand-up-the-sleeve bit."

Caitlin shushed him, then elbowed him in the ribs for good measure.

"WITNESS! MY! LEGERDEMAIN!" the man bellowed. His voice was much louder than it should have been, but Cisco didn't notice any sort of microphone or speaker.

With a wave of the wand, the man pointed to his own shoulder. A dove appeared there, twitching its wings in confusion before flying off. The crowd mumbled something appreciative.

The magician scowled. "PREPARE YOURSELVES!"

He tapped the wand against his head, then thrust out his empty hand. A gout of flames spurted forth with a roar.

"Are you kidding me?" Cisco moaned.

"Maybe he's just warming up," Caitlin offered.

"These tricks were old when my grandfather was a kid. Look," he said, waving his arms at the crowd around them, "no one else seems impressed."

"I bet he's building up to the big stuff."

The magician made a circle with his wand and shouted, "PRESTO!" Sparks danced in midair before dying out to the silence of the crowd.

"IT IS CUSTOMARY," the man boomed, "TO *APPLAUD* THE ART OF MAGIC!"

"Lame!" someone shouted.

"Go stuff a rabbit back into a hat!" someone else called. Laughter rippled through the crowd.

Fuming, the magician flexed his wand with both hands. "YOU *WILL* APPRECIATE THIS NEXT TRICK!" he cried, and then jabbed the air with the wand. Flowers popped out of the end of it. Cisco groaned, along with everyone else.

"I would call that old hat, but at least an old hat is useful," Cisco said.

"APPLAUD!" the magician yelled, puffing out his cheeks.

No one bothered. The crowd started to break up.

"APPLAUD!!!" he screamed again, this time gesticulating wildly with his wand.

And then something amazing happened: Everyone actually started . . . to clap.

It wasn't a polite little clap, either. People were slamming their palms together, stomping their feet, cheering and hooting and hollering at the top of their lungs. It was like a rock concert had suddenly broken out on the pier.

Much to his shock, Cisco found himself joining in. His palms stung with the repeated slaps against each other, but no matter how badly he wanted to stop, he just couldn't. It was as though his hands were no longer connected to his brain; they refused to obey his command to stop.

Caitlin, too, couldn't stop herself from applauding. Her palms were beet red, and even though she cried out in pain, she kept clapping anyway. Then she shouted, "Bravo! Encore! Encore!" No one was more surprised than she was to hear those words come out of her mouth; she hadn't meant to say anything at all.

Next to her, Cisco shouted, too. "Bravo! Bravo!" And then he let loose with a full-throated howl of delight that tore at his throat.

Even while he couldn't stop himself from clapping, Cisco turned and looked around. He was shocked to see that it wasn't just the people in the magician's immediate vicinity who were applauding.

All up and down the pier, as far as he could see in every direction, people were cheering and clapping, most of them with bewildered looks on their faces.

The magician set his lips into a grim, firm line, his face contorted into something resembling satisfaction. He sketched a complicated design in the air with his wand. Suddenly, there was a crack of thunder, a blinding flash of light, and he was gone.

Everyone stopped clapping. Most of the audience looked around at one another; then the crowd began to thin as people wandered away, embarrassed and confused. Caitlin and Cisco stayed right there, rooted to the spot, silent.

"Are you thinking what I'm thinking?" Caitlin finally asked, shaking out her sore arms and hands.

They turned to look at each other. At the same moment, they nodded and said, "Barry."

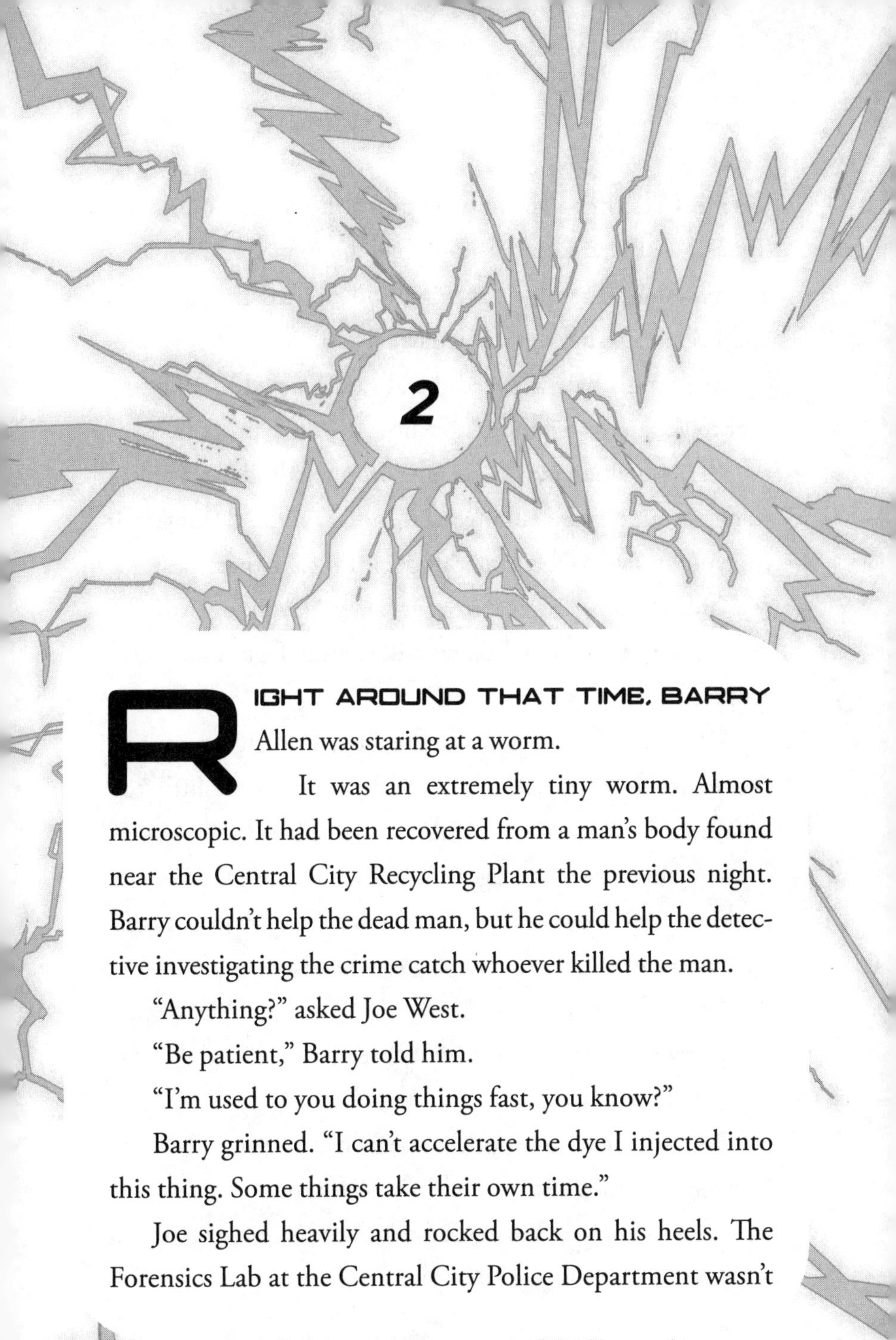

2

RIGHT AROUND THAT TIME, BARRY Allen was staring at a worm.

It was an extremely tiny worm. Almost microscopic. It had been recovered from a man's body found near the Central City Recycling Plant the previous night. Barry couldn't help the dead man, but he could help the detective investigating the crime catch whoever killed the man.

"Anything?" asked Joe West.

"Be patient," Barry told him.

"I'm used to you doing things fast, you know?"

Barry grinned. "I can't accelerate the dye I injected into this thing. Some things take their own time."

Joe sighed heavily and rocked back on his heels. The Forensics Lab at the Central City Police Department wasn't the most exciting place to hang out, although, he reminded himself, some exciting things had happened there. Like Barry being struck by lightning and doused in chemicals and becoming superhumanly fast.

But for all Barry's speed, he always seemed to take forever to get anything done. Like now.

"See, the thing is, this guy just dropped dead. And I need to figure out if we're talking some kind of natural thing or if it's, you know, maybe something a little *more* than natural," Joe said, wiggling his eyebrows at Barry. "Catch my drift?"

"You mean a meta?" Barry pulled away from the microscope and sat back.

"Will you be quiet?" Joe shushed, looking around to make sure they were alone. Barry always seemed a little too comfortable discussing metahumans in public for Joe's taste. "Just saying. Five years ago, weird deaths like this meant a lot of paperwork. These days, it means a guy whose fingernails are poison darts that he shoots whenever he's ticked off. And even *more* paperwork."

Barry frowned. "I don't remember a meta like that."

"I'm being inventive."

Barry opened his mouth to speak, but his phone buzzed. It was a text from Cisco: *At the pier. Get here!*

"I gotta go, Joe." Barry jumped up and prepared to speed away, but Joe grabbed him by the arm.

"Hey, you can't just Flash off in the middle of the day! I still need my report."

"Guy died of natural causes, Joe. That worm is *Toxoplasma gondii*. My bet is that once we get the full coroner's report in, you'll see that the guy had some sort of organ replacement."

"What do they have to do with each other?"

"*T. gondii* is harmless to most people, but if you're immunosuppressed—like you had an organ replaced—you're susceptible to the worm multiplying. That's what killed him. Not a meta with poison nail polish."

"I didn't say nail polish!" Joe protested, but Barry was already gone, a stack of papers flurrying about in his wake.

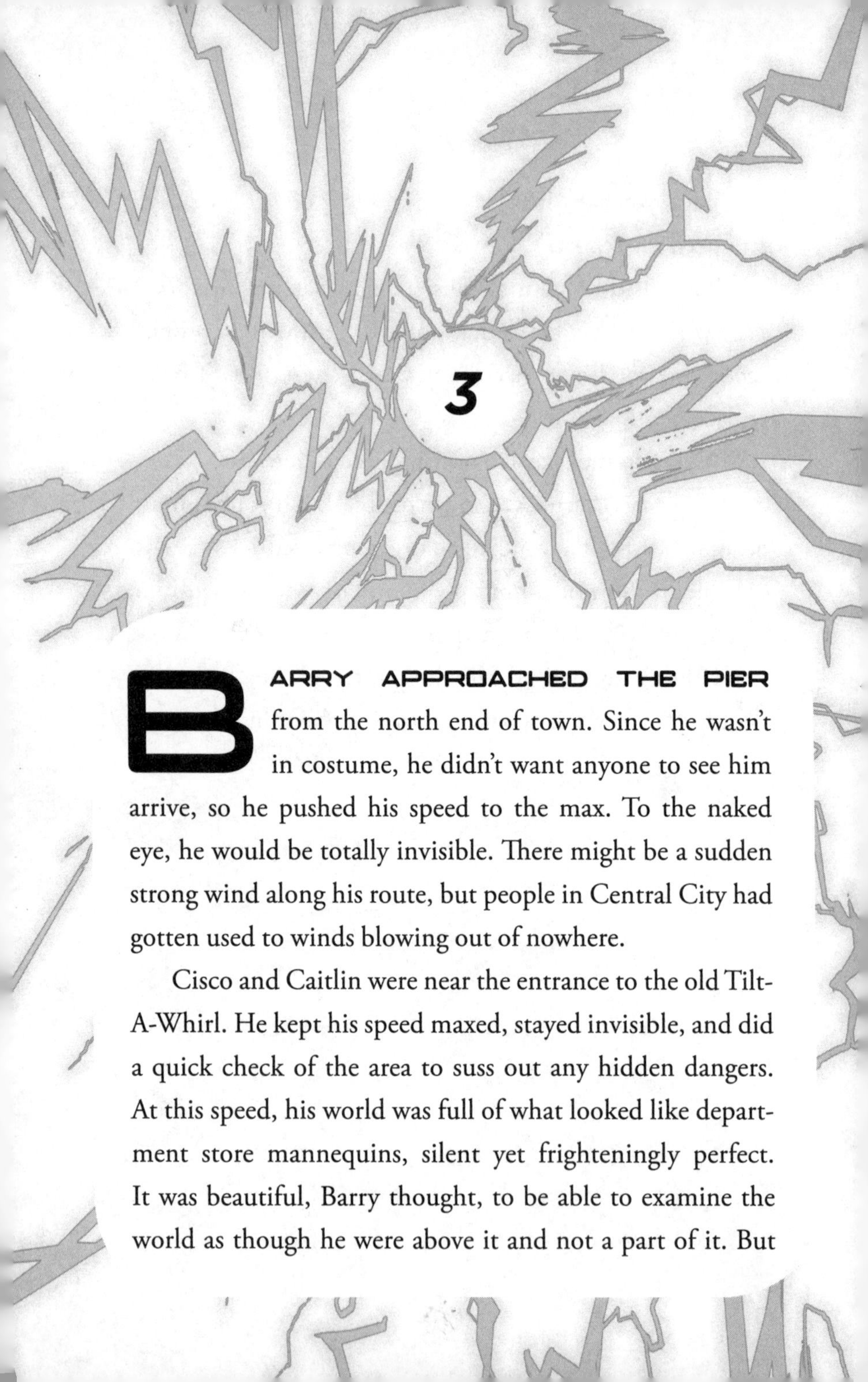

3

BARRY APPROACHED THE PIER from the north end of town. Since he wasn't in costume, he didn't want anyone to see him arrive, so he pushed his speed to the max. To the naked eye, he would be totally invisible. There might be a sudden strong wind along his route, but people in Central City had gotten used to winds blowing out of nowhere.

Cisco and Caitlin were near the entrance to the old Tilt-A-Whirl. He kept his speed maxed, stayed invisible, and did a quick check of the area to suss out any hidden dangers. At this speed, his world was full of what looked like department store mannequins, silent yet frighteningly perfect. It was beautiful, Barry thought, to be able to examine the world as though he were above it and not a part of it. But it also felt sterile and fragile. Looking at his friends—as he did now—frozen in time made him fear for a day when, inevitably, they would stop moving altogether, stop living. He would do so, too, he knew, but his powers made him the likeliest to live the longest.

He shook away the negativity. A few months ago, he'd been at his lowest point ever after his father's death. But things were better now; no point wallowing in the future. With renewed resolve, he swept up and down the pier, checking for trouble, hidden or obvious. Nothing concealed under the boardwalk, or stashed in any of the trash cans, or lurking behind the artificial palm trees that stood along the length of the pier. No one up to any blatant skulduggery. Just families and friends out enjoying the last warm day of the season.

Barry scooted over to Cisco and Caitlin. Cisco stood stock-still, his expression one of concern. Caitlin hugged herself as though cold, biting her lower lip.

Barry scoped out a spot behind a stand of bushes, made sure no one could see him, and slowed down. The world rushed back in on him—sound and motion and a soft breeze coming off the river. Somewhere in the distance, a baby cried, joined a moment later by an older sibling demanding cotton candy. The pier, which moments before had been as still as a sculpture garden, came alive with the bustle of families and couples moving up and down the boardwalk, and a solitary art student with her sketchbook, frowning in consternation as she moved back and forth along the same three feet of ground, looking for the perfect lighting and angle to capture the Ferris wheel.

Barry came around the bushes, tripped on a root, and almost spilled onto the boardwalk.

"There he is!" Cisco proclaimed. "What took you so long?"

It had been all of fifteen seconds since Barry had gotten the text.

"I stopped for pizza," Barry told him, ambling over to them. His eyes widened at the kettle corn. "I'm actually starving. Do you mind?" He didn't wait for an answer, but rather snatched the kettle corn and started eating.

"The machine needs fuel," Caitlin said with a bit of snark.

Barry couldn't speak through his handful of kettle corn.

"We didn't invite you here to eat our food," Cisco told him. "For which, by the way, you now owe me five bucks."

Swallowing, Barry said, "Why *did* you text me? Nothing's going on. Why the emergency?"

"We think we experienced a metahuman event," Caitlin said very seriously, though Barry detected a hint of excitement in her voice.

"Well," Barry said, checking over both shoulders that no one nearby was eavesdropping, "Cisco's a meta, so . . ."

"Not like that. It seemed to be a spontaneous area-wide psychosomatic trigger that completely overrode nominal conscious controls!" Caitlin's tone was slightly panicked, her speech rapid-fire.

"Wait, what?" It wasn't often that the Flash had to tell someone to *slow down*.

"Dude made us applaud for him!" Cisco exploded. As though to demonstrate, he clapped his hands and stomped his feet. "Street magician. Right over there." He pointed to the empty bench. "He told us all to applaud!"

Barry rolled his eyes. They'd taken him away from work for *this*? His boss, Captain Singh, was already annoyed enough at his seemingly endless string of absences and sudden disappearances. With his superspeed, he could do his job a lot faster than most people, but he still had to show up at the precinct if he didn't want the wrong people to start asking the right questions. And Joe could cover for him for only so long.

"Guys, there's no law against asking you to applaud."

"But then we *did*!" Cisco protested.

"That's not illegal, either," Barry pointed out.

"You don't understand." Caitlin took Barry's arm and locked her eyes on his. "This wasn't a request. It was a command. He *ordered* us to applaud, and we did. Everyone did. Everyone within earshot on the pier. Whether they wanted to or not."

"You can't be sure—"

"I didn't want to," Cisco said. "I so totally did not want to applaud for that guy's lame act. But I couldn't help myself. I had to."

Barry narrowed his eyes. "'Spontaneous area-wide psychosomatic trigger that completely overrode nominal conscious controls,' huh?"

Caitlin nodded and swallowed, her eyes wide. "Barry. He took over our *minds*."

The trio went back to STAR Labs together after Barry called the Central City Police Department and informed Captain Singh that he was pretty sure he'd left the iron on at home and that he would have to take a break to go home and check.

"Again?" Singh managed to sound annoyed, angry, and resigned all at the same time. "Allen, this is the third time this month you've left the iron on, and now you're taking a break before lunch. I'm not one to control my people's private lives, but maybe you need to think a little less about a crisp pleat in your khakis and a little more about your job."

"Yes, sir. You are totally right, Captain. I'll work on it, I promise."

STAR Labs was a massive complex in the heart of Central City, built years ago by the late Dr. Harrison Wells, who had actually—in a complicated series of events—turned out to be a villainous speedster from the future named Eobard Thawne, the Reverse-Flash. When Barry and his friends turned the tables on Thawne and defeated him, STAR Labs had—again, in a complicated series of events—ended up bequeathed to Barry.

The building looked something like an upside-down stool with only three legs—massive pylons jutting out from the circular main structure. It was Barry's home away from home, a workplace for Cisco and Caitlin, and the command center in a never-ending battle against evil metas, time travelers, and whatever else the universe (and the Multiverse) decided to throw at them.

If STAR Labs was their command center, then the Cortex, located in the middle of the building, was its beating heart, a large, open, circular chamber with computer workstations and satellite medical bays attached via short hallways. In one of those medical bays, they ran a series of tests on Caitlin and Cisco, checking for modifications to their brain chemistries—specifically the cerebral cortex, which controlled voluntary movements, and the cerebellum, which ensured smooth bodily motion.

The tests showed nothing.

Barry slumped a little lower in his chair. Cisco and Caitlin were peeling electrode leads off their skin. They would look at the results in a moment, but he'd spent enough time looking at weird or off-kilter medical tests to know that there was nothing wrong with Caitlin's or Cisco's brain. Not now, at least.

"Whatever he did to you guys, it didn't leave any lasting damage."

"I guess that's good news," Cisco said. "We're back in our right minds again."

"As right as yours gets, at least," Caitlin teased.

"Ouch."

"The truth hurts," she said, grinning. "But remember—it's the way our brains work that sets us apart from the rest of the world." She paused for a moment. "And the superpowers, for you guys."

"Do you guys think you could describe this magician to a police sketch artist?" Barry asked. "Maybe we could get a decent enough likeness to do some facial recognition and see if we can track him down."

"Track who down?" said a new voice coming from behind them.

They all turned to see H.R. enter the Cortex, wearing an expression of delight and carrying a small plastic bag.

"A possible new meta," Cisco said.

"He can control minds," Caitlin added.

"And he's a street magician," Barry said. "Sound like anyone from your Earth?"

A denizen of Earth 19, H.R. was an alternate version of the same Harrison Wells who'd turned out to be Reverse-Flash . . . *and* of the Harrison Wells from Earth 2 who'd helped them defeat Zoom. Despite their physical similarities, the three men could not have had more different personalities: H.R. lacked his doppelgangers' scientific acumen, but he made up for it (sometimes) with creativity and verve.

Right now, though, he merely frowned. "I don't quite understand how you do magic with a street or why anyone would want to watch it, but there are things about your world that I confess still confuse me."

"It's not a . . . Street magician doesn't mean . . ." Cisco threw his hands up in the air. "Never mind."

"Oh, good, we're moving on," H.R. said, his eyes dancing. "I have an announcement to make! I have discovered the purpose of life. Or at least the purpose of life on this specific Earth." He delved into the bag and produced a small brown bead, which he held out to them between his thumb and forefinger. "This!"

Cisco leaned in for a better look. With a fevered gasp, H.R. yanked the bauble away as though terrified for its safety.

"It's a coffee bean. Covered in a layer of peanut butter. And then further covered in a layer of dark chocolate. And then—as if the wizards of food preparation felt they had something to prove—coated in a hard chocolate shell. All evolution and social advancement on your Earth is clearly aimed at the endpoint of producing this specific delicacy. And can you believe they just sell them in stores for a mere pittance, with no ID necessary?" His eyes danced and he jiggled a little as he chomped the bean.

"How many of those things have you eaten?" Cisco asked, stepping away.

H.R. blinked rapidly. "Was I supposed to be counting?"

Cisco groaned. "Just what we need. Something to make him talk even faster. At this rate, pretty soon only Barry and Wally will be able to understand him."

"Did someone say my name?" Wally West blasted into the Cortex a little too fast and nearly collided with Cisco, who jumped out of the way and screamed a high, shrill scream.

"Kid Flash!" Cisco complained. "More like Skid Flash!"

"Still getting the hang of my speed," Wally admitted. "What's going on? Anything cool?" Kid Flash was so excited he was bouncing up and down on his toes, rubbing his hands together. "Need me to do something? Run somewhere? Fast? I'm getting a lot faster. I bet I can—"

"Slow your roll!" Cisco told him. "What are you even doing here?"

Barry checked his watch. "Don't you have class right now?"

Iris's younger brother, Wally, was a freshman in college, carrying a significant course load. He was also Central City's newest hero: Kid Flash. A few months ago, the team had been trying to restore Barry's powers in order to fight Zoom, and Wally had been caught up in the resulting wave of energy. Months later, he'd begun exhibiting superspeed, and now, even though he was still in training, he'd been given a costume and allowed to operate in public, albeit with Barry always looking out for him.

"My Fundamentals of Engineering class doesn't start for, like, five minutes," he told them, stretching out *five minutes* as though it were all the time in the world. "Plenty of time for me to do whatever. You guys ready for lunch? Want Thai food? From Thailand? I'll go get it. Who's up for drunken noodles?"

"Wally," Barry said very calmly. "Go back to school."

Wally grimaced and stopped bouncing. "C'mon. I'm pulling all A's in my classes right now. I want to Kid Flash it up."

"If you want to keep pulling all A's, you need to get to class. Trust me—we'll call you if we need you."

"But—"

Barry pointed to the door. "Go."

In a blur, Wally was gone.

"That kid needs to learn some control," Cisco said.

"I'll work with him," H.R. volunteered.

"Oh, *that's* a great idea!" Cisco said with withering sarcasm. "Overcaffeinated ADHD meets superspeedster. The two great tastes that taste great together."

"Can we focus on the issue at hand?" Caitlin asked. She tapped one of the screens. "Typical mind control involves alteration of brain waves and brain chemistry."

"I love that we live in a world where there's such a thing as *typical* mind control," Cisco said mordantly, slumping into a nearby chair.

"But in this case," Caitlin went on, "there's no evidence of such a thing in our brains. Even after the effect wears off, there should be markers in the cerebral cortex at the very least."

"Maybe they've faded by now," Barry suggested.

Worrying her bottom lip, Caitlin shook her head and scrolled through the data on her screen. "We got here and ran the tests really fast. We should be seeing *something*."

There was silence in the Cortex Bridge for several

moments as Barry, Cisco, and Caitlin all stared at their computer screens, as though the longer they stared, the more likely an answer was to appear.

Popping another bean into his mouth, H.R. broke the silence. "Have you considered," he asked, jittering from side to side, "that it might actually *be* magic?"

"There's no such thing as magic." Cisco did a double take. "Wait a sec. Is there magic on your world?"

"Not that I know of. Unless you count the magic of marketing. But no. Still, didn't the great Hemlock Holmes say that once you eliminate the impossible, whatever is left, no matter how improbable, must be the answer?"

"It's not Hemlock Holmes. It's Sherlock Holmes."

"Well, that's just ridiculous," H.R. said, and left.

"Guys, I'm not ready to call in Harry Houdini for a consult yet." Barry ran his hands through his hair as he glared at the screen. "We've seen a lot of weird stuff, sure, but all of it has been explainable in scientific terms. I don't think we're totally through the looking glass here. Not yet."

"Points for the literary reference," Cisco said somberly. "We'll keep crunching data here and see if we can learn anything. In the meantime, enjoy the park."

"What?"

Cisco pointed to a video image from a camera posted at Central City Park. On the grainy feed, the tuxedoed magician was standing amid a crowd of people, just beginning to wave his wand.

"Time to get speedy," Cisco said, and he grinned with delight.

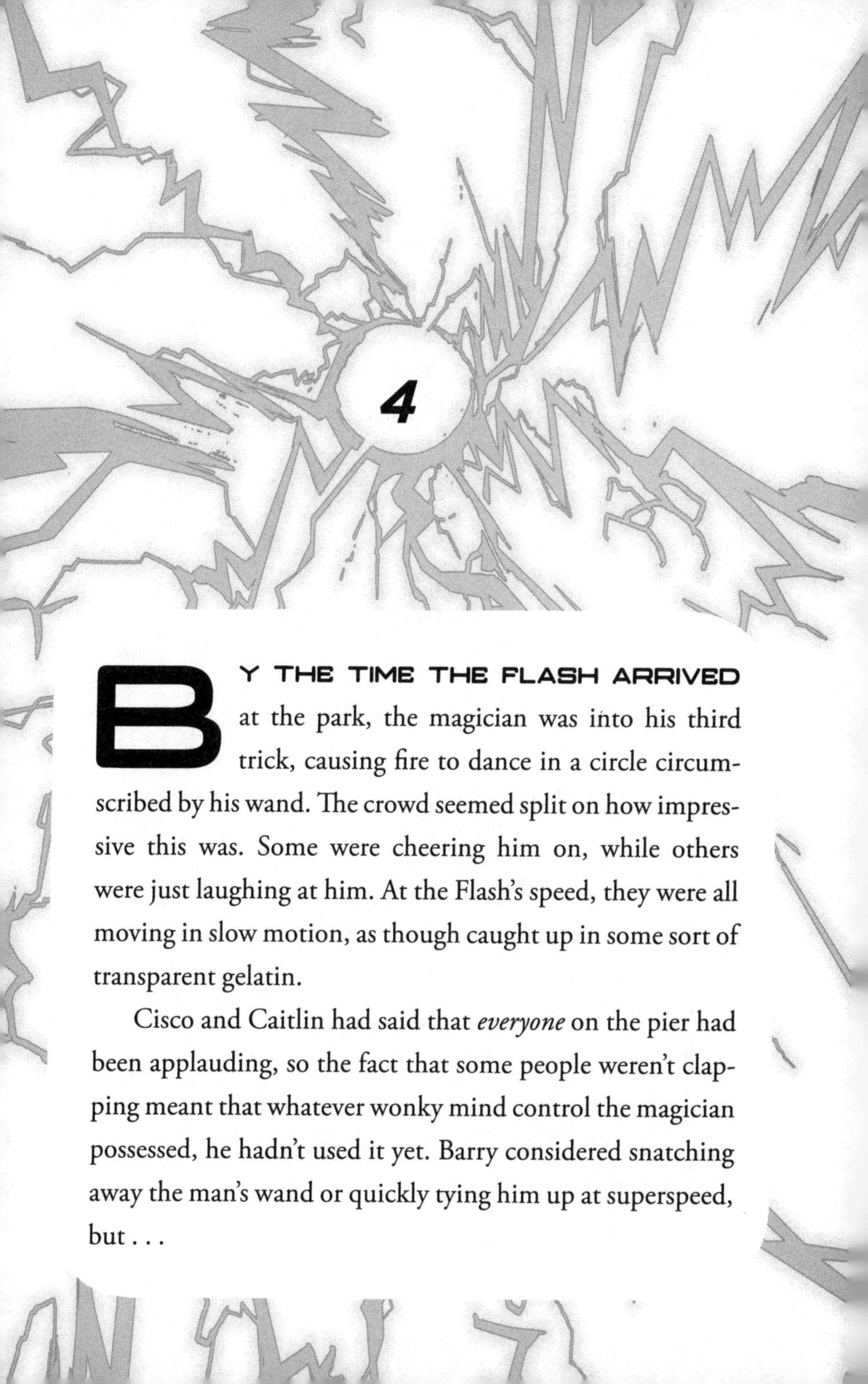

4

BY THE TIME THE FLASH ARRIVED at the park, the magician was into his third trick, causing fire to dance in a circle circumscribed by his wand. The crowd seemed split on how impressive this was. Some were cheering him on, while others were just laughing at him. At the Flash's speed, they were all moving in slow motion, as though caught up in some sort of transparent gelatin.

Cisco and Caitlin had said that *everyone* on the pier had been applauding, so the fact that some people weren't clapping meant that whatever wonky mind control the magician possessed, he hadn't used it yet. Barry considered snatching away the man's wand or quickly tying him up at superspeed, but . . .

The man hadn't actually done anything wrong, so far as Barry could tell. He couldn't let a man go around controlling people's minds willy-nilly, but it was entirely possible the magician didn't even know he had superpowers and was totally innocent in all of this. So Barry slowed down to normal speed, and the world rushed back in—sound roared at him, and everyone sped up to real time.

"FOR MY NEXT ACT," the magician boomed more loudly than should have been possible, "I'LL NEED A VOLUNTEER!" He scanned the crowd, stroking his immaculately styled goatee. "YOU, SIR! DRESSED SO JAUNTILY!"

How can he make his voice so loud? Barry wondered. And then he realized that the magician was pointing at him!

"No, thanks," the Flash told him. "But I'd like a moment of your time."

The magician offered an indulgent smile that teetered on the edge of a frown. "Perhaps after my act," he said in a normal voice.

Barry sped to the man's side in less than a blink of an eye. "Perhaps now?" he said.

The crowd, thrilled at the sight of the city's hero, began applauding. Barry offered a wave to his adoring public, then turned back to the magician.

Who was *furious.*

"YOU DARE . . ." His voice was as loud as a cannon again as he seethed at the crowd. "YOU DARE SEEK THE FAVOR OF THIS CRIMSON JACKANAPES?" Turning to the Flash, he twisted his face into a rictus of sheer rage. "AND YOU! YOU DARE UPSTAGE THE GREAT HOCUS POCUS?"

With that, he thrust his wand out over the crowd. The ground rumbled and suddenly split beneath their feet. People screamed and flung themselves away, but too many were caught off guard. The Flash didn't spare even a microsecond to think; he dashed away from the magician—the Great Hocus Pocus, as he called himself—and began sweeping people away from the path of the sudden chasm.

Moving people from danger was the Flash's top priority and also pretty much the most routine of his superpowered exploits. Someone was *always* in the path of danger, and there was *never* enough time to move, so the Flash was *always* yanking, shoving, and hauling people out of the danger zone. The problem, though, was that he was superfast, not superstrong. He could get to a two-hundred-pound grown man—like right now, for example—faster than the ground could open under the man's feet, but it wasn't like he could just pick the guy up and carry him away safely.

With kids and smaller people, sure, he'd grab them up, scoot them away, and take an aspirin later for his sore muscles. But physics was physics, gravity was gravity, and two hundred pounds were two hundred pounds that the Flash's muscles couldn't heft. So he ended up doing what he always did in these cases.

He used his momentum, lowered his shoulder, and knocked the guy ten feet away in the blink of an eye. Barry's shoulder throbbed, and the guy would probably have some light abrasions, but at least he was safe.

Barry always made sure to say, "Sorry!" when he had to knock someone out of the way like that, but since he was moving faster than the speed of sound, no one ever heard him. *Oh well—it's the thought that counts, right?*

He zipped around the park, knocking, carrying, and outright shoving where necessary, making sure no one fell into the crevasse that had formed. With a quick look over his shoulder, he noticed that Hocus Pocus was in the process of lowering his wand. So everyone should be safe for now. He had a few hundredths of a second left before the magician finished lowering it—a lifetime, really, in Flash terms—so Barry took that time to kick up some nearby loose dirt and fill in part of the gap in the ground.

"Are you insane?" he demanded, planting his fists on his hips. "You could have hurt someone!"

"ARE YOU NOT AMAZED BY MY POWER?" Hocus Pocus demanded. "DO YOU NOT RECOGNIZE YOUR SUPERIOR, THE MAGNIFICENT HOCUS POCUS?"

Barry had been fed up with Pocus's ego beforehand. Now that he saw how cavalier Hocus Pocus was with others' lives, he was more than ready to knock the magician out and drag him off to jail. Barry had given him the benefit of the doubt long enough.

Before he could move, Pocus shouted, "SHOW YOUR APPRECIATION!"

And everyone in the park . . .

. . . began to applaud.

Even the people who were still running from the gash that had been torn into the ground. They stopped. Turned. Clapped their hands enthusiastically. Cheered wildly!

Kids who'd been knocked down. Adults limping away. Everyone stopped what they were doing and applauded the madman in the white tux and cape.

Even the Flash.

At first he didn't even realize he was doing it. He was so shocked to find the crowd applauding the man who'd endangered them that it took a second or two for him to comprehend that his own hands were slapping together enthusiastically. In a moment of embarrassment and outrage, he heard himself project a high, piercing whistle of appreciation.

What the heck? This is exactly what happened to Caitlin and Cisco. How is he doing this?

Pocus caught the Flash's eye, smirked, and took a bow. Before the magician could stand upright again, Barry turned to the crowd and shouted, "Everyone! Run! Get out of here now!"

They listened. Of course they did—he was the Flash, the hero of Central City. He felt no gratification at that idea, but rather a flush of gratitude that people trusted him enough to obey, with no mind control (or whatever it was) required. Catching bad guys was one part of his job, and he was good at it. But protecting people was the most important part, and he had to be the *best* at it.

From behind him came a roar of anger, like that of a wounded and half-starved elephant. The Flash spun around, ready to charge at Hocus Pocus—but before he could move, the magician pointed his wand at a nearby tree.

And to Barry's complete shock, the tree *moved.*

Now, Barry could move at velocities that, up to this point, had never been experienced by any other human being. (Well, on this particular Earth, anyway.) But he *was* still a human being, and like all human beings, he could be shocked into inaction.

Seeing that tree move did exactly that. He was stunned.

The tree outstretched its branches like menacing arms and plucked up a pair of innocent bystanders, lifting them off the ground, clutching them with strong wooden limbs. It should have been impossible. Trees just couldn't move like that.

"Help!"

That first scream shook the Flash out of his reverie. He zipped over to the tree, but even as he did so, other nearby trees came to life and began snatching people up like kids grabbing marbles or jacks. "Guys!" he shouted into his communicator. "We've got a major problem here!"

"We're watching on the satellite feed," Caitlin's voice responded from the earpiece in his suit. "Are those trees *actually* moving?"

"Uh, yeah." He ran up one tree's trunk, deftly dodging its branches as they swiped at him. There was a little girl, maybe six years old, wailing her head off about fifteen feet above the ground, branches wrapped around her midsection and legs.

The tree was too strong for him to pry her loose, and in the cramped confines of the upper branches, his speed was practically useless—he couldn't move, because there was nowhere to go. Branches swiped at him, buckling and thrusting. One caught him across the chest and nearly sent him toppling out of the tree to the ground below. At the last instant, he snagged a knurl in the trunk and steadied himself even as the tree swayed.

"I don't know what to tell you, man." There was real panic in Cisco's voice. "I deal in tech, not trees. You need a botanist."

"Or a tree doctor," Caitlin offered.

"Not helping!" Barry snapped. He was close enough to the girl to witness the panic and terror rolling off her in waves. But try as he might, he couldn't pry the branch away from her. Pliable as it had impossibly become, it still had the sturdy strength of hefty wood.

The twists and turns of the branch kept him from inching out any farther—he couldn't get close enough to grab the girl and phase her out of harm's way. He had to do something to the branch itself.

Hmm . . . Phase her out of harm's way . . . He phased through solid matter by vibrating his molecules at a different resonance, such that the atoms of his body could slip past the space between the atoms of the thing he was phasing through.

Maybe he could use those vibrations differently. Properly applied, vibrations could shake solid matter to pieces. If he vibrated the branch just right, maybe it would weaken and lose its grip on the girl.

He laid both hands on the branch. He vibrated his right hand at one frequency and his left at another. The tree might be able to adjust to a single vibration, but two opposing vibrations would reinforce each other. They would attack the branch in two different ways at the same time, making it more vulnerable. That should, theoretically, make the branch weak enough to release the girl. Either that or it would shake to pieces. One way or the other, she'd be rescued.

Instead, the girl screamed higher and louder; he glanced over at her. No! The girl could feel the painful vibrations conducted through the tree branch. If he kept this up, he would scramble her insides!

Can't pull her out. Can't vibrate her out. Think, Allen! Think!

Whatever he came up with, it would have to be fast even for the Flash. There were at least a dozen people still in the park at this point, all of them in the clutches of suddenly mobile, deadly trees.

And the trees were squeezing.

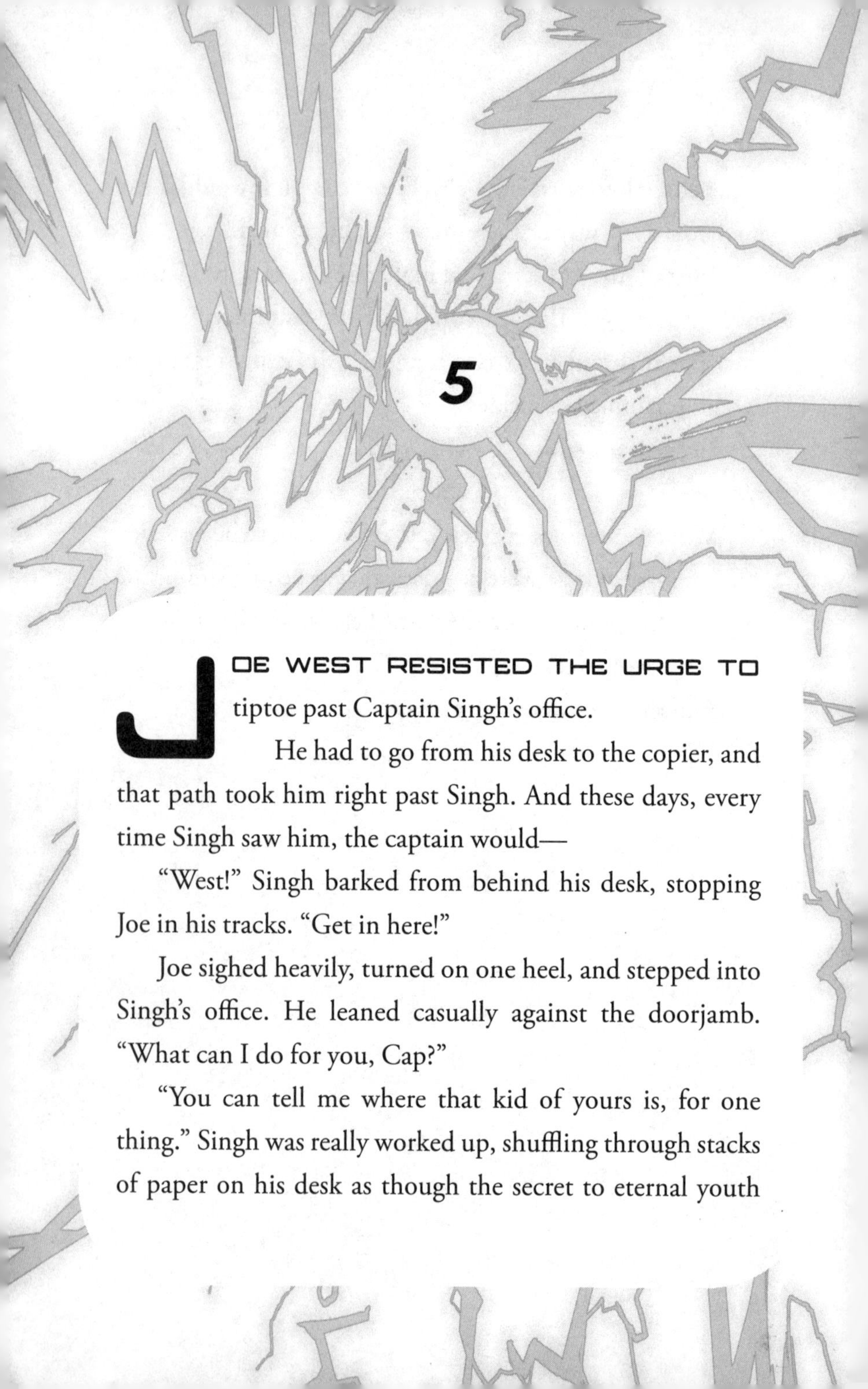

5

JOE WEST RESISTED THE URGE TO tiptoe past Captain Singh's office.

He had to go from his desk to the copier, and that path took him right past Singh. And these days, every time Singh saw him, the captain would—

"West!" Singh barked from behind his desk, stopping Joe in his tracks. "Get in here!"

Joe sighed heavily, turned on one heel, and stepped into Singh's office. He leaned casually against the doorjamb. "What can I do for you, Cap?"

"You can tell me where that kid of yours is, for one thing." Singh was really worked up, shuffling through stacks of paper on his desk as though the secret to eternal youth and calorie-free ice cream had been printed out and then left somewhere in the mess.

"Which kid?" Joe joked. "Iris is at work, and Wally's at school—"

"I'm in no mood for that thing you call your sense of humor, West." Singh gave up and dropped a stack of papers straight onto his desk. "Allen promised me six different reports first thing this morning. They were supposed to be on my desk, and they're not, and now he's off on the world's longest lunch break. Not answering his phone. Poof. Gone into thin air. I swear, he disappears so often, I'm going to file a missing-person report with my own department."

Joe pursed his lips and took in the chaos of Singh's desk. "All due respect, Cap, the reports *might* be there. Somewhere."

Singh stood up and planted his fists on the desktop. "Don't tell me how to keep house, West. Find Allen and tell him I need those reports five minutes ago—"

"Sir!" A uniformed cop burst through the door, almost knocking Joe down. "The 911 switchboard just blew up. There's something going on at the park!"

"Something?" Singh echoed irritably.

"We're not sure of the details yet, but the Flash has been sighted at the scene."

Joe's heart froze every time he heard of danger and the Flash in the same sentence. Some part of him knew that Barry was fast and powerful and almost ridiculously able to avoid harm. The kid could catch bullets in midair, for crying out loud! There wasn't much that could hurt him.

But another part of him—a much bigger part, the part that was a dad and a cop—knew that anything was possible, that even the fastest man alive could be caught off guard. Barry wasn't Joe's biological son, but he had a claim on Joe's heart just the same. And right now that heart was beating triple time in fear for what could happen to the Flash.

"Cap," Joe blurted out, "I should—"

"Get out of here!" Singh told him. "Get a team down to the park now!"

Joe shoved the uniformed cop out of his way and ran for the elevator. As he did so, he heard Singh shout after him, "And when you're done, get Allen in my office!"

Joe's phone rang on the way to the park. He was in a car with three other cops, all of whom looked at him with *Now? Are you kidding me?* expressions when he answered the phone. Here they were, barreling through the streets of Central City with sirens blaring, on their way to a supremely dangerous situation, and Joe was answering the phone like nothing was going on.

With a shrug, he explained, "It's my kid."

My kid could have meant any one of three, but in this case, it was Wally. Joe knew it would be Wally before he even looked at caller ID. That kid had a nose for trouble and for opportunities to use his new speed powers.

"Dad!" Wally exclaimed as soon as Joe answered. "There's something going on at the park! I'll meet you there!"

"No!" Joe told him. "Stay away from the park!"

"But Dad! I'm fast! I can—"

"We don't know what's going on there. Hang back until you hear from me."

"Dad!"

"This isn't a negotiation. I'm *telling* you, you understand?"

Wally said nothing. Which meant, Joe knew, that he was agreeing. And sulking. But agreeing, most important of all.

Joe hung up. One of the cops arched an eyebrow at him. "Your kid wants to go to the park? Now? He got a death wish or something?"

With a snort, Joe glanced at the speedometer. "You heading to church or to a crime in progress?"

"Uh—"

"Gas pedal is on the *right*," Joe told him, and he leaned back as they sped off.

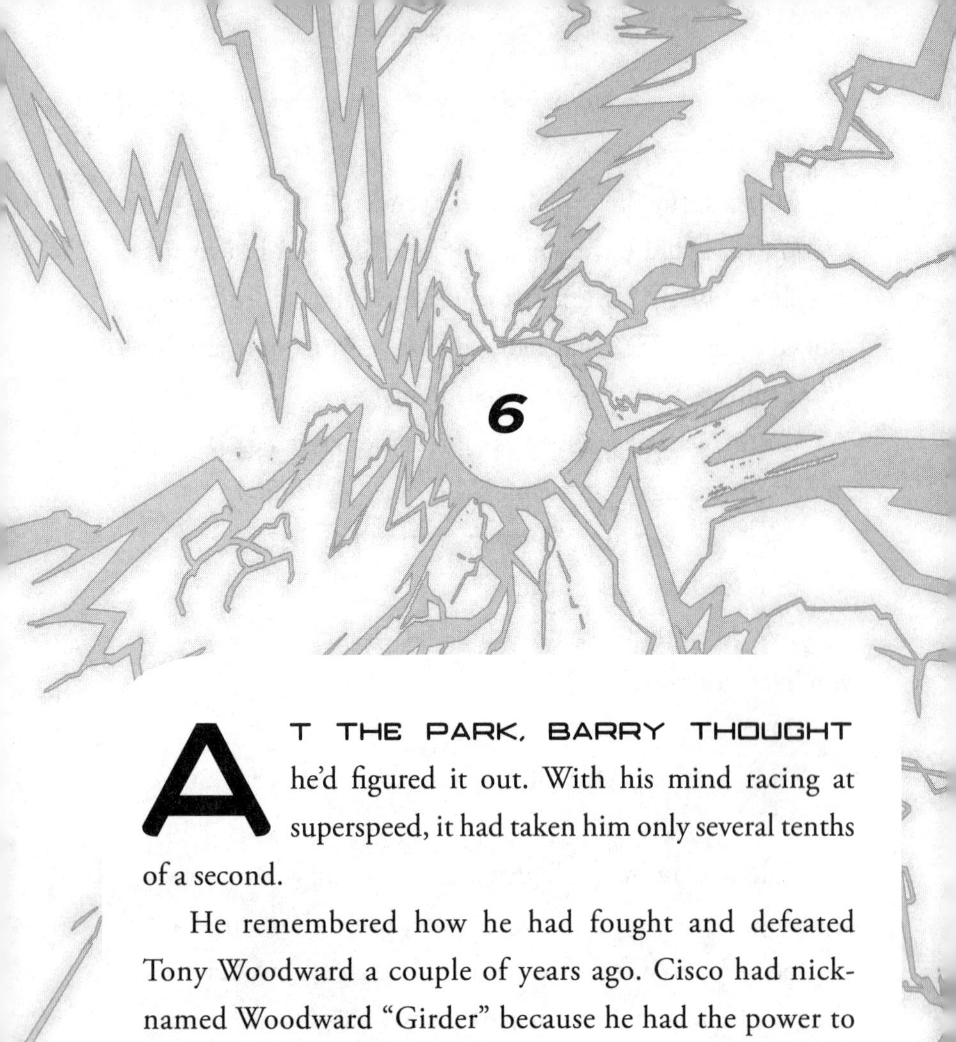

6

AT THE PARK, BARRY THOUGHT he'd figured it out. With his mind racing at superspeed, it had taken him only several tenths of a second.

He remembered how he had fought and defeated Tony Woodward a couple of years ago. Cisco had nicknamed Woodward "Girder" because he had the power to turn his body into flexible, nearly indestructible steel. No matter what Barry threw at him, Girder could just shrug it off. Barry had needed superstrength, which he couldn't acquire.

But he could fake it. With science.

F=ma. It was one of the most basic equations in all of science: Force equals mass times acceleration. Which basically meant that even something small and light can have a big impact if it's moving fast enough.

And *moving fast* was what the Flash did better than anyone else.

So he'd backed up about a mile and then run as fast as he could at Girder. The resulting superspeed punch came so fast that Tony never saw it coming, and all that force sent Girder into dreamland faster than a shot of methohexital (which Barry knew was a very popular medicine used to knock patients out for surgery . . . something Tony would never know).

He had to break through the tree branch. Speed alone wouldn't do the trick, but speed turned into force could.

"Stay calm!" he told the little girl, and then felt foolish. She was being crushed by a *tree*, and he was telling her to calm down! This was actually the perfect time to panic. "I've got this," he promised her. "Don't worry."

This is gonna hurt, he thought, and he raised his hand, then brought it down at superspeed, so blindingly fast that it happened in less time than it takes to even think about blinking.

There was a loud cracking sound, and then the branch split almost entirely through with the force of his chop. It twitched and slackened; the girl's eyes widened in horror as she realized she would fall, but before she could gasp, the Flash had launched himself at her and whisked her out of the tree. They dropped for a moment, and then he churned his legs, causing a cushion of air to break their fall, landing them safely on the ground.

Barry's hand throbbed, but it wasn't broken. He raced up into the other trees, pummeling the branches at superspeed until they released their captives. Pretty soon he had a dozen people safe on the ground.

Before he could even catch his breath, the magician gestured again and shouted, "WITNESS AND BELIEVE YOUR OWN EYES!" as the fountain at the center of the park suddenly shot a ten-foot-wide geyser of water thirty feet straight up.

That was just impossible. There wasn't enough water in the fountain or in its plumbing for it to shoot a column that wide, that high. For that matter, there wasn't enough pressure in the pipes, either.

The fountain didn't seem to care that it was offending both Barry's sensibilities and the laws of physics; it just geysered away. And then, as though everything going on around Barry wasn't insane enough, the column of water began to spin like a tornado and hopped out of the fountain, tearing a path across the park and bearing down on the innocent civilians the Flash had just rescued.

"Oh, come on!" Barry complained. He dug in his heels and took off, launching himself toward the oncoming water cyclone. As he closed in, it began throwing off mud and clods of grass, which he dodged easily. Then, juking quickly to his left, the Flash encircled the waterspout, racing counterclockwise against its natural torque. He'd done this trick with a genuine tornado before, setting up a counter-spin that unwound it. It had actually been his very first case as the Flash, fighting his very first metahuman: Clyde Mardon, who'd gained weather-controlling superpowers in the same accident as his brother, Mark. Barry had been terrified and unsure of himself, but he'd run full-tilt into the storm anyway. Mardon floated in the air at the center of the storm, controlling the winds. An average tornado produced something like sixty gigajoules of energy. The idea of being able to shut that down just by running seemed impossible, but Barry had done it anyway, pushing himself to what was his maximum speed at the time.

He'd been exhausted and thrilled at the same time. He'd fought nature . . . and won.

And now he figured the same thing should work with water, right?

Right! In just a few moments—and before the cyclone could get close enough to hurt anyone—the whole thing collapsed, soaking Barry and bringing him to his knees under the sheer weight of it all.

But there was no time to shake it off. He dried off by

superspeeding people out of the park entirely. Out on the street, he heard sirens—the police were on their way. Ambulances, too. Good. He didn't think anyone was badly hurt, but there would probably be some bumps and bruises and a few cases of shock to treat.

He had one more civilian to rescue before the park was empty. And then it would be him and Hocus Pocus, one-on-one.

When Barry got back into the park, he frowned and chided himself. The only remaining civilian was a young boy, maybe five years old, holding the string of a helium balloon that was emblazoned with the Flash's lightning logo. They sold them all over Central City. Barry had grabbed the kid's parents but left the kid for last. That wasn't right. He mentally kicked himself. *Come on, Allen. Kids first. Kids always first.* It had been a harrowing day, but that was no excuse.

Fortunately, it had taken him only a few seconds to empty the park, so the kid wasn't even really aware he was alone yet. The parents were probably just now realizing their son was missing, and by the time they could process it, the Flash would have delivered him safe and—

"FLY!" Hocus Pocus yelled, pointing his wand directly at the balloon.

It had been a day of impossibilities, so stuffed full of them that you'd think no more could fit. And yet as the Flash watched, the boy's balloon rapidly expanded, growing so quickly that Barry didn't have time to react. In no time at all, it had swollen to the size of a basketball, then a tire, then a . . .

And then it was the size of a car!

The balloon should have burst. It wasn't designed to handle that sort of stretching. And even if it could, it shouldn't be floating—it would have been sucking in air, which is too heavy. But it still floated, so somehow there was *more* helium being generated within, spontaneously!

Another impossibility. Barry was beginning to get tired of them.

The boy screamed as his feet left the ground. He should have let go of the balloon, but Barry realized he'd overlooked something—someone had tied the balloon to the boy's wrist. Probably his parents, to make sure it didn't float away. He was tethered to the balloon and flying up into the air.

The Flash looked over at Hocus Pocus, who was grinning maliciously.

Catch the crook or catch the kid. No contest.

He couldn't fly, but he didn't need to. He pinwheeled his arms at superspeed, setting up a strong wind that caught the balloon and jerked it to one side. The boy cried out again as the balloon headed for the top of a tree.

The trees had all stopped moving. This one swayed a bit in the wind Barry had created, but that was all.

The balloon scraped against a high branch, pushed with great force by the Flash's wind. Even down on the ground, the Flash could hear the loud *pop* of the balloon as its skin ruptured. The boy started to fall.

Barry darted beneath him and kept pinwheeling his arms at superspeed. The updraft he created cradled the boy, slowing his fall. The boy dropped safely and without a single scratch into the Flash's arms. Before the kid could thank him, Barry whisked him out of the park and over to his parents. The ambulances and the cops were closer now and could take care of the victims.

The Flash ran back into the park. Pocus would be gone, but Barry could still do a superspeed sweep for clues before CCPD started stepping all over the place.

Much to his shock, Pocus was still there, standing in the same place, fuming.

"You took my audience!" he cried out, fists clenched and shaking. "You took them from me!"

Barry couldn't believe his luck. *Saved the day. Now to grab the bad guy who's too dumb to run when he can.*

He sped over to Pocus as the magician fired beams from the wand at him, but he dodged the energy bolts easily. First order of business was that wand. The Flash reached out and grabbed it.

"LET GO!" Hocus Pocus boomed. "RELEASE ME!"

"Don't worry," the Flash told him, "we've got a nice comfortable cell waiting for you, and all the Big Belly Burgers you can eat."

Pocus's upper lip curled into a snarl. "STOP IT!" he bellowed as Barry reached out with his other hand. "FREEZE!"

There was an explosion of light, and when it cleared, Hocus Pocus had made his escape.

CCPD arrived on the scene in time to direct the park victims to the nearby ambulances and EMTs. As best Joe could tell, people were shaken, with the occasional bump or scrape, but there was no serious trauma. Joe smiled to himself. Barry had done a good job, as usual.

An Anti-Metahuman Task Force officer approached Joe. "Detective West, we've locked down the park. You want us to move in or what?"

Joe considered. The Flash had been seen at the park, which meant that the odds were, the whole thing was over already. "Keep your men back. I'll go in and see what's what. Stay in radio contact."

The AMTF officer nodded and headed off, barking orders into his radio. Joe stepped into the park. He remembered bringing Barry and Iris here when they were kids, teaching them to box on warm days, watching them run around the water fountain and climb too high in the trees.

The path to Barry was clear and easy to follow: Trees were bent in odd ways, as though they'd melted for an instant and then were refrozen in new positions. The ground was wet and torn. *Must've been one heck of a show*, thought Joe.

A familiar red glimmer caught Joe's eye. There, near a cluster of rocks, stood the Flash, all by himself. Joe resisted the urge to call out to him and jogged over instead.

Weirdly, even though he wasn't being quiet, Barry didn't turn to acknowledge him. He just stood there, his back to Joe, immobile.

Joe tapped him on the shoulder. "Hey, Bar. What happened here? You let the bad guy get away?"

Nothing.

Joe's cop instincts immediately took over. His gun was in his hand before he even realized it. He turned his back to Barry and stepped in a wide, slow circle around the Flash, carefully scrutinizing the area around him, looking for anything out of place or amiss or dangerous.

There seemed to be nothing there.

And then he heard Barry's voice.

Spinning back to the Flash, he realized that Barry hadn't moved a muscle. His expression was one of concentration, but there was terror in his eyes.

"Joe," he managed to say through his teeth, fighting for the syllables. *"I can't move!"*

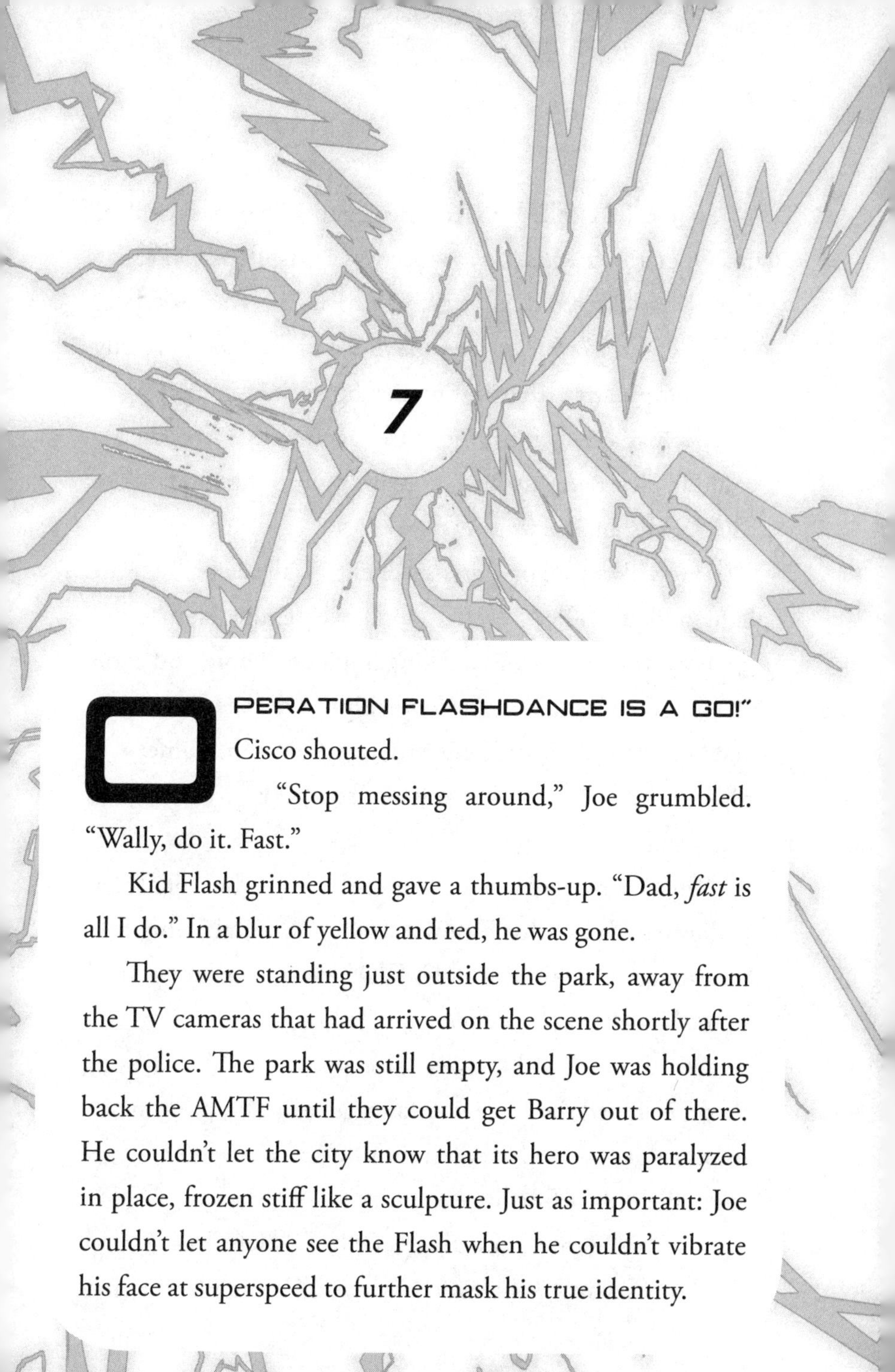

7

OPERATION FLASHDANCE IS A GO!" Cisco shouted.

"Stop messing around," Joe grumbled. "Wally, do it. Fast."

Kid Flash grinned and gave a thumbs-up. "Dad, *fast* is all I do." In a blur of yellow and red, he was gone.

They were standing just outside the park, away from the TV cameras that had arrived on the scene shortly after the police. The park was still empty, and Joe was holding back the AMTF until they could get Barry out of there. He couldn't let the city know that its hero was paralyzed in place, frozen stiff like a sculpture. Just as important: Joe couldn't let anyone see the Flash when he couldn't vibrate his face at superspeed to further mask his true identity.

So Joe had called STAR Labs, and Cisco had cooked up "Operation *Flashdance*," which was a ridiculous name, but that's what Cisco did, after all. The basic idea was *Get Barry out of the park before anyone knows what's happened.* Exactly how didn't matter. They just needed him out of there.

Wally dashed into the park at invisible speed. He couldn't pick Barry up and run with him all the way back to STAR Labs, but he wouldn't have to.

"Hey, Barry." For Barry's benefit, Wally kept his tone light and unruffled, even though seeing the Flash completely immobilized was freaking him out. Before he'd actually met the Flash, Wally had worshipped the speedster from afar. Finding out that Central City's Crimson Comet was his own adoptive brother was the second-best moment of Wally's life.

The best moment, of course, had been the accident that had gifted Wally with his own speed powers, allowing him to team up with his idol and be the hero he'd always wanted to be. Which. Was. *Awesome*.

But as much as he loved those powers and loved using them, he hated the current circumstances. He'd jump at any opportunity to use his speed, but he'd never wanted something like this before him.

"Wally," Barry said with great effort. "Help."

"That's what I'm here for. Cisco and Caitlin said the electronics in your suit aren't giving them any helpful readings. They shorted out during your fight. That's the bad news. The good news is, they have a theory anyway. They think your inertia's been interfered with on a molecular level. And an object at rest stays at rest, right?"

He sort of expected Barry to nod along with the science, but the Flash didn't budge. Still, Wally could tell from Barry's eyes that he was following along.

"So I'm here to give you a jump start. And then an object in motion will stay in motion. OK?"

Again, Kid Flash expected a nod. He shrugged and reminded himself it wouldn't happen.

He put his hands on Barry's shoulders. "I'm gonna run through a series of increasing vibrational patterns designed to literally shake off whatever's got you frozen in place." He hesitated before whispering, "Cisco told me to tell you he's calling this 'Operation *Flashdance*,' which I think sounds stupid, but anyway . . ."

Still no response. Too difficult to respond, no doubt.

"Let's do this," Wally said.

He ran through all the vibrations Cisco had instructed him to try. He started with some simple 1 Hz vibrations, touching Barry once per second, then added a counter-vibration, so that when one hand was touching Barry, the other was not, and vice versa. He increased the frequency all the way up to 100 Hz, touching over and over in the space of a single second.

He tried angular frequency. Spatial frequency. Rotation. Oscillation. Waves.

Nothing worked.

"Wally, how's it going in there?" Joe asked in his earpiece.

"Tell Cisco his idea has more than just a stupid name against it."

"I can't hold back the task force and the crime scene team much longer. You gotta get him outta there, one way or another."

Wally nodded and looked into Barry's eyes. "You trust me?" he asked, but didn't wait for an answer because

A. there wouldn't be one, and

B. it didn't really matter.

A whirlwind whipped into existence inside Central City Park, then moved swiftly to the edge of the park and beyond. It all happened so quickly that it was over before anyone even noticed, but if you could have watched it happen, you would have seen the Flash borne aloft on the wind, carried out of the park, and then somewhat bumpily dropped and moved into a STAR Labs van, which then cruised away from the scene, even as CCPD advanced.

"Sorry that was a little rough," Wally apologized as he helped Caitlin strap the immobile Barry onto a stretcher for the ride to STAR Labs. "Still figuring out how the laws of angular momentum apply when—" He broke off and bit down hard on his lower lip. Barry was just *lying* there, completely still. It felt ghoulish, standing over him like this.

"You're gonna help him, right?" Wally asked Caitlin. Since the Flash costume's built-in electronics had shorted out at some point during the fight, she was hooking up a portable EEG to Barry. "You guys can fix this, right?"

Caitlin took just a moment too long to answer, smiling brightly. "Of course," she said.

But she'd taken that moment. And to someone as fast as Kid Flash, that moment had lasted forever.

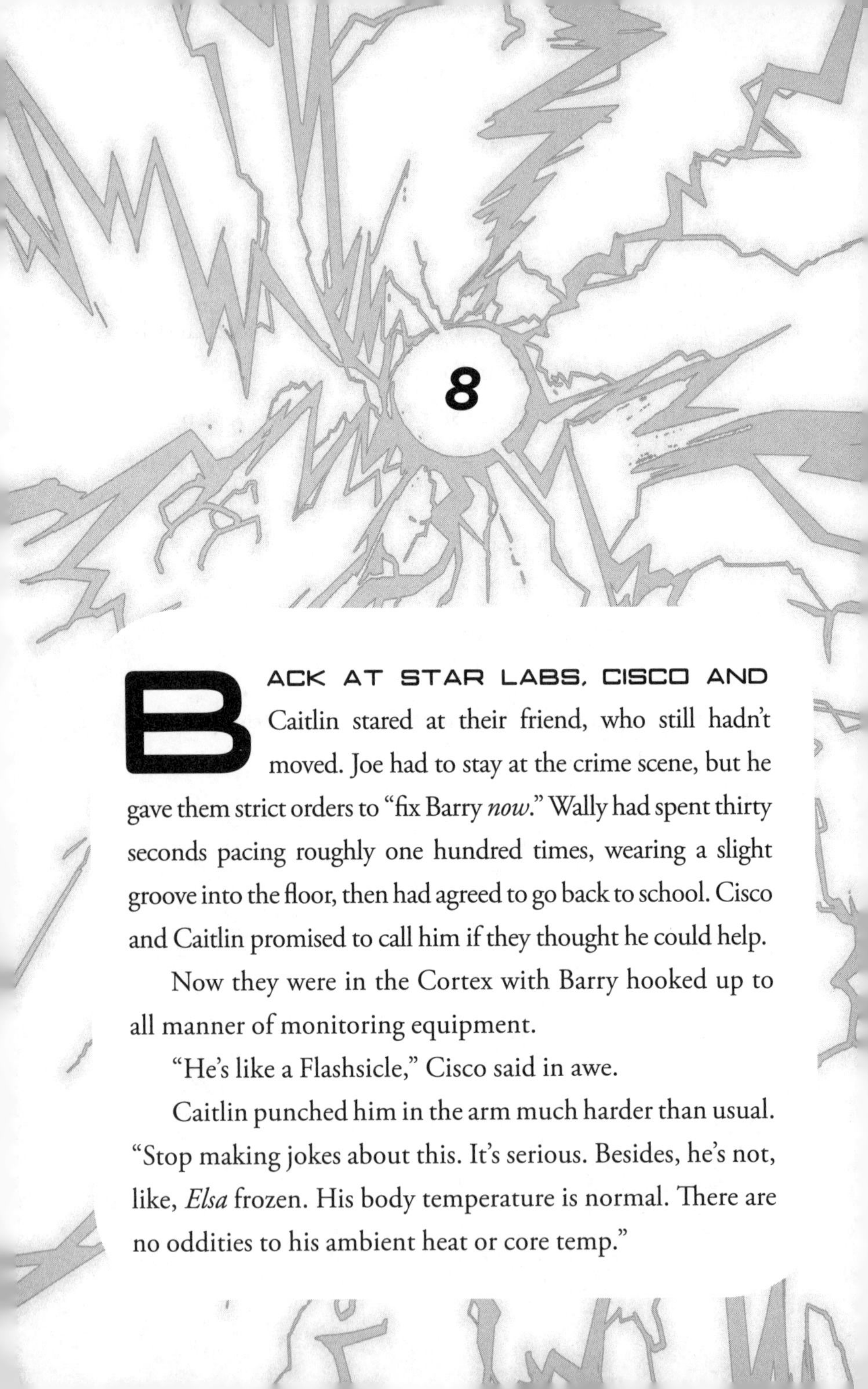

8

BACK AT STAR LABS, CISCO AND Caitlin stared at their friend, who still hadn't moved. Joe had to stay at the crime scene, but he gave them strict orders to "fix Barry *now*." Wally had spent thirty seconds pacing roughly one hundred times, wearing a slight groove into the floor, then had agreed to go back to school. Cisco and Caitlin promised to call him if they thought he could help.

Now they were in the Cortex with Barry hooked up to all manner of monitoring equipment.

"He's like a Flashsicle," Cisco said in awe.

Caitlin punched him in the arm much harder than usual. "Stop making jokes about this. It's serious. Besides, he's not, like, *Elsa* frozen. His body temperature is normal. There are no oddities to his ambient heat or core temp."

"Some kind of neuromuscular thing?" Cisco asked, frowning at a computer screen.

Caitlin clucked her tongue, thinking. "It could be some sort of artificially induced form of amyotrophic lateral sclerosis? Or maybe a souped-up version of vecuronium, the stuff they use to paralyze patients temporarily for surgery?"

She swiveled in her chair and moused around on the computer for a few moments. Cisco watched, gnawing at a knuckle on his right hand. "You think I could vibe him out of it?"

"If Wally couldn't . . . I mean, no offense."

"None taken. It's like being in a Flash wax museum." Cisco brightened for a moment. "Someone should totally build a Flash museum. How awesome would that be?"

"Maybe wait until . . . Darn!" Caitlin pushed away from the computer in frustration. "No markers for anything like ALS or vecuronium in his system."

They sat there, silent, gazing at the Flash, who had no choice but to gaze back.

Suddenly Cisco snapped his fingers. "Remember, the magician told us to clap, and we did. What if he told Barry not to move?"

Caitlin jumped up and ran to Barry. "Cisco, this isn't like before, when we couldn't check our own brains *while* we were under his control. Barry's *still* under his control."

She adjusted some of the monitor leads on the Flash's head. "There. Scan the cerebral cortex and the cerebellum. There should be some sort of chemical evidence this time."

But there was none.

"How is this even possible?" Cisco flung himself into his chair, which coasted back a couple of feet and collided with H.R., who had just stepped into the Cortex.

"Seriously, have you considered magic?" H.R. asked.

"I'm going to put you in a box and saw you in half," Cisco threatened. "How's that for magic?"

Suddenly, Barry shot up.

"Whoa!" Cisco cried.

"Barry!" Caitlin exclaimed, and ran to him.

"See?" H.R. said with smug satisfaction. "Magic!"

"Get your magic out of here!" Cisco ordered.

H.R. shrugged as he ambled out the door.

"Are you all right?" Caitlin asked Barry, helping him into a chair. He seemed shaken but otherwise OK.

"I'm not hurt, if that's what you mean." He passed a hand over his eyes. "It was the weirdest thing: I *wanted* to move, but I just couldn't. No matter how hard I tried."

"What, exactly, happened?" Cisco scooted his chair around. "What did—wait for it—Magic Man do to you?"

Barry chuckled. "He actually calls himself Hocus Pocus."

"I hate when they name themselves!" Now that Barry was out of danger, Cisco didn't hesitate to focus on what was really bothering him. "They need to leave that to the professionals."

Barry stood—a bit woozily, but waving off help from Caitlin—and walked to the big monitor screen, which showed a grainy satellite still from video of his fight with Hocus Pocus. "I grabbed for his wand, and there was a flash of light. He said, 'Freeze,' and I did. That's all."

"He headed north, and then we lost track of him," Caitlin said. "We think he might have turned invisible. Or creates some kind of illusion to screen himself."

"This makes no sense," Cisco complained. "He's doing all kinds of things that have no connection to one another. None of his powers seem related. We've encountered lots of metas in the past, but they usually have one deal, right?"

Caitlin nodded. "That's true. Barry's fast. He's not fast and, say, able to control the weather."

"Mirror Master can travel through mirrors, but he doesn't shoot lightning out of his butt, too," Cisco added.

Barry shrugged. "That hasn't been definitively proven yet, but based on the available evidence, you're right.

"But this guy," he went on, "this guy controls minds, shoots flames, makes trees come to life, can rip open the ground . . . The only other person with so many different powers I know is . . ." Barry broke off. "Nope, I don't even want to think it."

It took a moment, but then Caitlin realized what he was thinking: "Supergirl."

"She's not a meta," Cisco reminded them. "She's an alien. An alien from another universe, to boot."

"I know, Cisco. But what if this guy is the same?" Barry didn't want to think it, even if it was a possibility.

"An alien? Or from another universe?"

Barry shrugged. "Uh, both?"

"Or what if it's actually magic?" H.R. poked his head in from around the corner. "Why won't you at least consider that?"

"Because this is STAR Labs, not Hogwarts!" Cisco cracked. H.R. took the hint and ran back down the hall.

"Maybe we're overlooking the obvious here," Caitlin told them. "We assume he's a meta, but maybe we're not dealing with superpowers. Maybe it's tech. His wand."

Barry thought about it. It was true that pretty much every "magic trick" Pocus had pulled came with a flourish of his wand. "Could be. But still, to have something *that* small and compact be able to do so many different things . . ." He looked over at Cisco, who shrugged his shoulders.

"Everything is impossible until someone does it," Cisco said. "But, man, I don't know how you'd manage it. Like, I had to build something ten times bigger than that wand just to make Captain Cold's gun, and that's a one-trick pony that just freezes things." When Barry winced at the word *freezes*, he added, "Sorry. Too soon?"

Barry sighed heavily and stared down at his hands, flexing his fingers over and over, as though disbelieving that he was now able to do even this simple thing after being paralyzed. "Look, guys, I don't want to run out on you, but there's nothing I can do here for now. And I need to get back to work or Captain Singh is gonna run me through a meat grinder."

"We'll finish collating and analyzing all the data we just pulled from you. And check to see if the suit's backup buffer has anything we can use," Caitlin offered. "Maybe something will jump out at us."

"And we'll start matching up the video images of Magic Man—"

"Hocus Pocus."

Cisco grimaced. "Yeah, Hocus Pocus, OK, fine. I'll see if I can get any hits from the CCPD database."

"Thanks, guys." In an instant, the Flash costume was back on its storage mannequin and Barry was gone, leaving only wind in his wake.

At his lab, Barry blew through the reports Captain Singh needed. Not for the first time since the accident that had given him his powers, he wondered how it was possible that he could be the fastest man alive and yet still manage to be late all the time.

His cell phone buzzed in his pocket. It was Iris, so he picked up immediately. He could hear sirens and crowd babble in the background.

"Honey, where are you? I can barely hear you."

She raised her voice. "I'm at the park, covering a story. I understand someone else was here, too."

"Yeah, that's what I hear."

"Are you OK?" she asked. "Dad called and said—"

"I'm fine." Just then, his desk phone rang. Caller ID said Captain Singh. "I'm just behind the eight ball right now."

"As usual."

"Gotta go."

"Take care, baby."

His desk phone rang again, and before the ring could finish, he was downstairs, just outside Captain Singh's office. Singh, phone in his hand, looked up and did a double take.

"Why are you winded, Allen? Did you run here?"

"No, sir."

"You should have." Singh grunted and gestured with his phone. "I was just calling up to the lab. Those reports—"

"Are done, sir." Barry stepped inside and handed them over.

"Get that home situation under control?"

"Yes, sir. It's all ironed out." He offered a weak chuckle.

Singh didn't so much as twitch. "Don't go anywhere. Close the door."

Well, *that* wasn't good. As Barry closed the door to Singh's office, he caught a glimpse of some of the cops out in the bullpen. Detective Patterson winced sympathetically at him.

Singh pointed to a chair, signaling for Barry to sit; Singh didn't need any magic powers to make Barry follow his order. Singh remained standing. He tapped the stack of reports on his desk. "You're a smart guy, Allen. And I like you a lot. We've had our differences and our troubles, but I like to think we respect each other."

"Sir, I totally respect you. I know I've been a little out of it lately. There's a lot going on right now, and I'm doing my best to juggle everything."

"I know that. I believe you. That's part of the problem: I believe you. But I can't *rely* on you. I'm sorry about your father, but this is a police department. We have responsibilities."

Barry had been in this position before. Being the Flash made his regular life so much more difficult; even superspeed couldn't always smooth over the bumps and rough patches. "Sir, I realize that I've been cutting it close lately, but I always get the job done—"

"And you get it done well," Singh admitted. He turned to look out his window, hands clasped behind his back. "But you're always rushing, always harried. One of these days, you're going to cut it *too* close. One of these days, you're going to be so panicked, pushing yourself so fast that you make a big mistake. And in our line of work, that can be absolutely tragic." He paused. "Do you hear me, Allen? Is this getting through to you?"

When Captain Singh turned around, Barry Allen was gone.

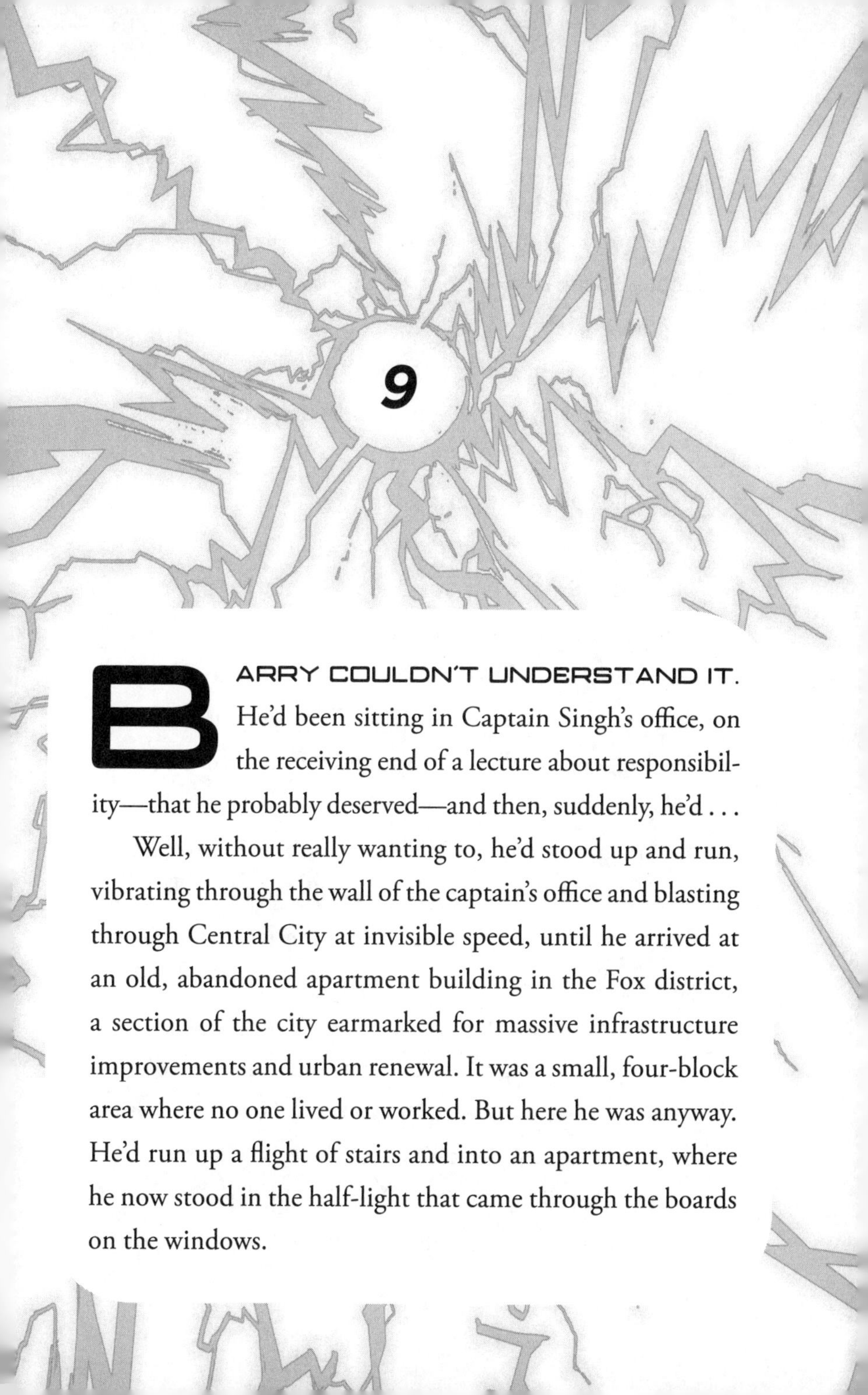

9

BARRY COULDN'T UNDERSTAND IT. He'd been sitting in Captain Singh's office, on the receiving end of a lecture about responsibility—that he probably deserved—and then, suddenly, he'd . . .

Well, without really wanting to, he'd stood up and run, vibrating through the wall of the captain's office and blasting through Central City at invisible speed, until he arrived at an old, abandoned apartment building in the Fox district, a section of the city earmarked for massive infrastructure improvements and urban renewal. It was a small, four-block area where no one lived or worked. But here he was anyway. He'd run up a flight of stairs and into an apartment, where he now stood in the half-light that came through the boards on the windows.

What the heck is going on?

"Welcome, my puppet," said an all-too-familiar voice.

Hocus Pocus stepped out of the shadows, leering and stroking his goatee.

Barry moved quickly, but not quickly enough; Pocus shook his head and said, "Stop," and Barry stood perfectly still.

Just as he had at the park.

We thought it wore off, whatever he did to me. But it didn't!

"So . . . this is what you look like under the mask," Pocus mused. He took Barry's chin in his hand and tilted his head this way and that. "Nothing exceptional. Nothing exciting. Nothing even memorable. Why do you hide your face behind a mask, Flash? I thought perhaps you were disfigured."

The truth was that he hid his face so that jerks like Pocus couldn't strike at him through his family and friends, most of whom were more vulnerable than the Flash. Ironically, right now all his friends and family were perfectly safe—Barry was the one in danger.

Not just "in danger"—he was also absolutely helpless. He couldn't move a muscle. Hocus Pocus could shoot him, stab him, punch him, kick him . . .

If Barry could have shivered, he would have. He wasn't afraid of Pocus, but he suddenly relived a stark, potent memory. He remembered the last time he'd been this vulnerable. Years ago. As a child.

The playground at Carmichael Elementary School. Recess time. A couple of months after his father, wrongly convicted for the murder of his mother, had been thrown into prison at Iron Heights. Joe, who'd become his guardian during the trial, had kept Barry out of school while his father was being tried, so Barry had just returned.

It was the worst, lowest time of his life. His mother was dead, and his father had been blamed for it. Barry knew his father was innocent, but no one would listen to a kid. So he'd watched in horror as his father went off to jail.

Back in school, he kept to himself, not even talking to Iris. He wanted to fold in on himself and vanish forever, but that was impossible.

And then came the playground that day. A mob of kids. Some older than him. Mocking him.

Your dad's a murderer!

You ain't got a mommy!

Your daddy's in jail!

When they kill your old man in jail, you're gonna be an orphan!

He'd done his best to ignore their taunts, their terrible jibes. But he was a child, and he could only take so much, and eventually he'd lashed out at them, swinging his fists manically, unable to see his targets through the tears in his eyes.

They'd retaliated, of course. Held him down. Punched and kicked him. Spit on him.

The worst, most humiliating moment of his life. He'd been outnumbered, completely overwhelmed. Utterly at their mercy.

Like he was now. In the thrall of Hocus Pocus, unable to help himself or anyone else.

He shoved away the memories. The fears. The pain. "What have you done to me?" Barry demanded. At least this time Pocus was letting him speak, which was good.

"Our earlier . . . encounter has left me famished," Pocus said. "Bring me some food."

Before Barry could retort, he realized that he'd run to Carmine's, his and Iris's favorite restaurant. So fast that no one could see, he zoomed through the kitchen, piling a plate with risotto, eggplant Parmesan, and garlic bread. In less than half a second, he was back at Pocus's apartment. The magician had settled into an old armchair. Barry presented the plate.

Pocus curled his lip. "Am I supposed to eat with my hands?"

Again, against his will, Barry ran back to the restaurant, grabbed some silverware, and returned in the blink of an eye.

Pocus nodded approvingly and tucked into the meal with gusto, pulling out a large napkin from his sleeve and laying it over his lap with a flourish. Barry thought he'd never seen someone enjoy a meal so much.

"Where I come from," Pocus told him, "food like this . . . Well, you just can't get it. One more reason I'm glad I came here."

"Where are you from?" Barry couldn't move, but he could still think. Sometimes he thought his greatest superpower wasn't his speed, but rather his ability to reason. Knowledge was power, and he was gathering it now. He knew where Pocus's hideout was, for one thing. And now he knew that Pocus wasn't from Central City.

"Where?" Pocus chuckled. "I was born not far from here, geographically speaking. But I don't expect you to understand, and I'm not here to explain myself to you. I don't need to explain anything to you, my little puppet. I command; you obey. It's very simple."

"How did you do this to me?" Barry asked.

Pocus licked some sauce from his fork and set the plate on the floor. "You are, shall we say, under my spell." Pocus leaned back and steepled his fingers together. "Yes, under my spell is the perfect way to describe it. My will is your will. My wish is your command. Now, begone, you speedy little gnat. When I need you again, I will summon you."

Still under Pocus's spell, Barry ran out the door and down the street before he regained control of his body. But once he had, Barry immediately made a U-turn and blasted back to the apartment building.

Hocus Pocus, of course, was gone.

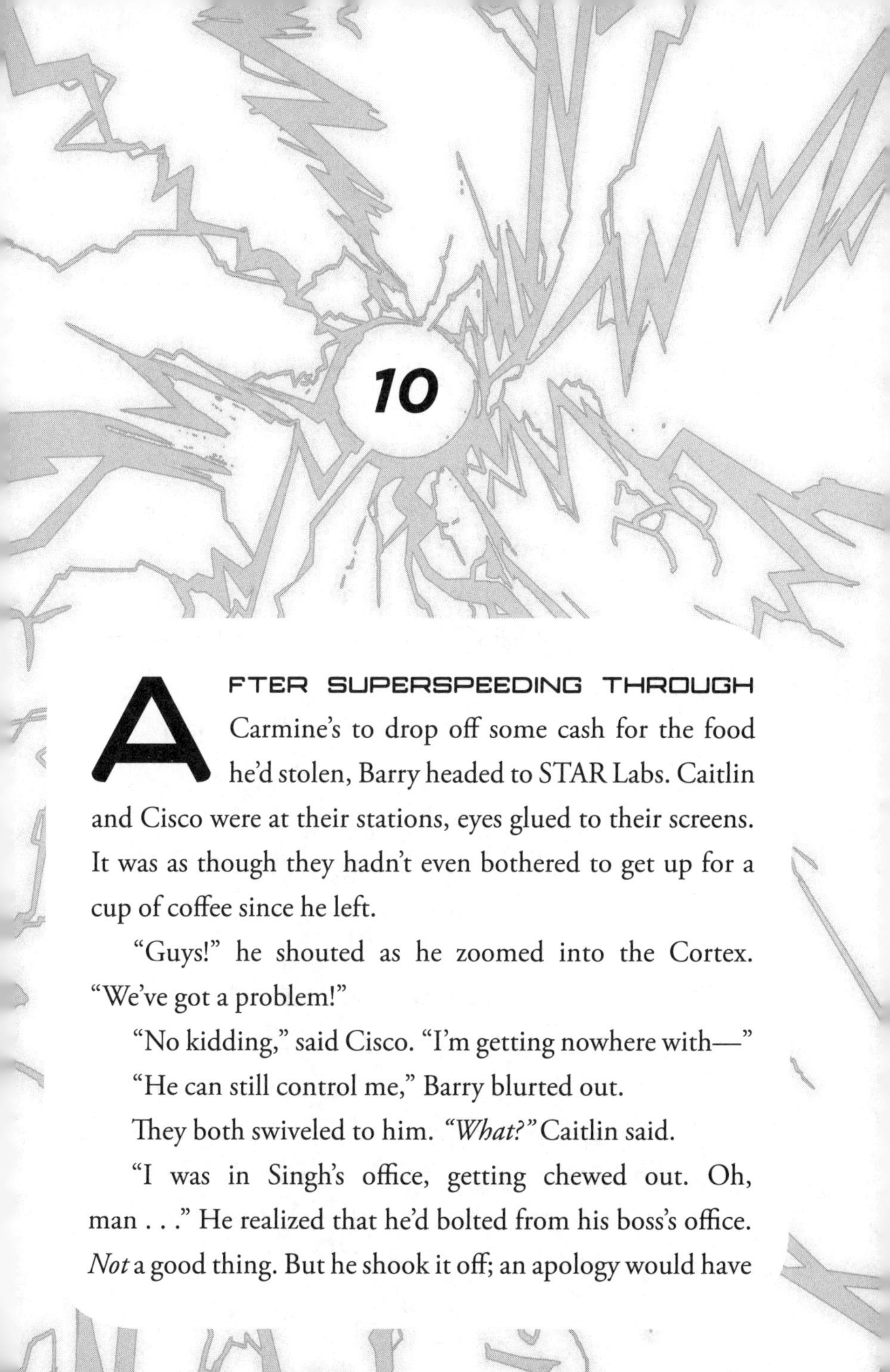

10

AFTER SUPERSPEEDING THROUGH Carmine's to drop off some cash for the food he'd stolen, Barry headed to STAR Labs. Caitlin and Cisco were at their stations, eyes glued to their screens. It was as though they hadn't even bothered to get up for a cup of coffee since he left.

"Guys!" he shouted as he zoomed into the Cortex. "We've got a problem!"

"No kidding," said Cisco. "I'm getting nowhere with—"

"He can still control me," Barry blurted out.

They both swiveled to him. *"What?"* Caitlin said.

"I was in Singh's office, getting chewed out. Oh, man . . ." He realized that he'd bolted from his boss's office. *Not* a good thing. But he shook it off; an apology would have to come later. Pocus was more important at the moment. "Anyway, next thing I know, I'm running to some old run-down apartment . . ." He quickly filled them in on what had happened and what Pocus had said.

"It really shook me up, guys," Barry confessed. "I can't lie. I wasn't in control."

"Hey, we get it," Cisco said, prompting a supportive nod from Caitlin, who added, "We couldn't stop clapping, no matter how much we wanted to."

"This is different. It's like he's in my head now. What if I can't get him out? What if he's always out there somewhere, tugging on my strings?"

"That's not going to happen," Caitlin assured him. "We'll figure out a way to stop him. We always do."

"What do we have so far?"

"Not much. He said he's from around here?" Cisco asked, puzzled.

"Born nearby, yeah."

"Well, he must have left town as a baby, then, because facial recognition is getting *nothing* on this guy. No driver's license or photo ID card in any database. No hits at all. If he lives in Central City, he's the only person here who's never stood at an ATM and gotten his picture taken."

"He doesn't seem to need cash," Barry said ruefully, thinking of the meal he'd swiped. "I don't know what he's after."

"Sure you do!" H.R. breezed in.

Cisco bristled. H.R. just rubbed him the wrong way. But before he could snark something, Caitlin held up a hand. "Enlighten us."

"He wants attention," H.R. said.

"That's ridic—"

Barry jumped up, interrupting Cisco mid-word. "No! It isn't! H.R., I think you've nailed it!"

H.R. bowed. "I live to serve."

"The one element in common across both of Pocus's appearances is that he compelled people to applaud for him," Barry reminded them. "He made everyone at the pier clap. He did the same thing at the park. He didn't really get ticked off until I took his audience away. That's when he started messing with the laws of nature."

"So he's an egotist with superpowers?" Caitlin asked.

"Dude's obsessed with having people get their worship on. He needs a reality TV show or something."

"Or he could run for president," Caitlin said.

"Don't even joke about that."

Barry drummed his fingers on the table. Before he realized it, he was tapping so fast that the table was vibrating. He stopped before Cisco could remonstrate him.

"I bet the wand is the source of his powers," he mused. "But there might be some other gadgets on him, too. Like something to amplify his voice when he wants attention." He slammed his fist down. "We need to figure out how he's controlling me!"

"If I may . . ." H.R. said.

"Don't start with magic again." Cisco sounded weary. "We have enough problems. We don't need to add mastery of the dark arts to our list."

"No, no," H.R. promised. "I've been thinking. And I've been reading up on this cerebral cortex and cerebellum you were all so exercised about before. It seems to me that they're kind of like cars on the road, no?"

"Not exactly," Caitlin ventured.

"Please. I'm a writer. Let me have my metaphors."

"That was technically a simile," Barry said, cracking a smile for the first time since he'd been called down to Singh's office.

"Very well, then—a simile. My point: You've been looking for someone who took the steering wheel, but maybe you should be looking for someone who hijacked the traffic lights instead."

"Well, that clears everything up!" Cisco said sardonically.

"No, wait." Caitlin clucked her tongue, thinking. "There's more than one way to control a car."

"How is that helpful?" Cisco asked.

"I think H.R. and Caitlin are on to something," Barry said. "Think about it: You can control a car directly with the steering wheel, like H.R. said."

"Or you can control it indirectly through the traffic signals," Caitlin told them. "The car is still stopping and starting, but for different reasons. So that means we should be looking at . . ."

"The thalamus!" Barry and Caitlin cried at the same moment.

"Sure, that," H.R. said cheerfully.

Cisco, who was pacing the Cortex, grunted. "OK, sure, that makes some kind of sense."

"Your praise is like fine sugar in my Moroccan blend," H.R. said. "And *that* is a metaphor."

"Still a simile," Barry told him, then jumped up. "Guys, hook me up again. We have to check my thalamus."

Truthfully, he knew, they should have done that from the beginning. The thalamus acted as a go-between between brain hemispheres, but it also filtered data and was instrumental in perception. All sensory data except for smell—sight, hearing, taste, and touch—went through the thalamus. If you controlled a gateway like that, what *couldn't* you make someone do?

In moments, they had him hooked up to the EEG and strapped into a series of MRI cables. Soon after, they had a 3-D model of his thalamus on the screens.

“Whoa . . .” Cisco breathed.

“What is *that*?” Caitlin shook her head and tapped at the keyboard.

Barry ripped off the wires and leads and zipped over to them. “What have we got?”

On the screen, his thalamus was etched in glowing blue lines. At this angle, it looked something like a soft boxing glove with a light bulb hanging off its rear. So far, so normal.

What was *not* normal at all were the tiny specks moving along it. Almost as if dust had been trapped in his brain and was being blown around. But dust couldn’t get into his brain, and neither could wind.

“Nanites,” Cisco said with authority.

“Little microscopic machines?” Barry said. “In my head?” It was crazy, but now it was almost as though he could feel them, itching their way through his head. He wanted to rip his skull open and scratch his brain fiercely.

“I’ve never seen anything like this before,” Cisco said, leaning in, awestruck. “I mean, sure, I’ve seen nanites. I’ve *made* nanites. But these are, like . . .”

“Light-years ahead of yours?”

“Light-years? More like parsecs.” It took a lot for Cisco to admit that someone had out-engineered him. But the evidence was right there in front of them. “This isn’t just beyond anything I’ve ever seen—this is beyond anything *anyone* has ever seen. Our 'magician' is actually the world's greatest scientist."

They all mulled that over for a moment. It wasn't a terribly comforting notion. They were used to outthinking their adversaries, exploiting their scientific acumen to leapfrog the bad guys. This time, they were the ones being outthought. They were the ones being leapfrogged over.

"He doesn't seem like a scientific genius," Barry said after a moment. "I'm not basing that on anything but a gut feeling. He just seems like a regular guy trying to be a magician."

"Maybe he stole this tech, then."

"Guys," Caitlin said, "we're forgetting something really important." Before they could respond, she'd marched over to the analysis station and started connecting leads to her head.

"Oh man!" Cisco slapped a hand over his mouth. "What if these things are still inside *us*, too?"

Once Caitlin had hooked herself up, Cisco ran his hands over the control board. Soon they were looking at a 3-D scan of her thalamus. It looked blessedly normal. A little boring, even, without all the nanites swarming its surface. Barry felt relief and a little flush of jealous anger at the same time.

They tested Cisco, too. He was similarly clean of nanites.

"I don't understand." Cisco forced past a lot of pride to say those words. "Why are they still in Barry, but not in us?"

"Because I touched the wand?" Barry leaned back in his chair, fingers steepled in front of him. It was still a chore to ignore the creepy-crawlies in his brain, but he was making his best effort. "Maybe that gave me an extra shot of—"

"Nanite juice?" Caitlin said.

"Gross," Cisco opined. "But better than what I was gonna say."

"Which was?"

Cisco looked away in shame and mumbled, "Nanite . . . stuff."

His mortification was given a reprieve by the chirping of Barry's cell phone. It was Joe.

"Barry, Singh's on the warpath . . ."

"Flash stuff is going down, Joe," he said. "I'll handle it."

"I don't think you get it. He's—"

"I'll handle it. Singh and I have a rapport these days."

"I wouldn't count on that. And I would get here *fast*. Even for you."

Barry grumbled in annoyance as he hung up. "I have to go, and come up with an excuse for why I left Singh's office on the way. In the meantime, you guys . . ." He waggled his hands all around the Cortex. "Y'know—science it up. Get these things out of my head." Something occurred to him. "Is Wally still going on patrol later?"

"Every day when his classes are over," Caitlin said.

"Whatever you do, don't let him go after Pocus, OK? The last thing we need is another speedster under this guy's control."

"Right," Cisco said, "we'll just stop the kid who can move at the speed of light."

"Be persuasive," Barry told him, and zipped away.

On his way to CCPD, he came up with an excuse. He rehearsed it to himself at Mach 2.

"'So sorry, Captain Singh . . . Got a text that my landlord smelled gas coming from my apartment . . . Had to go . . . I could swear I said something to you . . . Maybe you didn't hear me?' Yeah, that sounds good."

He raced into the building and then emerged from the fire stairs as regular, harried Barry Allen. Something was strange, though. As he walked through the normally buzzing, busy, loud precinct, everyone went silent around him. Joe, standing in a corner chatting with Detective Patterson, caught sight of Barry. His expression immediately turned sad. What was going on?

He sidled into Captain Singh's office. Singh was on the phone but looked up as Barry entered. "Oh," Singh said into the phone. "He just walked in. Uh-huh. OK, great." He hung up without so much as a "see ya" to the person on the other end.

"Close the door, Allen."

Barry did so. "Captain, I'm so sorry I disappeared before. I got a text from—"

"Save it." Singh held out a hand. "Say no more. Wait."

Barry shifted his weight from one foot to the other. He was unaccustomed to standing still like this. The last time he'd done it, well, had been when Hocus Pocus zapped him. Ugh. He didn't want to think about that. He had to mollify Singh, then figure out how to get the nanites out of his head, then stop Pocus. His days were usually crazy busy, but this one was more jam-packed than usual.

A knock at the door interrupted his contemplation. Singh waved in a stocky, gray-haired man wearing an expression that demanded to know who'd stolen his lunch and carrying an old, beaten briefcase. He focused his alert, flashing blue eyes on Barry, then closed the door with finality.

"You Allen?" he asked in a voice that communicated that he would use as few syllables as possible. Maybe fewer.

"Uh, yeah."

The man grunted and sat down. He slapped his briefcase on his lap and snapped it open. "Well?" he asked Singh.

Singh gestured to the newcomer. "Allen, this is Darrel Frye. He's your union rep."

Union rep. It took Barry a moment to make the connection. The police officers' union. They got involved only in serious disciplinary situations. Like firings.

"Captain Singh!" Barry came right up to the desk. "Sir, I know I've been a little off lately, but my work is *always*—"

"Allen!" Singh slapped a hand on his desk; Barry jumped back. "There comes a time when I don't care *how* good your work is. You've been erratic. Unavailable. And then, while I was in the middle of giving you a lecture about how you were on your last chance with me, you just up and left the office!"

Barry realized he was trembling. Then again, Singh was, too. In his seat, Frye yawned. He was the only one not upset.

"Sir," Barry tried again, "I'm really sorry that—"

"It's past time for sorry, Allen." Singh shook his head. "I'm sorry, too. But I have a responsibility to this precinct, this department, and this city. As I've said: I like you, but I can't rely on you." He took a deep breath. "I'm officially placing you on administrative leave, indefinitely, without pay, until a review of your employment status can be completed."

Barry sat for a moment, still trembling, choosing his next words very carefully.

"What . . . what exactly does that mean?" Barry asked. He thought he knew, but his mind was spinning.

"It means," Frye said, "that you're on ice until he figures out how to fire you."

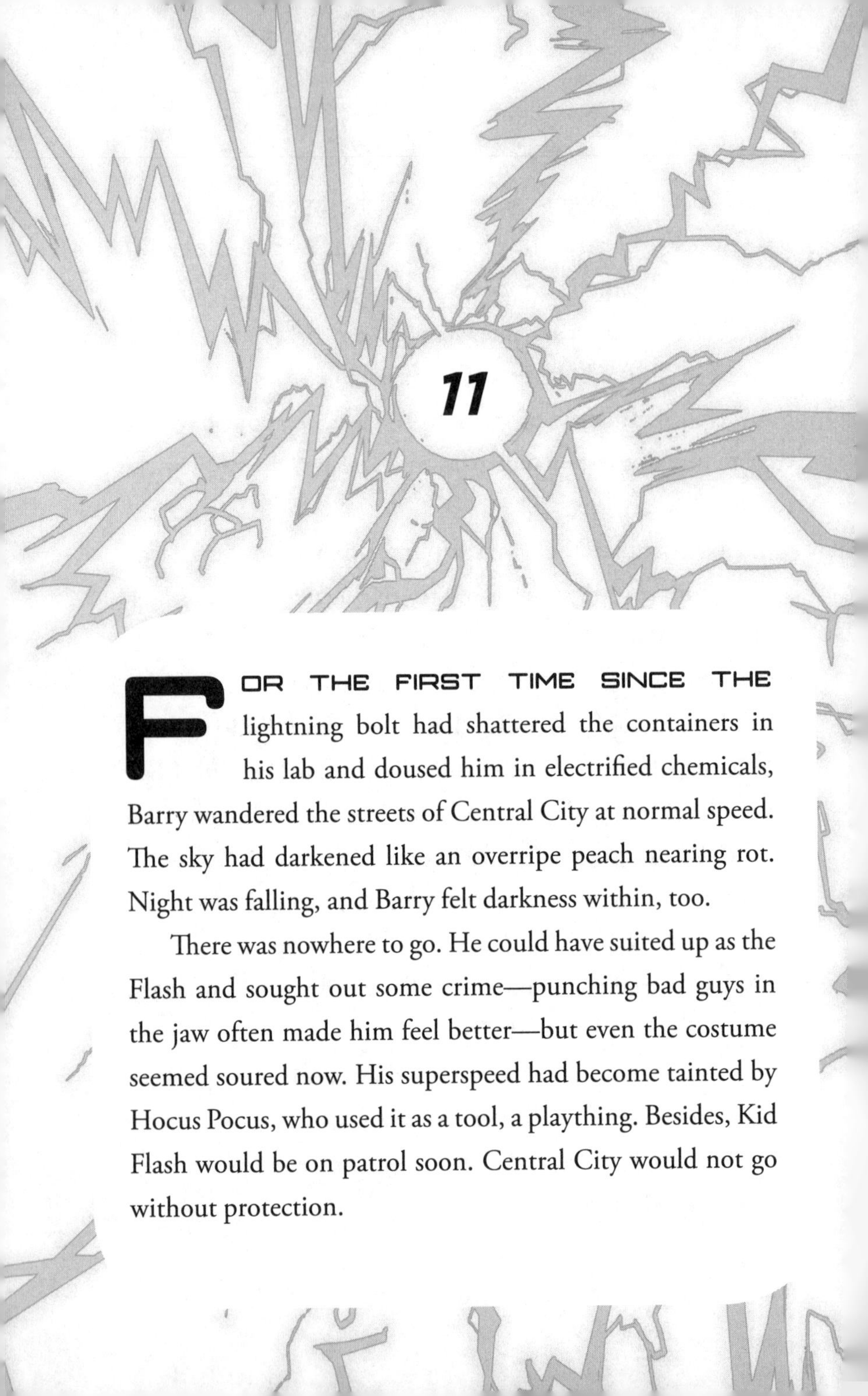

11

FOR THE FIRST TIME SINCE THE lightning bolt had shattered the containers in his lab and doused him in electrified chemicals, Barry wandered the streets of Central City at normal speed. The sky had darkened like an overripe peach nearing rot. Night was falling, and Barry felt darkness within, too.

There was nowhere to go. He could have suited up as the Flash and sought out some crime—punching bad guys in the jaw often made him feel better—but even the costume seemed soured now. His superspeed had become tainted by Hocus Pocus, who used it as a tool, a plaything. Besides, Kid Flash would be on patrol soon. Central City would not go without protection.

He turned up the collar of his coat against a late-summer chill. He'd found himself down by the pier, where it all started. He shivered at the breeze coming off the river and at the thought of Pocus walking the same boards he now walked. Magician, meta, scientist, opportunist—did it really matter which one (or how many) Pocus was? If Cisco and Caitlin couldn't figure out a way to purge the nanites from his thalamus, he would be Pocus's puppet for life. Never mind losing his job—he would lose *everything*. How could he be close to Iris, knowing that at any moment Pocus could order him to do something horrible?

Iris. He hadn't even called her yet to tell her he was going to lose his job. On his way out of the precinct, Joe had approached him, but he'd brushed Joe off and dashed outside. He knew Joe would offer fatherly comfort, and right now Barry couldn't bear that.

Deep down, he knew he didn't deserve it. He'd spent his entire life working to be a crime scene investigator. It was the perfect melding of his love of science, his thirst for justice, and his urge to use his gifts responsibly. In fact, now that he thought about it, those three traits each came from one of the three people he was so proud to call a parent: Henry, his doctor father; Joe, his adoptive cop dad; Nora, his real estate agent mother who'd turned her successful business into urban renewal as a way of giving back to the city. They'd blended together to create . . .

A failure.

He kicked a tin can and watched it roll along the boardwalk. Some part of his brain—the part that, even before he became the Flash, was always racing—calculated its trajectory, momentum, and velocity. The can would stop rolling right about . . .

The can bumped into something. A dip in the boards? A protruding knot of wood? It spun slightly, changing direction. Much to Barry's surprise, the can kept rolling in the new direction. Bemused, he tracked its progress with his eyes until it landed in a tiny crevasse created by the intersection of a walkway with the boardwalk.

The walkway was made of old cobblestone and ran for six or seven feet from the boardwalk to a concrete step that led up to a ramshackle, stucco building, a squat little one-and-a-half-story cottage jammed between a closed soft-serve ice-cream shop and a closed T-shirt store. The paint, a sick yellow, peeled like snakeskin. A sign on the door said OPEN, and a larger sign over the doorway read MADAME XANADU.

On any normal day—and on most abnormal ones—Barry would scoff at the idea of a fortune-teller and walk on. Today, he still scoffed but found himself meandering up the walkway. Why not? Nothing else was working for him today. Maybe the (fake) spirit world would have some advice for him.

A tiny bell rang as he opened the door. Within, the space was dark and cramped. The scent of incense hung in the motionless air. Wall-mounted shelves ran along the perimeter, cluttered with bottles, trays, candles, and knickknacks that seemed to have come from some bizarre Indiana Jones movie. And jars. Row upon row of old mason jars, their contents murky and somehow in motion. Toward the back, black curtains hung from the ceiling, so stiff and still that he'd thought them part of the wall at first. He set one foot over the threshold and hesitated.

"Enter freely," said a woman's voice, "and unafraid."

He'd missed the table, somehow. It was small and round, like a bistro set, with two chairs arranged at opposite sides, facing each other. In one chair sat a woman, her elbows on the table, long fingers clasped before her. She was tall and slender, wearing a sleeveless dress, her wrists a jangle of golden bracelets of all shapes and sizes. Her face was long and narrow, tapering to a sharp chin just below a knowing grin of a mouth. Her hair spilled around her shoulders, so black that it shimmered a midnight blue in the light of a nearby candle.

"Sorry," Barry said. "I thought you were open."

"And so I am." She gestured to the empty chair with one elegant hand. The motion seemed to take forever, but Barry was mesmerized by it, unable to look away. Her eyes seemed almost too large for her face; they were an unearthly green that caught the candlelight and tamed it into submission.

He made his decision and sat down. "How much?" he asked her.

She threw her head back and laughed a throaty laugh. Tears clustered in her eyes, and Barry blushed, wondering how he'd managed to offend her.

"Let us first see how I can help you," she said. "How else can we assign worth to my work?"

That made more sense than Barry had considered. He wiped his palms, suddenly damp, on his jeans. "I've never been to a fortune-teller before. How do we start?" He still felt silly doing this, but at the very least, it was an opportunity to talk about what was going on with someone who was a neutral observer. Everyone he knew—Joe, Iris, Cisco, Caitlin, Wally, even H.R.—would sympathize and empathize and pat him on the back. Maybe he needed some cold, hard tough love.

She laid a single, immaculately manicured finger along her cheek. The nail was polished a shining dark blue, with an almost glowing red X painted into it. "You are here seeking direction."

Barry didn't find her assessment all that impressive. Most people coming here were probably looking for advice, so it was a good guess. "Sure, I suppose."

She nodded. From somewhere in the hidden folds of her dress, she produced a deck of cards. It was larger than a typical deck, both wider and taller. The backs of the cards showed a pattern of stars and moons that seemed to move on their own as she rapidly shuffled the deck.

Cartomancy. "Magic" from cards. Barry had read about the tarot once for a case where a serial killer had left tarot cards on his victims. This had been a while ago, before he'd been the Flash, when he'd just started at CCPD. The idea was that there were different cards than in a regular deck. Instead of kings, queens, jacks, and aces, there were the "major arcana." And instead of tens down to deuces, there were the "minor arcana." Allegedly, by dealing out the cards, the cartomancer could read minds, see the future, and perform all sorts of magic.

It was all fake, of course. But Hocus Pocus was a fake, too, so maybe it would be helpful to have some fake magic on his side for a change, Barry decided.

She finished her shuffle with a little flourish and fanned out the cards on the table before him. He half expected her to yelp in the nasal patois of a carnival barker: *Pick a cahd, any cahd!* Instead, she said absolutely nothing, sitting with her hands folded primly on the table.

With nothing but silence hanging in the air between them, Barry took one of the cards and laid it faceup on the table. On it was a painting of a knight in black armor, hoisting a poleax over his head. He stood on the neck of what appeared to be a dragon.

"The Knight," Barry said.

Madame Xanadu shook her head. "No."

He looked again. At the bottom of the card, written in a Gothic font, were these words:

the Hero.

Now Madame Xanadu drew a card. She laid it perpendicular to the Hero. This card showed a leering face with a too-wide grin, bloodred lips, teeth sharp and shiny. A bell from a jester's cap dangled over one eye. The image creeped Barry out. It read:

the Impostor.

"Not a clown or a fool?" he asked.

Madame Xanadu said nothing. Barry figured it was his turn again, so he drew another card and laid it down next to the Hero. It depicted a riderless black horse rearing up on its hind legs. Its front hooves pawed at the sky. Flames shot out of the horse's nostrils. This one was called:

the Steed.

“This doesn’t look like any set of tarot cards I’ve ever seen,” Barry said, confused, thinking back to his experience on the case.

“I never said these were tarot cards.” She drew another and butted it up against the Steed. The card showed a man dressed in old Enlightenment garb—breeches, doublet, a veritable Shakespeare play condensed into one guy—gazing at himself in a mirror:

eht Gnikool Ssalg.

Madame Xanadu swept up the remaining cards and tucked them back into whatever mysterious pocket whence they’d come. She stared at Barry for long, uncomfortable seconds; her eyes seemed to change shades of green as he watched.

After what felt like hours, Barry pushed back from the table. “What’s going on here?”

“You’ve suffered a setback,” she said to him.

He glanced at the table, unsure how she got that from these four cards. Then again, his demeanor probably made it obvious.

“Yeah,” he admitted. “It looks like I’m losing my job . . .”

Madame Xanadu went on, still staring at him. “And there is someone new in your life. Someone who makes you feel helpless. Someone controlling.”

This was getting weird. Barry gestured to the cards

spread out between them. "How are you getting *that* from the cards?"

She tilted her head, her expression that of a woman who had just learned an interesting bit of trivia. "I haven't read the cards yet."

"What?"

Before he could go on, she scrutinized the cards, nodding to herself. "You drew the first card. Therefore, it describes you. The Hero."

"I never said I was—"

"Your destiny says you are. I drew the second card, the Impostor, so it refers not to you, but to someone else. I laid it on its side, so it is someone in opposition to you. Someone fighting you is not what he or she claims to be."

Pocus. Pretending to be a magician.

"You drew the Steed," she went on, tapping it with a long fingernail, "and placed it next to the Hero. So the Steed is the solution to your problem."

He looked again at the card. Black horse. Rearing up. Fire from nostrils. Speed? Well, sure. Speed was always the answer for the Flash.

But she didn't know he was the Flash. And neither did the cards.

"And then the Looking Glass," she said, tapping the strangely named card, "next to the Steed. It modifies the Steed. Your solution can be found at their intersection."

Barry snorted a laugh. "How is this supposed to get my job back?"

Madame Xanadu stood, gathering the remaining cards. With a knowing grin, she quipped, "Who said this was about getting your job back, Barry?"

And she disappeared through the black curtains.

Barry sat in silence for a moment, replaying everything that had just happened. He'd always thought that people who believed in fortune-telling were too gullible for their own good, but now he was beginning to understand how they got lured into their faith. Charlatans like Madame Xanadu were students of human emotion; they knew how to get into your head and feed you what you wanted to hear. For people who were desperate, it was a seductive possibility. Here was someone who seemed to know you better than you knew yourself. Someone who was connected to a higher power with all the answers. All you had to do was to believe, and your trials and tribulations would end.

What a load of garbage!

With a short laugh and a shake of his head, Barry left. A fortune-teller! What in the world had he been thinking?

He was half a block away before he realized: She'd called him *Barry*, but he'd never told her his name.

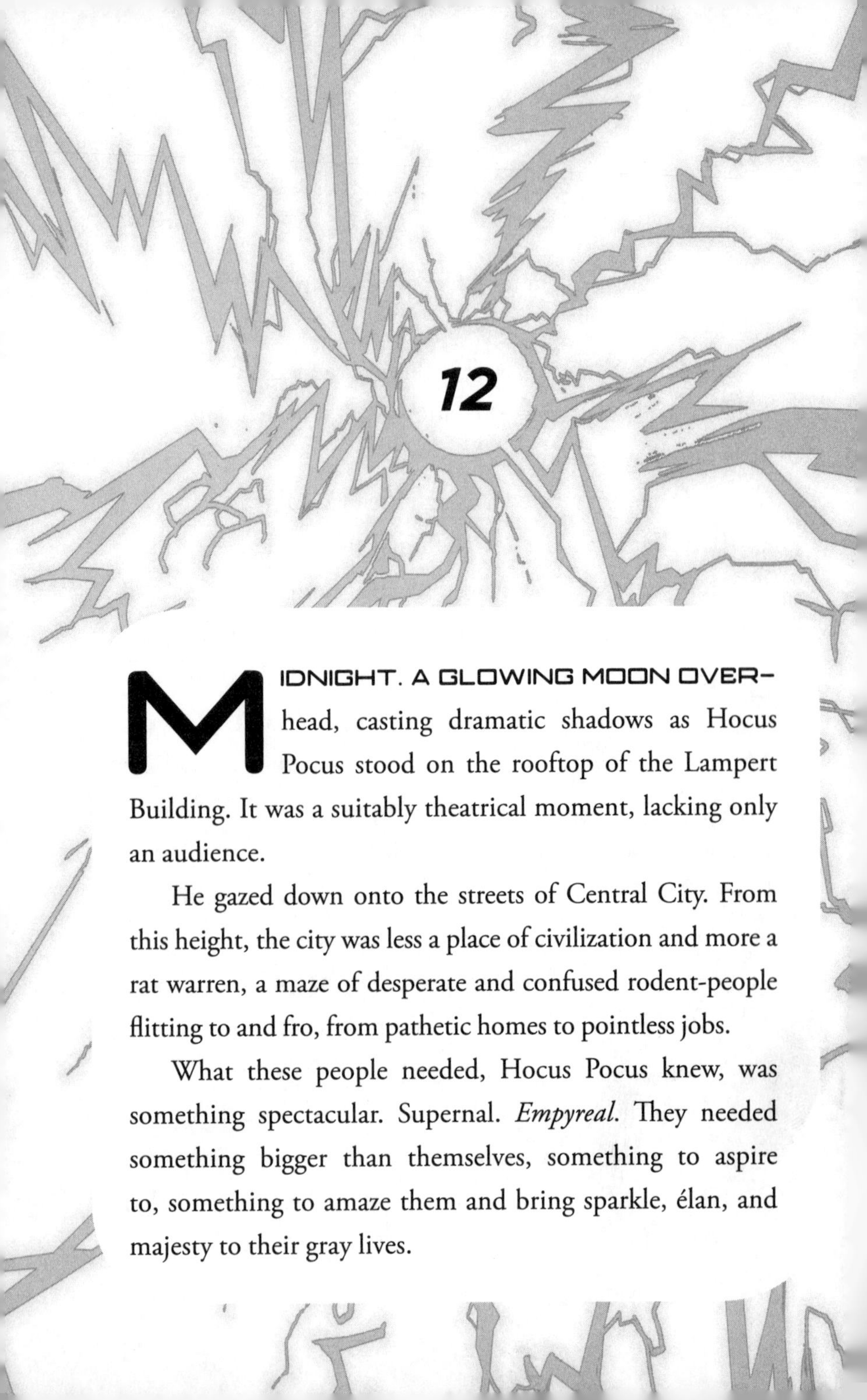

12

MIDNIGHT. A GLOWING MOON OVERhead, casting dramatic shadows as Hocus Pocus stood on the rooftop of the Lampert Building. It was a suitably theatrical moment, lacking only an audience.

He gazed down onto the streets of Central City. From this height, the city was less a place of civilization and more a rat warren, a maze of desperate and confused rodent-people flitting to and fro, from pathetic homes to pointless jobs.

What these people needed, Hocus Pocus knew, was something spectacular. Supernal. *Empyreal.* They needed something bigger than themselves, something to aspire to, something to amaze them and bring sparkle, élan, and majesty to their gray lives.

They needed *magic*.

And Hocus Pocus needed a triumph.

He grinned, the points of his immaculately groomed mustache quivering. With a wave of his wand, he could control weather, physics, *people*. This city and he . . . they were in a symbiotic relationship. They needed each other. He could bring joy and wonder into the lives of every man, woman, and child in Central City. And all they had to give him in return was their enthusiastic love and appreciation.

Easy enough. A simple trade. The city would be his, and he would love it and care for it and make it perfect in his image.

He had come here to prove himself. To rise from his station and show his erstwhile master that he, Hocus Pocus, was the superior magician and the superior villain. Along the way, he'd discovered that his love of the approbation of the crowd did not mean he had to change his goals or even his methods. He could have his victory, crush his old mentor, *and* have the love of the people of Central City.

He. Could. Have. It. *All!*

Only the Flash stood in his way.

Hocus Pocus laughed until he nearly choked on his own mirth. The Flash. The Flash was no challenge at all. He already knew precisely how to defeat him, and the time was *now*.

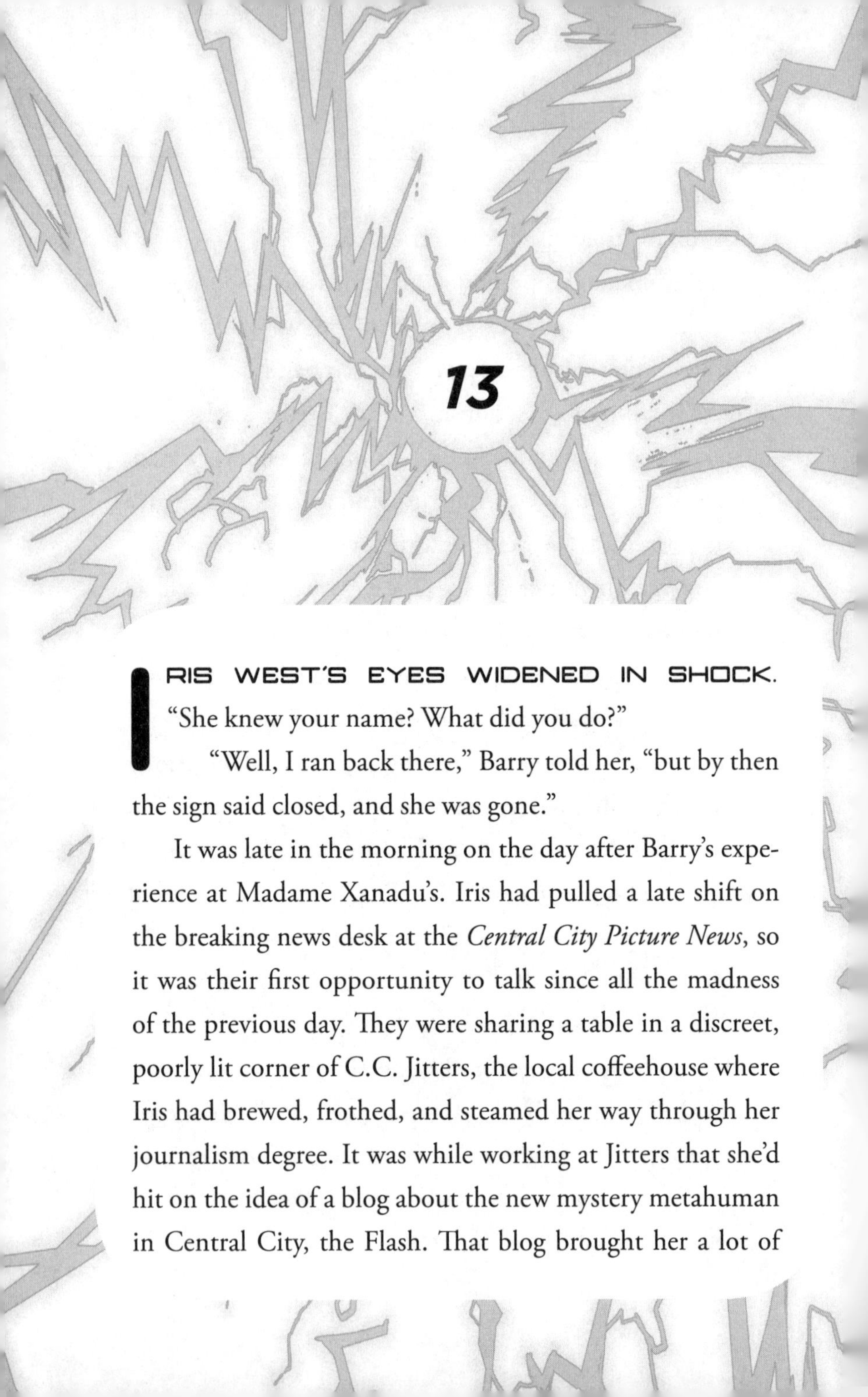

13

IRIS WEST'S EYES WIDENED IN SHOCK. "She knew your name? What did you do?"

"Well, I ran back there," Barry told her, "but by then the sign said closed, and she was gone."

It was late in the morning on the day after Barry's experience at Madame Xanadu's. Iris had pulled a late shift on the breaking news desk at the *Central City Picture News*, so it was their first opportunity to talk since all the madness of the previous day. They were sharing a table in a discreet, poorly lit corner of C.C. Jitters, the local coffeehouse where Iris had brewed, frothed, and steamed her way through her journalism degree. It was while working at Jitters that she'd hit on the idea of a blog about the new mystery metahuman in Central City, the Flash. That blog brought her a lot of grief, but it also garnered the attention that landed her a job at the city's oldest and most prestigious newspaper.

"I don't even remember there being a place called Madame Xanadu's on the boardwalk," Iris said. "I did a piece on phony fortune-tellers for the paper last summer, and I spent a *ton* of time down there. I'd remember a name like that."

Barry shrugged. "I'm not in the market for an investigative reporter right now. Just a sympathetic girlfriend."

"You've got that." She reached across the table and took his hand. "We're going to figure this out. All of it. Singh, Hocus Pocus . . ."

Barry sighed with contentment at her touch. She had saved him emotionally . . . and maybe existentially. Months ago, he'd had a mad, impulsive plan to change history as a way of ending his grief. No one could know what the ripple effects of such a change would be, but he'd been too wretched to think it through. Who knew what horrors she'd prevented?

If he had changed the past, he realized, he would have been avoiding processing his grief over his father's death. And maybe he never would have recovered from it. By staying in the present, he was able to live with the pain, understand it, and move past it. He had Iris to thank for that.

"What did I do to deserve you?" he asked.

She chuckled and squeezed his hand. "I don't know. Twenty years of being an awesome guy and best friend?"

"Is that all it took?"

"Hey, kids." Joe came in and pulled over a chair, swung it around, and sat on it backward. "Honey." He pecked Iris on the cheek.

"So, look," he said without pause, "I've been thinking about this whole firing thing. It's nonsense. Singh's out of his mind. You're the best CSI we've got. Best I've ever worked with."

"Thanks, Joe," Barry said somewhat ruefully, "but I'm not 100 percent sure he's wrong."

"What?" Both Joe and Iris stared at him, their expressions those of people who've just bitten into a tuna-infused chocolate bar.

Barry strummed his fingers along the side of his rapidly cooling coffee cup. "Listen to me: Singh's right. He hasn't said anything false at all. I'm erratic. Unreliable. The quality of my work is great, sure, but a cop who shows up at the last possible minute?" He shook his head. "That might be a relief, but it's not a cop you can count on, is it?"

"I can't believe you're talking like this," Iris said.

Joe checked over both shoulders to make sure no one was listening in, then leaned in close and said in a low whisper, "Is this Pocus talking? Is he controlling you again? Blink twice if yes."

Barry snorted laughter. "Joe, if Pocus were controlling me, he would just make me blink twice."

Joe leaned back and crossed his arms over his chest. "This just doesn't sound like you. Giving up like this."

"You think I *want* to lose my job?" Barry ran his hands through his hair, gripping his head as though he could squeeze an answer out if only he could press hard enough. "I just don't see a way out. And maybe this way I can spend more time as the Flash and at STAR Labs and—"

"Maybe it's time to tell Singh," Iris said abruptly.

"Tell him what?" Barry asked.

She tilted her head and glared in that way she had when he was missing the obvious.

"Oh! You mean tell him about . . ." He ran his forefinger and middle finger along the table like little bodiless legs.

"Bad idea," Joe said, shaking his head. "Singh digs the Flash these days, but he does *not* like being lied to."

"I agree," Barry said. "I mean, the time for that has passed. Maybe a year ago, but now? I don't think so."

"Let me see what I can do," Joe insisted. "I have some weight in the department. *And* I knew Singh when he was just a rookie. He owes me more than a few favors."

“Joe, thanks, but . . . no. It’ll just look like a dad trying to help his kid.”

“But—”

“And it’ll look that way because that’s what it is.” Barry held Joe’s gaze until the older man relented. “This is my mistake, my mess. I need to be the one to clean it up.”

A buzzing sound kept anyone from saying anything else. Joe checked his phone and jumped to his feet. “Oh man. Dead body. Gotta go. Barry, let’s . . .” He sighed, realizing what he was saying. “I guess you’re not riding with me on this one, are you?”

“Not this time,” Barry said with a sad smile.

As soon as Joe cleared the door to Jitters, Barry stood. “I have to get going.”

Iris did a double take. “But you just said—”

“Barry Allen has no business at a crime scene. But a certain Crimson Comet does.”

“I prefer Scarlet Speedster.”

“Red Racer? Vermilion Velocitor?”

She slapped his arm. “Get going, you goofball.”

Chuckling, he turned to go but then spun around again, his expression suddenly serious. “I really appreciate this. You taking the time after a long night at the office.”

“Of course!”

"As long as you're with me, even my worst days aren't so bad."

Iris groaned and rolled her eyes. "That is *such* a cliché. Did you get super-cornball powers, too?"

"Sometimes things are clichés because they're true." He grinned and kissed her lightly on the lips. "Everything will work out. Somehow. Trust me."

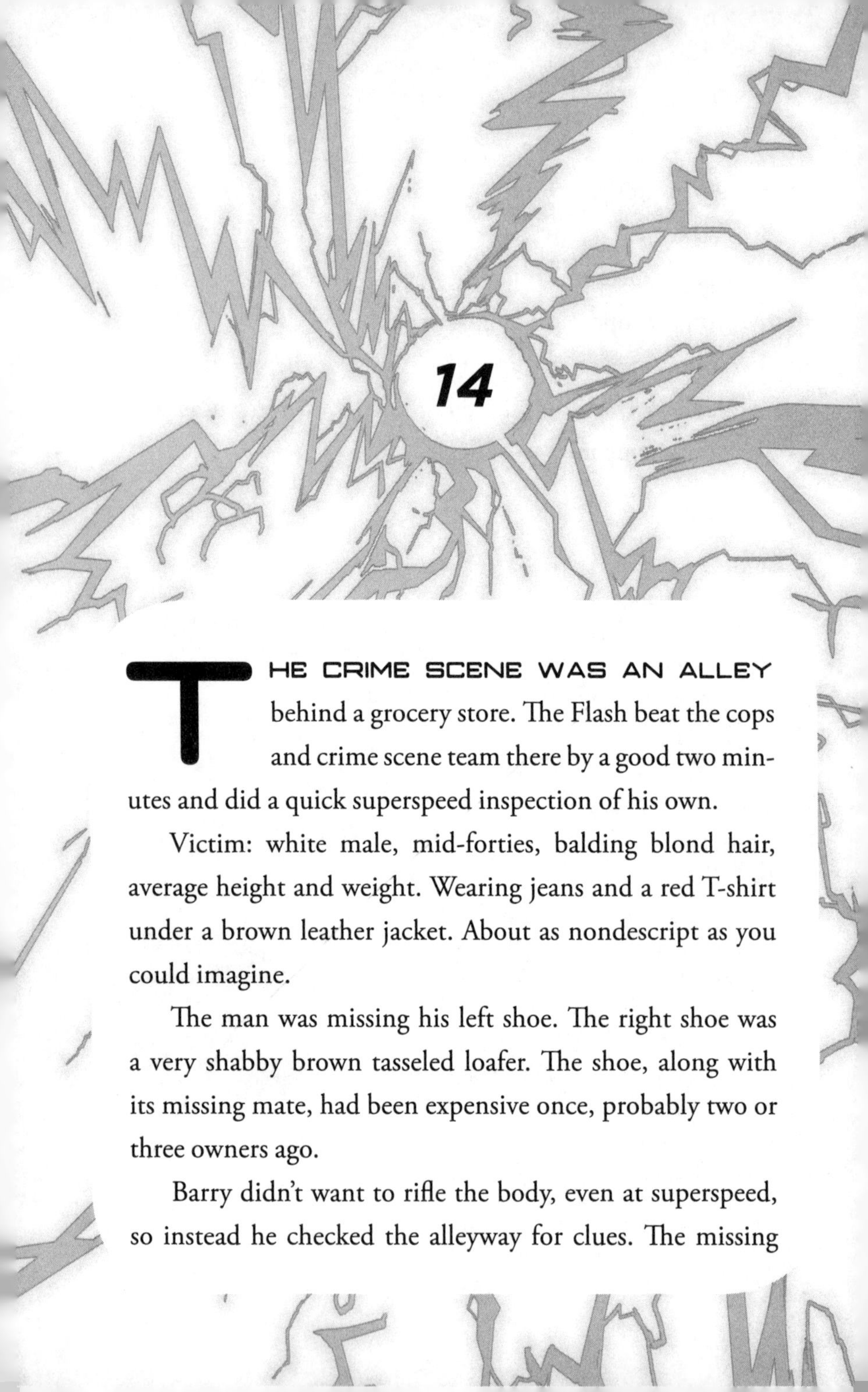

14

THE CRIME SCENE WAS AN ALLEY behind a grocery store. The Flash beat the cops and crime scene team there by a good two minutes and did a quick superspeed inspection of his own.

Victim: white male, mid-forties, balding blond hair, average height and weight. Wearing jeans and a red T-shirt under a brown leather jacket. About as nondescript as you could imagine.

The man was missing his left shoe. The right shoe was a very shabby brown tasseled loafer. The shoe, along with its missing mate, had been expensive once, probably two or three owners ago.

Barry didn't want to rifle the body, even at superspeed, so instead he checked the alleyway for clues. The missing shoe was nowhere nearby. There was a garbage-fragrant puddle at one end of the alley and, he noticed, a nearly dry water stain on the upper thigh of the victim's left jean leg. So the guy had been dragged from one end of the alley and had partially rolled into the puddle. Good to know.

In that direction, the alley opened onto Waid Avenue, about a block south of Wieringo Street. The Flash zipped up and down the avenue, looking for anything that might indicate from which direction the body had been dragged.

Nothing.

By now, the cops were in the alley. The Flash vibrated so fast that he was invisible and darted into the alley, carefully sidestepping the array of cops. Joe stood over the body, fists planted on his hips, staring down at the corpse as though he was just fed up with bodies in his city.

Barry knew he was.

He ran up the side of the grocery store and grabbed hold of a fire escape, swinging himself up onto a balcony. From this vantage point, he could watch the cops as they processed the scene.

The CSI who should have been Barry Allen did a fine job, he had to admit. Then again, this wasn't a particularly difficult scene to process.

Each time something new would come up, the Flash dashed down the side of the building and checked it out at superspeed before running back up to his hiding spot. Wallet out of the pocket? Flash zoomed down and read off the ID: Mitchell MacDonald. Prescription bottle turned out of hip pocket? Flash zapped by and read off the drug name: prednisone.

And then, when the CSI tech flagrantly ignored department protocol and decided to take a blood sample from the body right there at the scene? Well, the Flash sped on down and—in the split microseconds before the blood flowed into the test tube—swapped out an empty test tube and gathered a tiny bit of blood for his own analysis before superspeeding back to STAR Labs.

He couldn't use the lab at CCPD while on administrative leave, but one of the world's best medical laboratories in the world was at STAR Labs. It was right there in the name, really.

Caitlin was hard at work poring over the results of Barry's MRI and EEG. Cisco was nowhere to be seen, probably in his workshop trying to figure out how to extract a nanite from Barry's brain and then perform an autopsy on something so small, it was measured in millionths of a millimeter.

"Nothing yet," Caitlin said mournfully as Barry skidded to a stop in the medical lab. She didn't even look up from her screen. "I'm trying to figure out if there's a way to redirect the Speed Force in your system into the nanites as a way of accelerating their natural corrosion. But the nature of the blood-brain barrier is—"

"It's OK. I'm not here to push you. I just need to borrow a microscope." He waggled the test tube at her. Caitlin pointed to an empty lab table, and he got to work.

Some things couldn't be done at superspeed. Like, say, preparing a slide. You couldn't just slap a drop of blood onto a slide and then look at it under a microscope.

(Well, actually, you could. And you would see some interesting things. But for Barry's purposes, that wasn't enough.)

First, Barry put the blood on the slide. Then he added a stain so that certain elements in the sample would stand out. That was the part that took time, because he had to wait for the blood and the stain to mix; otherwise he'd see nothing.

It took only a few seconds, but to Barry—when he was in a hurry—seconds felt like years.

He slipped a cover over the mixture of blood and stain, waited the requisite few seconds, then peered into the microscope.

"What are you looking for?" Caitlin had come up behind him.

“Checking a blood sample from a crime scene.”

“Correct me if I’m wrong, but . . . don’t you have a lab at work?”

Barry sighed. He considered pulling rank—since he owned STAR Labs, he was technically Caitlin’s boss—but decided on telling the truth. Quickly, he filled her in on his meeting with Singh and Frye.

“Oh, Barry,” she said. “I’m so sorry.”

“It’s OK. Or, well, actually, it’ll *be* OK. I’ll figure it out somehow. Right now, though, I need to get back to . . .” He pointed to the microscope.

“But didn’t you just say you’re on leave?”

“Yep.” He tightened a knob on the microscope, zooming in further.

“Then aren’t you working for free?” She thought for a moment. “And, more importantly, isn’t what you’re doing illegal?”

“Technically, a masked vigilante running around the city beating up bad guys is also illegal.” Barry pulled away from the lenses and leaned against the table, arms folded over his chest. “I don’t stop trying to help people just because I’m not officially on the job anymore, Caitlin.”

“If you say something about having an unquenchable thirst for justice, I’ll punch you,” she said.

"What about a bottomless pit in my stomach that can only be filled by doing the right thing?" He held up his hands in self-defense and pretended to recoil in fear.

She laughed. "I'll let you get away with that one, but only because it's so incredibly lame."

"I knew my lousy sense of humor would come in handy someday."

"But seriously, Barry." Caitlin touched his shoulder, then held him firmly for a moment. "If you need to talk about what's going on . . ."

"I'll be OK." He sounded braver than he felt. So brave that he almost convinced himself.

"You—"

"Guys!" Cisco rushed in before Caitlin could get any further. "Pocus's back!"

The hacked police and security camera footage showed a truly bizarre scene that was, sadly, just another extraordinary event that had become ordinary.

Jewelers Row, in downtown Central City: During the day, it was a busy and bustling four-block square of retail shops and higher-end financial firms. Usually, the crowds at lunchtime were men and women in business attire, grabbing quick meals at the food carts or, if they had the time, lounging at an outdoor café.

Not today.

A crowd of hundreds had gathered in front of Broome & Son, the city's premier jewelry store. Broome & Son dated back decades, passed down through generations of Broomes. They were quite famous, especially known for the iconic bright pink boxes they used to package the jewelry. Standing before the crowd, his every movement a flourish, was Hocus Pocus, who was performing some minor feats of sleight of hand. Considering the simplistic nature of his tricks, the reaction of the crowd was drastically out of proportion. They applauded and hollered as though they'd never witnessed a simple card shuffle before.

The Flash arrived in seconds, moving so fast that no one could see him coming. But somehow Hocus Pocus knew—before Barry could grab the villain's wand, he felt himself slowing down, becoming visible to the naked eye. And then, quite against his will . . .

He dashed into Broome & Son and started gathering up those famous pink boxes, tossing them out the door as fast as he could. An elderly woman—an employee of the store—gasped in shock as her stock literally flew outside.

When he'd thrown about a thousand of them, the compulsion wore off and he dared to emerge onto the street. The boxes hung effortlessly in the air, spinning into an enormous, flashing circle—a Ferris wheel of expensive ornaments and gemstones in their packaging. The wheel revolved in front of Hocus Pocus, who stood on a street-side bench near the store, gesturing in a wide circle with his wand.

The crowd, of course, was cheering like mad, no doubt under Pocus's control.

"HELLO, AGAIN, FLASH!" he boomed with a curl to his upper lip. "PERHAPS NOW YOU WILL LEARN NOT TO DEFY THE GLORIOUS HOCUS POCUS!"

Defy? Ha! Barry *wished* he could defy the magician. Try as he might, he was under Pocus's control.

Except . . . not right now. The magician wasn't actually controlling him, so Barry was free . . .

Free to attack!

He raced forward—but in a split second felt his self-control vanish again. At Pocus's command, he veered left, running straight into the crowd. People dodged and leaped aside before he could plow into them at superspeed.

"CENTRAL CITY! THIS MAN YOU'VE GIVEN YOUR HEART TO . . . DOES NOT RECIPROCATE!"

Barry spun around, still under Pocus's control. The crowd had turned ugly, people pointing and snarling at him. He opened his mouth to say that it wasn't his fault, but no sound came out. Pocus.

"DID YOU REALLY THINK I WOULD LET YOU GET AWAY WITH STEALING THESE VALUABLES

FROM THAT STORE?" Pocus twirled his wand again and sent all the boxes of jewelry into a neat pile before him. "I WON'T LET YOU EXERCISE YOUR VILLAINY ON THE PEOPLE OF THIS CITY!"

And suddenly Barry was free again. He kicked into high gear, running at Hocus Pocus as fast as he could . . .

Only to come to a jarring stop a few feet from Hocus Pocus, who tut-tutted and waggled a shame finger. "PEOPLE OF CENTRAL CITY! YOUR NEW SUPER VILLAIN STANDS BEFORE YOU—THE FLASH! REVEALED AS A PERNICIOUS THIEF AND SCOUNDREL BY NONE OTHER THAN I, HOCUS POCUS!"

"I'll stop you!" Barry managed to say through gritted teeth.

Pocus raised one immaculately styled eyebrow. "DID YOU NOT LEARN YOUR LESSON LAST TIME? NOW . . . DANCE!"

Suddenly, the Flash felt an irresistible urge to dance. The only dance move he could do at all was the robot, so soon he was popping and locking, moving herky-jerky back and forth along a half block of concrete. The assembled crowd hooted and hollered in rapturous joy.

"DANCE!" Pocus commanded again, and this time Barry was horrified to find himself attempting an Irish jig, hopping from foot to foot in time to music no one could hear. The crowd guffawed and chortled.

"DANCE!" Pocus roared out.

And Barry, to his utter shock and shame, started to crunk. He wasn't really any good at it, but he was doing it anyway, contorting his body into new shapes, thrusting out his chest, flinging his arms and legs around. The audience's approval mounted even higher, the din of the crowd deafening him.

"You can do whatever you like to me," the Flash said, "but I'm not going to let you loot my city!"

After a humiliating few minutes, Pocus ordered Barry to stop. Breathing heavily, the Flash stared up at the magician as a slow smile worked its way across Hocus Pocus's face, followed by a low, appreciative chuckle. "You're right," he said in a low voice, just for Barry. "I will not loot the city." His smile became a sinister leer. "*You* will!"

Before he could stop himself, Barry had gathered up the boxes and tossed them into a large bag that Pocus seemed to conjure from thin air. Then he ran back into Broome & Son. The poor elderly employee—having suffered two serious shocks, one after the other—passed out in a dead faint. Barry caught her before she could hit the ground . . .

. . . and then swept through the rest of the store at superspeed, gathering up everything of value and tossing it into the bag. He even raced into the back room and rifled through the drawers and boxes there for sparkling gemstones and the gleam of precious metals, all of which went into Pocus's increasingly heavy bag.

I can't believe I'm doing this! His heart was sick at it, but he couldn't stop himself. Soon, he'd plundered the entire store, then dashed outside.

"WHAT DO YOU THINK, CENTRAL CITY?" Hocus Pocus cried. "SHOULD I LET HIM STEAL FROM THESE PEOPLE?"

The crowd's response was a deafening roar. Individual words were nearly impossible to discern, but the upshot was: *No way! We're on your side, Hocus Pocus!*

The sense of control over his mind faded again. Once more in control of his own body, Barry launched himself at Hocus Pocus. One punch! That's all it would take. One punch and he'd knock out the magician and not have to worry about being controlled again.

But just before he could land that punch, he felt his body acting on its own. He slowed down just enough that Hocus Pocus could dodge the blow, to the gasping amazement of the crowd. He threw another punch; this one, too, was too late. Pocus was playing with him, dancing around, expertly making it appear as though they were actually fighting, when Pocus himself was actually controlling both sides of the conflict. Barry helplessly flailed away at the magician, missing by a hair each time, his punches becoming more and more savage. The crowd muttered ugly imprecations as Pocus seemed to luckily dodge each devastating blow. The magician made it appear as though he were the underdog, barely holding his own against a cruelly violent Flash.

Finally, when he tired of the game, Hocus Pocus gestured with his free hand. A deck of cards appeared there, and then he flicked his wrist. As Barry watched, the cards spun into the air, multiplying as they were flung at him. What had been fifty-two cards became a hundred and four, then two hundred and eight, then more. The air filled with a blizzard of playing cards, zipping about as if they had lives and motivations of their own. Barry felt Pocus's control on him slacken and disappear as the thick cloud of cards neared him.

With a cry of triumph, he sped through the cards, deftly dodging them as he went. They were more than just cards, he realized—each one was rimmed with a sharp, steel edge. He ducked, bobbed, and weaved, running almost blind through the thicket of cards, intent on one thing and one thing only: catching the magician on the other side of the cloud. He slipped between queens and kings, batted aside a flurry of deuces, one-eyed jacks, and aces. Hearts, clubs, spades, and diamonds fluttered in the air around him—a storm of playing cards.

When he emerged on the other side, Hocus Pocus was nowhere to be seen.

But he *did* see a cluster of CCPD cops, their cruisers parked at angles on the street. Two uniformed cops were ushering civilians behind the cars, as a phalanx of armed and armored tech officers fanned out. They had complicated rifles aimed at him.

"FLASH!" one of them called out through a bullhorn. "DROP THE STOLEN GOODS AND PUT YOUR HANDS IN THE AIR!"

And much to Barry's shock, he felt something heavy in his hand. He looked down to realize that somehow he had picked up the bag of stolen merchandise. No matter how hard he tried, he couldn't drop it.

"Do you see that?" he heard someone saying.

"The Flash robbed the store!"

"He stole *everything*—"

"I thought he was a hero—"

The crowd had turned into an angry mob, and they were angry at him. He couldn't really blame them.

"What are you up to?" someone called out from behind the police barricade.

"You're supposed to be a good guy!" someone else yelled.

Barry dodged to his left just in time to avoid a sandwich someone had flung at him. An instant later, as he kicked into superspeed, the air around him went thick with pitas, water bottles, cans of soda, hot dogs, and more as the mob began pelting him with food and crying out at his villainy.

No doubt triggered by his becoming a blur, the cops started firing. Barry didn't know what kind of bullets they were using—maybe they were just rubber—but he didn't want to find out the hard way, either. He still had one free hand, and he pointed that hand at the cops. He started spinning it around and around, until the speed and friction of his motion generated a whirlwind that knocked several cops off their feet.

"STAND DOWN!" the cop with the bullhorn commanded. "FLASH! STAND DOWN IMMEDIATELY!"

How had he gotten to this point? How had he ended up fighting his fellow law enforcement officers?

But he knew the answer. He knew it was all Hocus Pocus.

Bullets started flying again. He dodged and weaved, still clinging to the bag. Somewhere, Hocus Pocus was still commanding him, ordering him to hold on to it. It slowed him down, but just a little. He was still faster than bullets, fast enough to step between gunshots, then sweep out with the heavy bag, knocking down a row of cops like bowling pins.

He wanted to explain to them what was happening, but what would he say? How could he convince them? He couldn't, he knew.

So he did what he always did: He ran.

He ran away.

Running was what he was best at, but it had never felt so cowardly before. He couldn't help it, though. He had to escape. From the accusations and anger of the crowd. From his own shame at attacking the cops. From all of it.

Moments into his run, he felt the mental tug of Hocus Pocus's yoke, yanking him in a certain direction. On the outskirts of town, near a stand of trees by the highway, he found the magician waiting for him.

"Kneel," came the command.

Gritting his teeth, the Flash dropped to one knee before the magician, his head lowered in supplication.

"If I had planned it all out before coming here," Hocus Pocus said, chortling, "it *still* would not have worked out half so well. The true magician must always be prepared to improvise."

"You're no magician," Barry snarled. "You're just a crook with a gimmick."

Hocus Pocus drew himself up to his full height. His eyes flashed with venom and righteous anger. "I am one of a lineage of magicians, you jackanapes! I have come here to do what others could not, to destroy the Flash once and for all and claim the title of Most Exalted Abra Kadabra from my master. I will let nothing and no one stand in my way!" he thundered.

"I'll stop you," Barry promised.

With a flourish that was practically Shakespearean, Hocus Pocus executed a long, slow, complicated bow that brought his eyes level with Barry's. The Flash felt the magician's breath wash over him and longed to slug him. But he couldn't move.

"Good luck, puppet," Pocus murmured. "I look forward to our continued . . . engagements."

And then he patted the Flash on the head. Like a master with a loyal yet stupid puppy.

"Why did you have me take the jewelry?" the Flash asked. "What are you going to do with it?"

"Hmm. I don't really have any plans. I just wanted everyone in the city to know that *you* took it all. After I'm gone, you can go dump it in the ocean before returning to your pathetic excuse for a life."

And then Pocus walked away. Barry wanted to watch, to see where he was going, but he couldn't move until long after the last footsteps had faded.

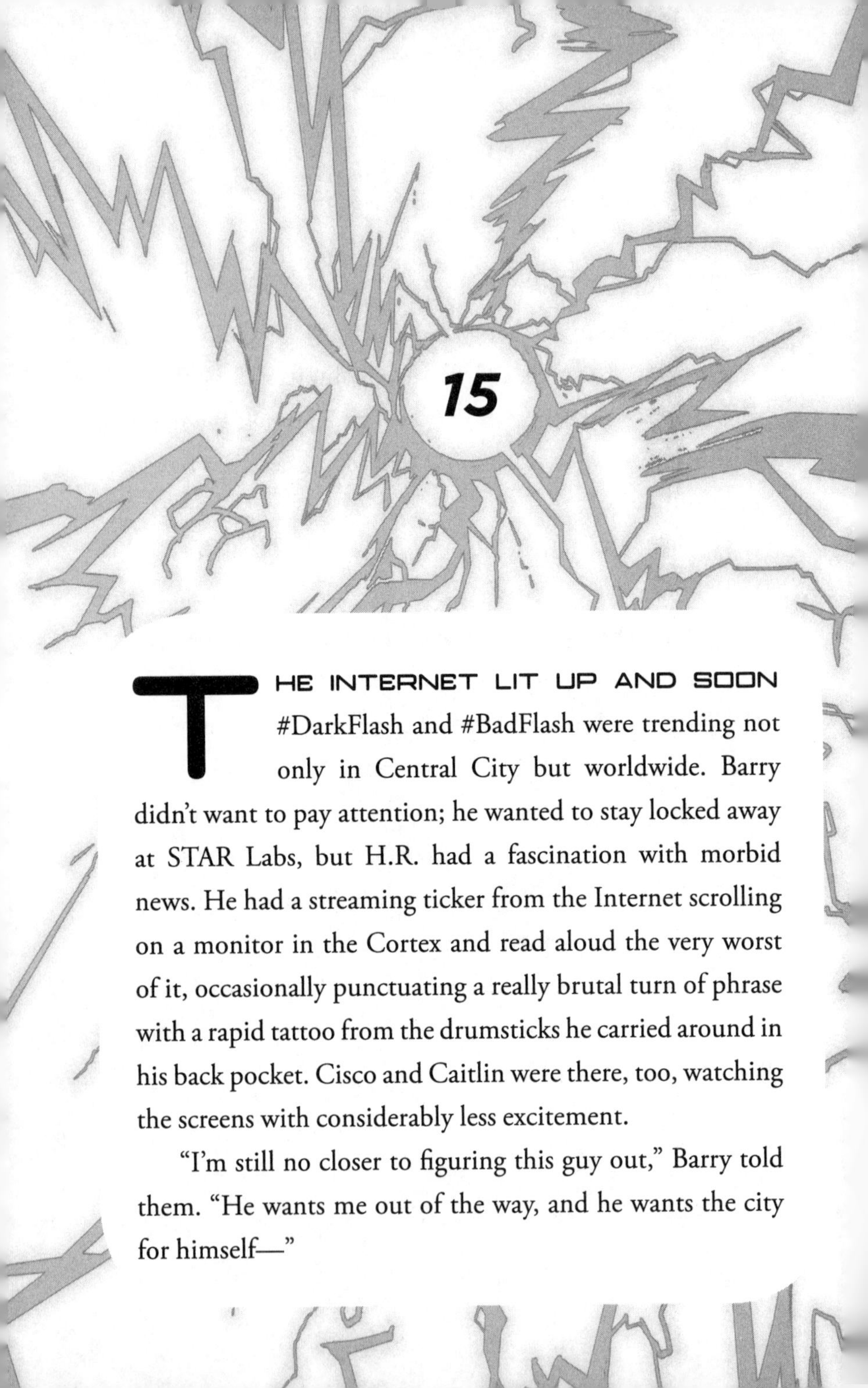

15

THE INTERNET LIT UP AND SOON #DarkFlash and #BadFlash were trending not only in Central City but worldwide. Barry didn't want to pay attention; he wanted to stay locked away at STAR Labs, but H.R. had a fascination with morbid news. He had a streaming ticker from the Internet scrolling on a monitor in the Cortex and read aloud the very worst of it, occasionally punctuating a really brutal turn of phrase with a rapid tattoo from the drumsticks he carried around in his back pocket. Cisco and Caitlin were there, too, watching the screens with considerably less excitement.

"I'm still no closer to figuring this guy out," Barry told them. "He wants me out of the way, and he wants the city for himself—"

"Standard bad-guy stuff," Cisco put in.

"*—and*," Barry went on, "he wants to do all of this so that he can supplant some guy he calls the *Most Exalted Abra Kadabra*. The idea that there're more like this one out there—"

"Uhhh . . ." Cisco's eyes glazed over. "Did you say *Abra Kadabra*?"

Barry glanced at him curiously. "Yeah. Are you OK?"

Cisco licked his lips nervously. "Yeah. Yeah, I think so. I thought I . . ." He trailed off. Blinked rapidly. "I thought I, uh, vibed something for a second there." He shook his head and shivered all over. "Man, it's all that caffeine I've been mainlining to work on this case. It's making me see things now."

"#BadFlash should run out to sea and drown!" H.R. barked, clicking his sticks together. "Actually, you could just run on the water, couldn't you? So, that's kind of a waste of a burn."

"Please stop it, H.R." Barry slumped at a desk, his head buried in his arms.

"It's important to see what people are thinking," H.R. admonished him.

"A bunch of brainwashed yahoos?" Cisco had recovered from his momentary lapse. "Don't care."

H.R. became very serious, pointing his sticks at Cisco in a vaguely threatening manner. "Hey. Those yahoos—lovely word, BTW—are our fellow citizens. They've been manipulated by Pocus, and they deserve our help."

Cisco shrugged, somewhat embarrassed. "Whatever," he mumbled defensively.

"At the pier, when we snapped out of it, we knew *something* was wrong," Caitlin said. Why don't they realize they were being manipulated?"

"Because he's gotten more subtle," Barry said, remembering. "He jump-started them by controlling them, but then put on a show. The Flash versus Hocus Pocus. Made me look like a thief. Made me fight cops. Made me fight *him*. He made himself look good so that no one would think it was weird to applaud for him and hate me."

"For once this is a problem that falls squarely in my wheelhouse." H.R. tucked the sticks into his pocket, stepped behind Barry, and began massaging his shoulders. "Listen up, Barry Allen. Your problem is no longer scientific. It is now an issue of marketing. Of *public relations*, as it were. And that's my bailiwick. My zone. My area of expertise."

"Marketing?" Barry looked up and shrugged H.R.'s hands off.

"Observe." H.R. switched one of the screens to the local news channel. A reporter stood downtown, just outside Broome & Son.

"—scene where Central City's hero, the Flash, performed what some are calling a 'heel turn.' According to eyewitnesses, the Flash entered the store, only to emerge moments later with a bag stuffed full of what we can only assume was jewelry. Owner Jason Broome tells NewsChannel 52 that every item of value had been stolen."

The screen cut to a haggard man identified in the caption as "Jason Broome, Owner—Broome & Son."

"We've been picked clean," Broome said in a voice hoarse with grief and shock.

Back to the reporter. "With hundreds of eyewitnesses to the theft, the Flash has quite a bit of explaining to do," she said seriously. "Back to you in the studio."

"Oh man," Barry mumbled.

The video feed switched to the studio. A middle-aged anchorman gazed sternly out from the TV screen. "No one knows why Central City's Scarlet Speedster would suddenly turn evil," he intoned, "but this turn of events could prove disastrous. No word yet on whether or not Kid Flash is similarly compromised, but if not, he may be our only hope against a speedster run amok."

They cut to a commercial. Cisco muted the TV.

"'A speedster run amok'?" Barry moaned. "Are you kidding me?"

"It's a decent enough play on words," H.R. told him. "But really, this is an issue of perception now. You have a story—a good one—to get out there. You were controlled by a madman."

Caitlin had been silent this whole time, but now she finally spoke. "I don't know, H.R. This is different from anything we've ever faced before. I don't know if we can explain mind control and nanites to people in any way that's convincing. Not on a large scale."

"But Barry's not the only one controlled," Cisco said. "All those people in the crowd, applauding. Wouldn't they be inclined to believe us?"

Caitlin shrugged. "Remember the pier? No one seemed thrown off when they applauded. They seemed a little embarrassed afterward, that's all. I think his control is very subtle. It makes people do things in such an artful way that they don't feel compelled. They just *do it*. As long as it's nothing outlandish, they don't really notice they're being controlled."

"She's right," Barry told them. "It's not like he's hammering away in my head. I just do these things before I even realize it. If I didn't know for a fact I was being controlled, I might think this was all my idea."

Deflated, Cisco sank into a chair next to Barry. "I'm sorry, man. I really am. I've been studying those nanites 24-7 and I'm nowhere. I wish I had better news."

Barry cradled his head in his hands. Once again, it was as though he could feel the nanites in there, even though he knew that was impossible. He was the fastest man alive, but he was frozen into inaction by his own brain.

"I don't know what to do," he admitted.

"Never fear!" H.R. chortled. "I'm on it!" Before anyone could respond, he vanished down the hall, clacking his drumsticks along the walls as he went.

"Well, *that's* comforting," Cisco joked darkly.

"I'll take all the help I can get," Barry confessed.

"I do have a tiny bit of good news," Caitlin said, fidgeting. "Not about your brain, but about your case."

"What case? I'm on leave."

"That blood sample you brought in?"

"Oh, right. I forgot." It had only been an hour or so, but it felt like an eternity.

"It seemed important to you," Caitlin said, tapping at her tablet to bring up some graphs, "so I ran some tests on it while you were gone. Here."

She handed over the tablet, and Barry examined the results. "You ran a TORCH panel to test for different kinds of infections?" he said.

"Well, yeah. I mean, I didn't know who the sample was from, and it might have been an infant or a pregnant woman, so I figured why not, and I found—"

"*T. gondii*," Barry whispered.

Caitlin blinked. "How did you guess? That's on the next screen."

Barry handed the tablet back to her. "I have to call Joe."

"Whoa, hold up!" Cisco pointed the remote at the TV and cranked the volume.

The reporter from earlier was now standing in front of CCPD. A wind stirred her hair. "—being told at this hour," she said, "that CCPD is issuing an all-points bulletin, that's an APB, for the Flash. Here's Captain Singh of the Central City Police Department."

The screen switched to an image of the press briefing room inside the precinct. Flashbulbs popped and voices overlapped as Captain Singh, looking distinctly uncomfortable behind the podium, read from a sheet of paper.

"As of noon today, I have issued an APB for the costumed vigilante commonly known as the Flash. All units and officers are advised that the Flash should be apprehended if seen. Due to his superpowers, the Flash is considered armed and dangerous. Our Tech Unit, with the help of our friends at STAR Labs, will outfit officers with appropriate gear to assist in the arrest." He sighed and rubbed his forehead, then spoke like a man being sent to the electric chair. "I'll take a few questions."

The assembled reporters went wild.

Cisco muted the TV again. "Don't worry, Barry. I'm not going to give them anything that would *actually* help them catch you. No matter what kind of deal we have with the city."

Barry shook his head and watched a muted Singh field questions. "He's ruining both of my lives. That's got to be some kind of record." He turned to Cisco. "And don't you *dare* weaken any of the countermeasures requested by CCPD."

"Are you nuts? You want them to be able to catch you?"

"Let me worry about that. But what if Pocus goes beyond making me his waiter and personal valet? What if he has me do something really bad?"

Caitlin swallowed hard. "I guess then . . . I guess then we really *do* want the police to be able to stop you."

Joe ducked out of the press conference when his phone started buzzing in his pocket. He was grateful for the excuse. He both liked and respected Singh as a man, as a cop, and as a boss. But he couldn't stand watching him sully the Flash's good name and put out an order for the hero's arrest. Was it justified? Probably, based on what little Singh knew, but it still stung for Joe.

He liked to think he would feel the same way even if Barry wasn't his son in every way but genetically.

Before the phone got to the third ring, he'd made it into a hallway just off the press room and answered, "Detective West."

"Joe, it's Barry."

"You seeing this on TV?" Joe checked to make sure no one was eavesdropping. "I'm sorry, Barry. I found out right before he called the press conference, and he wanted me in the room. I couldn't call to give you a heads-up."

"It's OK, Joe." Barry sounded like it wasn't exactly OK, but he wasn't nearly as broken up as Joe expected him to be. "I'm calling about Mitchell MacDonald."

"Who?"

"MacDonald. The guy in the alley this morning, off Waid."

Joe paused at the elevator. Cops milled about. Too open and exposed. He ducked into the fire stairs.

"How do you know his name?" he demanded. "You're off the job."

"Never mind. You need to have the coroner check for an organ transplant. See who prescribed him that prednisone—it's an immunosuppressant."

"Barry . . ."

"We found *T. gondii* antibodies in his blood, Joe." Barry's voice was low and worried. Despite the topic and the circumstances, Joe couldn't suppress a flush of pride. Barry's life was falling apart, and all he cared about was serving justice. "It might actually be a coincidence, because a lot of people walk around with *T. gondii* in their bodies and show no symptoms, but you need to have the coroner confirm whether or not he died from it."

"Right." Joe made a mental note to call the coroner right away, then realized something. "Wait. Wait. How'd you get a blood sample from this dude?"

"Can you really not imagine how?"

Joe blew out his breath. "Man, that's technically illegal. And a violation of the chain of evidence."

"Just think of it as me putting in unpaid overtime, if that helps assuage your conscience. Get on it, OK?"

"You think this is intentional? You think someone has weaponized this worm?"

"I don't know. Can't say without more data. Could be that or could be someone's hunting people who are immunosuppressed for some reason."

Joe nodded. "OK, I'm on it. But Barry—no more stunts like this, you understand? And stay out of the red jammies for a while, at least until we can sort out this Hocus Pocus mess and put this APB to bed."

"I can't make any promises. If people are in trouble—"

"—you're gonna help them. I know. Damn, you're annoying. Where'd you get that stubborn streak?"

Barry chuckled down the phone line. "Look in the mirror sometime, Joe," he said, and hung up.

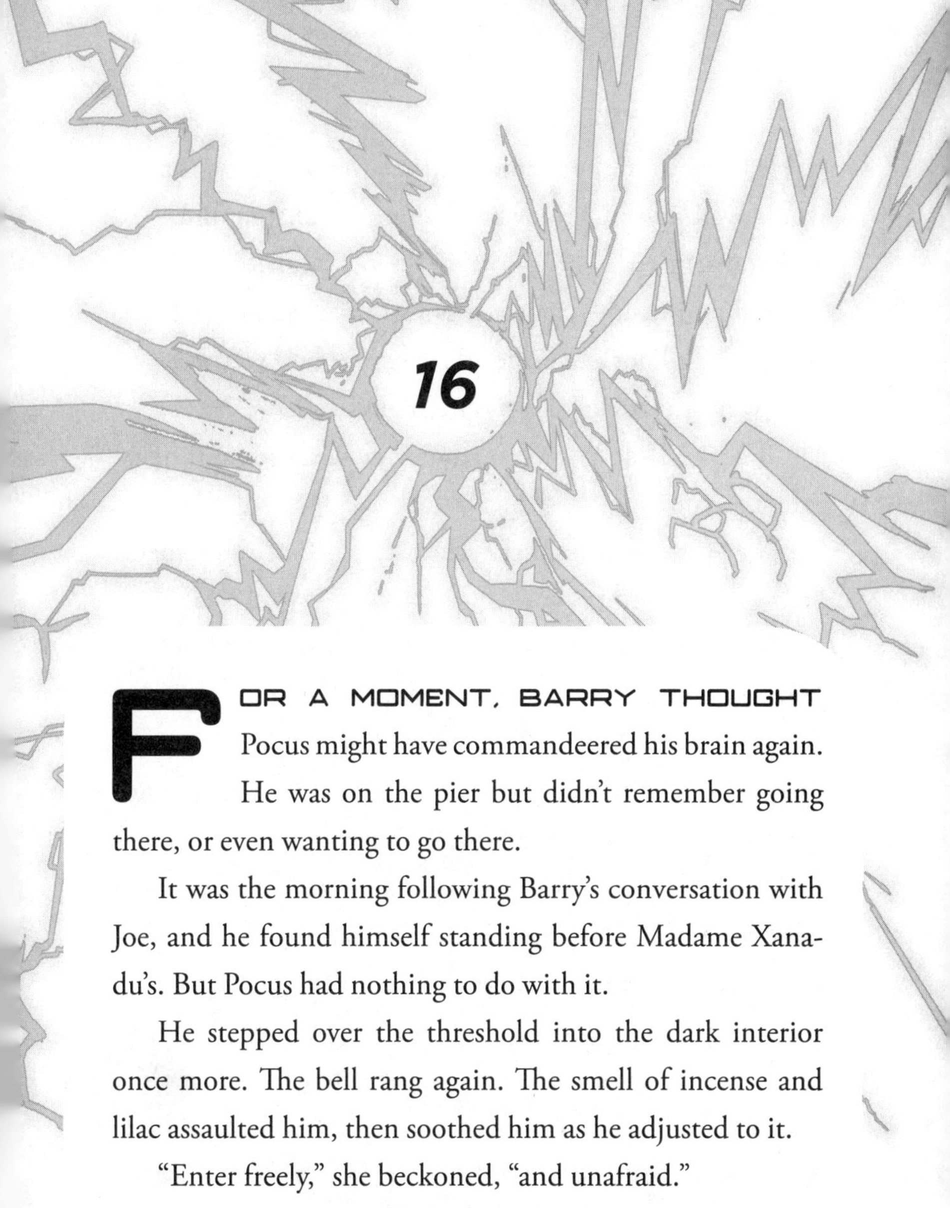

16

FOR A MOMENT, BARRY THOUGHT Pocus might have commandeered his brain again. He was on the pier but didn't remember going there, or even wanting to go there.

It was the morning following Barry's conversation with Joe, and he found himself standing before Madame Xanadu's. But Pocus had nothing to do with it.

He stepped over the threshold into the dark interior once more. The bell rang again. The smell of incense and lilac assaulted him, then soothed him as he adjusted to it.

"Enter freely," she beckoned, "and unafraid."

A part of Barry screamed at him to turn and run, to get away from Madame Xanadu and her craziness, her sheer irrationality. But that part was small and weak, and he knew it. He knew from the moment he saw the OPEN sign that he would walk in and sit down. Nothing could stop him. Not even himself.

Sliding into the chair across from her, he noticed that she'd changed not at all since the last time he'd seen her.

"Welcome back," she said in total sincerity.

"How did you know my name?" he demanded. "I never told it to you."

She pursed her lips; her eyebrows arched in amusement. "How do you think?"

Barry knew quite a bit about so-called mind reading. He'd studied it for a case years ago involving a hypnotist. There was something called cold reading, when a "psychic" used very subtle conversational cues and verbal manipulations to get people to reveal things about themselves without realizing it. For example, one technique was called "shotgunning" because it relied on spreading a lot of information over a large area, much like a shotgun blast. So a so-called psychic might say to a group of people, "I see with my third eye that someone here has a conflict with an older woman." Most people had an older woman in their lives. And *conflict* could be anything from *I hate her* to *She ate the last of the cold cereal this morning*. The "psychic" fires a blast like that, and a bunch of people think, *She's talking about me!*

Even one-on-one, using vague, probing statements—"I sense you are dissatisfied"—and then carefully studying the subject's responses helped a phony psychic fine-tune his or her patter and zero in on the mark's specifics. There were so many ways to "read someone's mind," all of which involved deception, none of which involved actual magic. The more you gave away, the easier it was for the "psychic" to get you to reveal even more. A vicious cycle.

"I can think of a couple ways that don't involve the supernatural," he told her.

"Then surely one of them is your answer."

Her calm and measured tone infuriated him. Yes, there were ways she could have gleaned his name. A hidden camera somewhere with facial recognition software, for example. But it wasn't likely. She had some kind of trick up her sleeve, Barry knew.

"I don't believe in magic," he told her. "I'm a scientist."

"I don't believe in magic, either."

He gestured to encompass the entirety of the inside of her shop—the candles and the cards, the mason jars and the eerie knickknacks. "Then what's all this?"

She mimicked his gesture. "*All this* is how we converse. It is a metaphor. Was there literally a Big Bang at the beginning of the universe, or is that just a convenient way for you to understand the origin of our world?"

He pondered that for a moment. "Were you in Central City a few years ago, when the particle accelerator blew?" If she was a meta, that could explain a lot.

"I wander and roam." She leaned forward intently, those green eyes captivating him. "Discussing my past and my future is, I promise you, vastly less interesting than discussing yours. Isn't that why you've come here?

He sat back and folded his arms over his chest. Before he could stop himself, he told her the truth: "I don't know why I'm here, honestly. But there's nowhere else to go. Not right now."

"You have friends." It was half statement, half accusation.

"I have the greatest friends in the world. But they've done everything they can for me." Cisco and Caitlin were trying to crack the nanite problem. Iris was his rock, his port in the storm that Pocus had created. Wally was patrolling the city as Kid Flash. And Joe was probably even now conspiring to persuade Singh to give that crazy, unreliable Barry Allen another chance. He couldn't ask for better, more committed friends. If all it took was the love of good people to solve his current crop of problems, the knots would have been untangled more quickly than the Flash could run.

"You rely on your friends a great deal."

Xanadu's tone was neutral, but Barry felt recrimination in her words. He sat upright. "Don't most people?" he said defensively. "You don't know my friends. They're some of the most accomplished, passionate people in the world. They—"

"I meant no insult, to them or to you," she said, holding up a hand to quiet him. "I am simply looking for the root of your problem and its solution. If your friends are as capable as you say they are, yet they cannot help you, then what does that tell you about your current predicament?"

Barry worried his lower lip, thinking. What was she getting at? His "current predicament" was something they'd never encountered before. It was hardly the fault of the crew at STAR Labs that Hocus Pocus had mastered a technology so advanced that they couldn't figure out its weakness—or even *if* it had a weakness.

A sharp trill of panic crackled through him like electricity. It *had* to have a weakness, right?

"I'm not sure what you're getting at," he told her. "Shouldn't we just try your cards again?"

"Are you so desperate that you'll try the magic you claim not to believe in?" She favored him with a knowing grin, her eyes sparkling.

Barry blushed. *Was* he that desperate? Or maybe he was just looking for some kind of affirmation. He knew how these boardwalk psychics worked: They told you what you wanted to hear. If you felt guilty because you never got the chance to tell your grandmother how much you loved her before she died, the psychic would conveniently "channel" your grandmother's "spirit" and tell you Grandma had known all along and everything is fine, and blah blah blah, and you can go on with your life guilt free.

In that moment Barry realized just how far he'd fallen. He was seeking solace and succor from a promenade huckster, from this "Madame Xanadu," whose real name was probably Jane Smith. Those crazy, almost glowing green eyes were probably contact lenses. If he turned on the lights in this place, he'd probably see that all the spooky accoutrements were nothing more than cheap plastic baubles bought half off at an after-Halloween sale.

"Thanks for your time," he said finally, rising, "but this was a mistake."

She didn't move a muscle. Didn't even look up at him. Staring down at the table, she said, "You always try to go faster."

Halfway to the door, Barry paused. "What did you say?"

Still she did not move. "You always try to go faster."

"What do you mean by that?" It was true. As the Flash, more speed was always uppermost in his mind. How could he move faster, go harder, save more people, wring more efficiency out of every last microsecond?

She said nothing, gave no answer. Just kept her gaze fixed on the table.

"What are you talking about?" he demanded. "How much do you actually know about me? Who *are* you?"

Still nothing. Fuming, Barry pulled out his chair and flung himself into it. "What's going on here?" His tone, belligerent, shocked even him.

With grinding slowness, Madame Xanadu raised her eyes to his. The green spun from emerald to forest to a glowing sort of lime that entranced him. "What's going on here?" he asked again, this time quietly and with great respect.

"You seek greater speed," she told him. "Always running. Always looking for the quickest path to the horizon."

"That's just . . . what I do." He didn't know what she was getting at. The equation was so simple that it needed no explanation: *Flash = speed.* No variables. Only constants.

"And perhaps now is the time to forsake that."

"And do what? Stop trying to be so fast? How does that help? What does that solve?"

"Go further. Dig deeper."

He pondered. What was *further* or *deeper* than not trying to be faster? It occurred to him instantly but seemed so ridiculous that he was mortified even to say it out loud. Finally, with a good dose of confusion, he said, "You want me to try to . . . be *slow*?"

Lips quirked into something like a smile, Madame Xanadu produced her deck of cards. As she gave them a thorough shuffling, she said, "You wanted to see your future, correct?"

"Why are you changing the topic?"

"Am I?"

Barry groaned, annoyed. But when Madame Xanadu extended the fan of cards to him, he reached for one anyway.

"Only one this time," she admonished.

He hesitated, his fingers hovering at the spread of cards. "Why?"

"You get only one future."

"That's not how I understand it. There are many possible futures, depending on the choices we make."

"Many futures *may* happen," she said with a shrug, "but only one *will* happen."

Barry surprised himself by being nervous about which card to pick. *Stop being an idiot, Allen. She's a carnival trick, that's all. She's not determining your future.*

He chose a card and laid it faceup on the table between them. The card made a dry, authoritative *snap!* as he placed it.

Madame Xanadu closed the remaining cards into a deck and tucked it away. Together, they gazed at the card Barry had chosen.

It was bordered in black and silver, pipes of color twining around each other as they ran the perimeter of the card.

The rest of the card was a bright, clean white, save for a tiny pinprick of black at the very center.

"What does it mean?" Barry asked after a protracted silence. He was captivated by the card. It seemed both familiar and unknowable at once, as though he'd dreamed it and the dream had almost come true.

There was more silence, so he asked again: "What does it mean?" And when Madame Xanadu did not answer, he looked up at her; her face was frozen not in terror, but rather in whatever precedes terror, as though she were about to realize something deeply horrific. "Madame Xanadu? What does this card—"

"I've . . . I've never seen that card before." She barely got the words out, gagging on them.

"You *what*?" Barry threw his hands into the air. "How is that even possible? Isn't this your deck of cards?"

Madame Xanadu chewed at her lower lip and tapped a fingernail next to the card. It was the first time he'd seen her express something like an emotion or a concern. "The deck is complicated. I admit I can't be certain what this means."

"I thought the whole point was that you were seeing my future."

"Some futures cannot be seen. They are too turbulent. Too distant."

"How is that supposed to help me?" When she didn't answer, he waved a hand before her eyes, which were locked on the card. She blinked and gazed up at him as though she'd just woken from a deep slumber.

"Who says it helps you at all? Perhaps the lesson you learn here is that you still control your own destiny."

"I sort of figured that before I got here. I—"

"And now it's time for you to go, Barry."

"Why?"

"Because." With one long, elegantly manicured finger, Madame Xanadu pointed at his pocket.

At that exact moment, Barry's phone rang.

HP sighting! said the text, along with a set of GPS coordinates.

HP was their shorthand for Hocus Pocus, of course. That was bad enough. The next text, though, really made Barry's blood run cold.

It read: *KF en route.*

KF meant Kid Flash.

No, no, no! Barry thought as he fumbled his phone back into his pocket. Without so much as a farewell or a chummy wave to Madame Xanadu, he ran outside. No one was around. No one was looking. He took off at top speed.

STAR Labs was on the other side of the river. There were no boats nearby to be affected by his wake, so Barry took a shortcut, running across the water. He zoomed inside the building and into the Cortex, threw on his Flash costume, and was out the door again before anyone knew he'd been there. Poor Caitlin and Cisco lived in a world in which mysterious gusts scattered their work at a moment's notice. Never mind what he did to their hair on a regular basis, blowing past them all the time.

Wally was almost as fast as Barry was, and he had a head start on his way to confront Pocus. But Barry had an advantage Wally didn't have: Barry had grown up in Central City. Wally had grown up across the bridge in Keystone. Barry knew every street, every avenue, and every alleyway in town.

He intercepted Wally a block away from Hocus Pocus, who was using his mysterious powers/technology to warp a statue of Central City's founder into a larger-than-life statue of himself. A crowd had gathered to cheer him on, of course.

Wally was a yellow streak burning down Gardner Way toward the statue. Barry came up on his left from the central business district, blowing past cars on Fox Boulevard. He grabbed Wally by the crook of his elbow and screeched to a halt, dragging Kid Flash along with him.

"What the—!" Wally spun around and swung a fist blindly. Barry ducked out of the way at the last instant. Lightning crackled over his head.

"Barry!" Wally exclaimed, realizing who'd stopped him. "What are you *doing*, man? I was about to—"

They weren't far from Pocus, and Barry didn't want the magician to see them. In the space of time it took for Wally to say the next word—*get*—he grabbed Kid Flash's hand and ran off at superspeed, dragging the younger man along. Wally was reluctant but reflexively started running, too. Soon, they were exploding out of the Central City limits, onto the open highway that led upstate.

"What are you doing?" Wally asked. "I know you can't get near the guy, but—"

"We're keeping you away from him for a reason, Wally." It had been a few seconds. Pretty soon, they'd hit the Canadian border. Barry turned left; Wally followed suit.

"What reason? Let me kick his butt and sort you out."

"We don't know if kicking his butt will fix me or not. For all we know, he might have some kind of fail-safe in place in case he gets caught. He's got bugs in my brain, Wally." Barry tapped his temple to drive the point home.

They crossed the Rocky Mountains, perfectly warm in the cocoon of their speed. Snow melted, then refroze into silvery footpaths in their wakes.

"I didn't think of that," Wally said, chagrined. "I'm sorry."

"It's not just that," Barry told him. "It's that we can't risk him getting his claws into another speedster. Bad enough he's got me. If he has me do something *really* bad, you're the only one who can stop me."

Wally took four or five seconds to think about that. At their speed, that was a considerable time. They ran so fast that the sun reversed its motion, sliding from west to east. By the time Wally spoke again, they'd crossed the Golden Gate Bridge and run up the Pacific Coast to a bluff overlooking the ocean. A trail of kicked-up dust, grass, and pollen settled slowly behind them.

"Do you really think I can stop you?" Wally's voice quivered with a mixture of pride, anxiety, and a touch of guilt. He stared out at the ocean as the waves rolled in, battering themselves against the shore.

Barry put his hand on Wally's shoulder. "I'm counting on it, Kid Flash."

"So we just let Hocus Pocus keep doing what he's doing? We don't even *try* to stop him?" Wally clenched his fists.

It rubbed Barry the wrong way, too, but he'd already thought about it and come to his decision. "For now? Yeah. Look, so far he's only tried to hurt people when he's been challenged. Everything else he does is just getting attention."

"Or stealing from people," Wally pointed out. "That jewelry store isn't going to be able to stay in business."

"We'll find a way to get their stuff back once we stop him," Barry assured him. "If he starts hurting people, we'll revisit our strategy. But for now, we stay clear. We observe. We try to outthink him and flank him where he doesn't expect it." He slapped Wally on the back. "You're my secret weapon, man. Don't go off too soon, OK?"

Wally kept gazing out at the ocean, at its relentless, hypnotic surge and ebb. Barry was so proud of him, of the way he'd already moved so far along on the transition from impetuous, speed-obsessed kid to becoming a man. Someday, if the information Barry had stumbled upon early in his career was correct, the Flash would disappear from Central City during its time of need, during a great crisis.

It was good to know that his city and his people would have Kid Flash, should that day come.

Wally sucked in his breath, held it, then blew it out. When he turned to Barry, he was grinning. "OK, got it. Race you back to Central?"

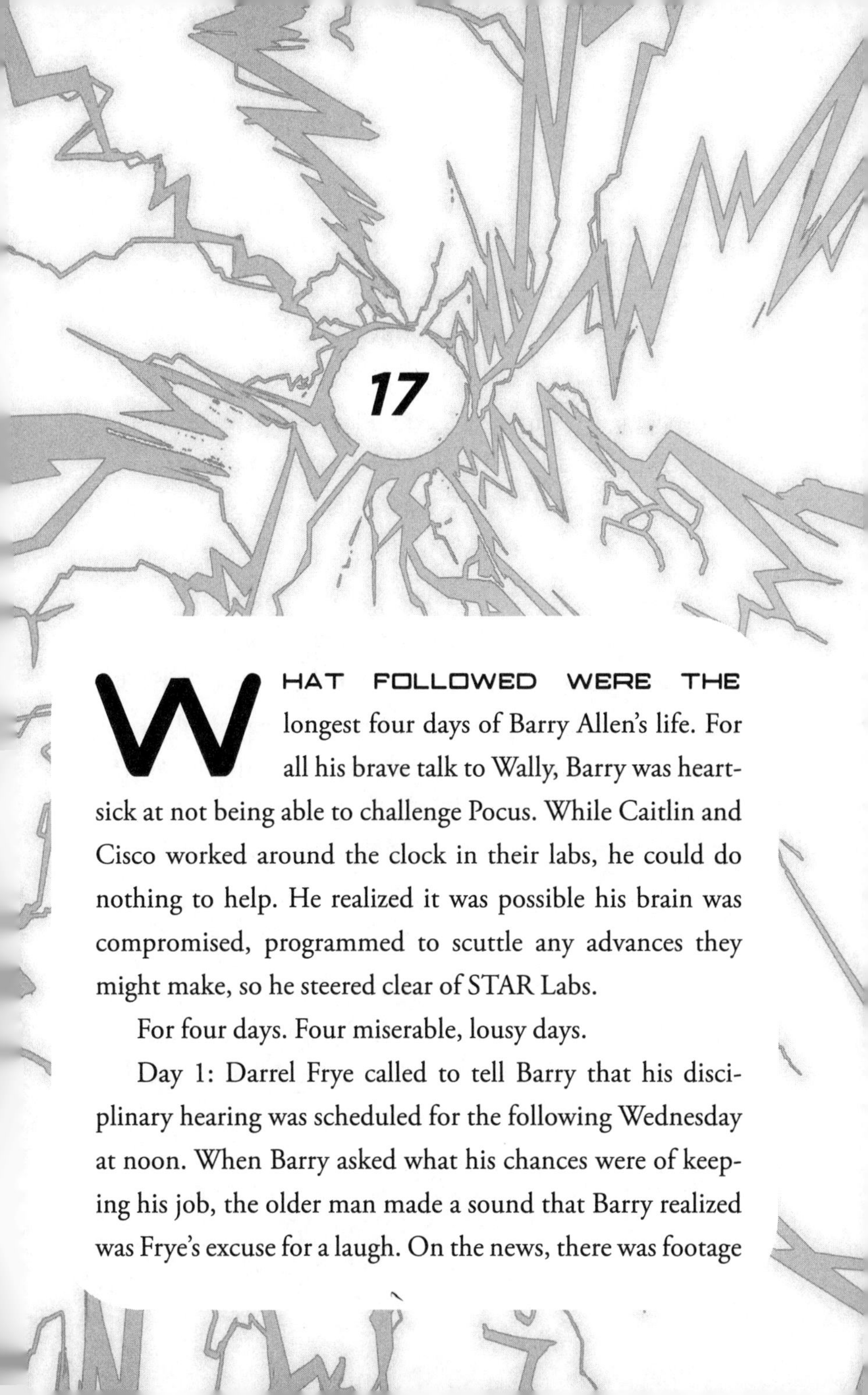

17

WHAT FOLLOWED WERE THE longest four days of Barry Allen's life. For all his brave talk to Wally, Barry was heartsick at not being able to challenge Pocus. While Caitlin and Cisco worked around the clock in their labs, he could do nothing to help. He realized it was possible his brain was compromised, programmed to scuttle any advances they might make, so he steered clear of STAR Labs.

For four days. Four miserable, lousy days.

Day 1: Darrel Frye called to tell Barry that his disciplinary hearing was scheduled for the following Wednesday at noon. When Barry asked what his chances were of keeping his job, the older man made a sound that Barry realized was Frye's excuse for a laugh. On the news, there was footage of Hocus Pocus strolling down Waid Avenue, a crowd following him like the Pied Piper of Hamelin. Pocus pointed the wand at parking meters, and they erupted into blazing bouquets of flame. Applause, applause.

Day 2: CCPD accidentally fired STAR Labs–designed anti-speedster weapons at Kid Flash as he was pulling injured victims from a bus crash near the park. For six seconds—an eternity to a speedster—he was disoriented and couldn't find his footing. With a heroic effort, he managed to save the last victim and then escape from the police, who later issued an apology. "He was moving so fast, he was just a blur," one officer explained. "We thought he was the Flash." On that same day, Hocus Pocus turned a series of billboards on the highway wending past Central City into animated movies promoting his "ASTOUNDING, ASTONISHING FEATS OF THAUMATURGY!" Traffic jams and sixteen accidents ensued as drivers applauded. Fortunately, no one was badly hurt.

Day 3: Pocus hijacked Channel 52's noon news broadcast, making the anchors dance, sing, and perform skits about the glory of his sorcery. He also did about ten minutes of truly lame card tricks, live on the air. Barry buried his head in his hands and moaned.

Day 4: Joe called.

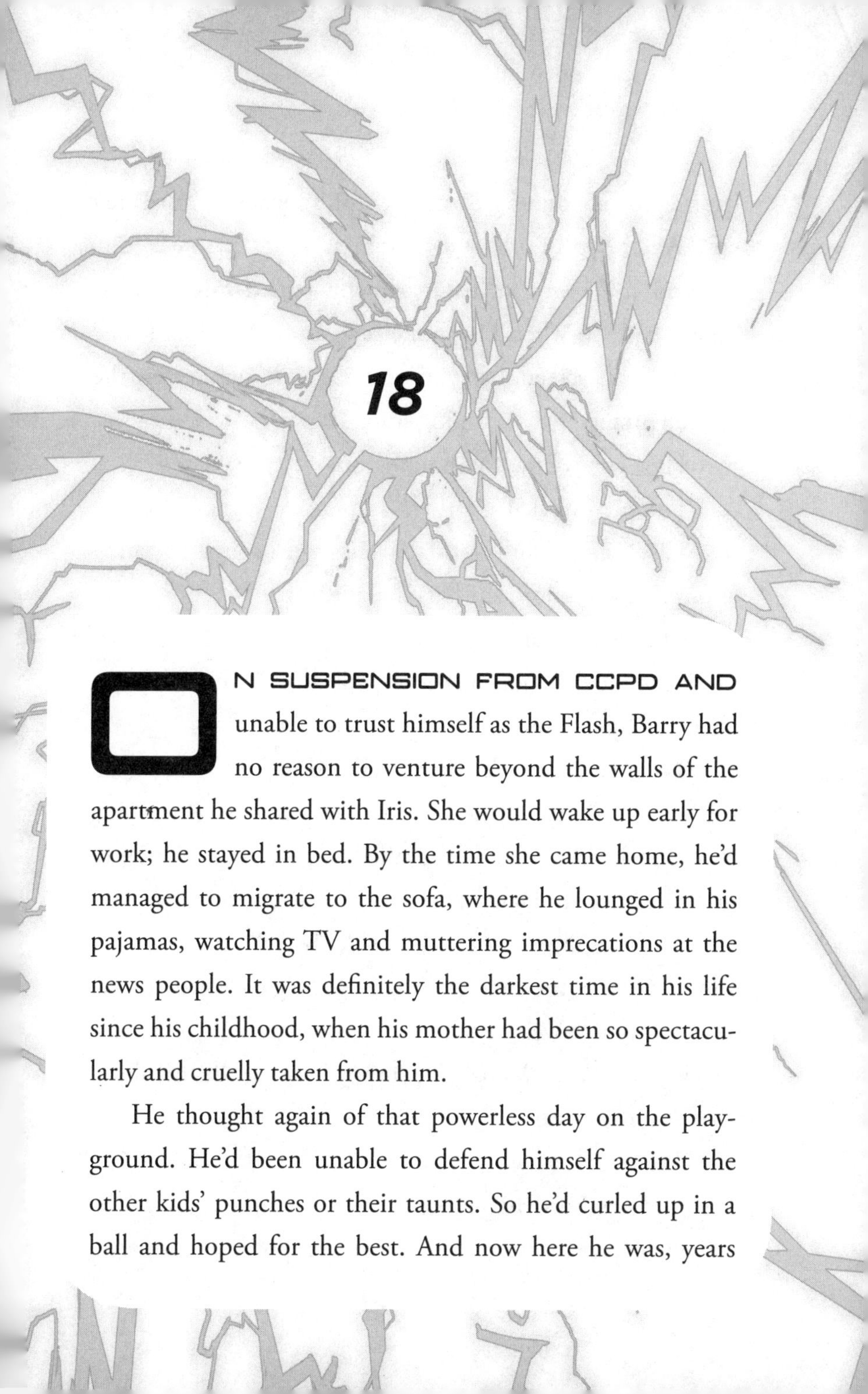

18

On suspension from CCPD and unable to trust himself as the Flash, Barry had no reason to venture beyond the walls of the apartment he shared with Iris. She would wake up early for work; he stayed in bed. By the time she came home, he'd managed to migrate to the sofa, where he lounged in his pajamas, watching TV and muttering imprecations at the news people. It was definitely the darkest time in his life since his childhood, when his mother had been so spectacularly and cruelly taken from him.

He thought again of that powerless day on the playground. He'd been unable to defend himself against the other kids' punches or their taunts. So he'd curled up in a ball and hoped for the best. And now here he was, years later, a grown man. A grown man with superspeed, for Pete's sake! And he still couldn't defend himself.

And so he was in his apartment, curled into a metaphoric ball. So when his phone rang and a picture of Joe's face lit up the screen, Barry dived for it as though it were the last life preserver on a sinking ship.

"Hey, Barry, how you holding up?"

"I'm fine," he lied.

"Cisco and Caitlin still haven't figured out anything about the, you know, the bats in your belfry?"

"They're not bats. And no."

He felt Joe's hesitation through the line. "Well, I was just checking up on you—"

"Nah, you can ask Iris how I'm doing. Why did you really call?" Barry got up from the sofa and started pacing the floor. Maybe Joe had prevailed upon Captain Singh to give him another chance . . .

"It's nothing," Joe said, suddenly self-conscious. "I shouldn't be bothering you. You've got bigger issues to deal with than some weird bodies."

Weird bodies. "Whoa!" He stopped pacing. "Is this about the *T. gondii* deaths?"

"Yeah, but . . ."

Barry grabbed his laptop and slid into a chair at the kitchen bar. He flipped open the computer and opened some files. "I'm on this. Give me what you've got. If I can help, I will."

"Seems like a lot of work."

"It's the easiest thing in the world."

"You must be really desperate for something to take your mind off things," Joe told him.

Barry grunted something noncommittal in order to avoid agreeing. "What have you got?"

Joe took a long, deep breath and then sighed for so long that Barry thought it would never end. At last, he said, "All right, all right, here's the deal: Coroner looked at the new guy, MacDonald, and also the first victim."

Barry had the file open on his computer already. "Ryan Paulson, right?"

"Yep. Hey, wait." Joe's voice went stern. "Do you have backup copies of official police files on your personal computer? That's against—"

"Just a good memory," Barry said, scrolling. "So, the coroner?"

"Oh yeah. Right." He could hear Joe shuffling some papers, could see him—in his mind's eye—flipping pages in his battered old cop's notebook. "So Paulson had a hip replacement but wasn't immunosuppressed at the time of death. MacDonald had no surgeries on record at all—looks like the prednisone we found on him was for bronchitis."

Barry tapped his fingers on the laptop. "That doesn't make any sense. *T. gondii* isn't fatal for most—"

"Wait up. There's more. I said MacDonald had no surgeries *on record.* But the medical examiner found a big ol' surgical scar on his side, and when they opened him up, guess what they found?"

Realization dawned on him like a harsh interrogation room light. "More like what they *didn't* find. A kidney, am I right?"

"Got it in one guess," Joe said. "Missing a kidney. M.E. says it was a decent enough removal, not a butcher job, but there's zero record anywhere of MacDonald having a kidney removed."

Barry stood up and started pacing again. "So someone must have done it illegally."

"And then patched the guy up and sent him out into the world. And get this: Paulson had a scar over his abdomen. Barry: his *stomach* was missing. I don't even know how that's possible!"

"Well, in some extreme cases, surgeons bypass the stomach entirely and connect the small intestine right to the esophagus." It was called a total gastrectomy, and it usually happened only when the patient had advanced stomach cancer. But that wasn't the point, Barry realized, because no one would perform such an operation and then let the patient wander off. "Where was Paulson found? Near the recycling plant, right?"

"Yep. How did we miss this?"

Barry scrolled through his files. "Well, we were going too fast . . ." He stopped himself even as the words tumbled out of his mouth.

You always try to go faster. That's what Madame Xanadu had said, and she'd made it sound like a bad thing. Which had befuddled him, but now Barry thought maybe he was beginning to understand.

"We moved too quickly," he said. "I got the blood samples from Paulson so fast and checked them . . . I saw something strange and assumed it was the answer, not just a clue."

"And then when you saw the same thing in MacDonald . . ."

"Confirmation bias," Barry admitted. "Seeing what I wanted to see, not what was actually there. If we'd waited for the M.E.'s report first, I might have gone into it with a different perspective. But the M.E. is always backed up, and I always think I can figure it out faster, don't I?" He slammed a fist on the table. "I'm such an idiot! Singh is totally right to fire me!"

"Hey!" Joe snapped at him. "I don't want to hear that kind of talk from you! You got me?"

Barry said nothing, fuming at himself.

“You goofed,” Joe said. “It happens. But what sets you apart from other people, Barry, is that when you get evidence to the contrary, you don’t just charge ahead with your original thought. You actually change your mind. And that’s a rare thing in this world.”

He didn’t want to admit that Joe could be right. It seemed easier to wallow in self-pity and anger. But what Joe described was nothing more than the scientific method, the basis of Barry’s entire life. You propose a hypothesis. You test it. If it’s right, great. If it’s wrong, you adjust and keep testing. You don’t stick to a wrong hypothesis just because you like it or because you’re invested in it. You let the world be the world and change your mind to fit the facts, not the other way around.

That’s what he’d done all his life. And that’s what he would keep doing.

“So let’s think about this,” he said. “Paulson was found at the recycling plant.” He closed his eyes. “And MacDonald was found at—”

“In the alleyway,” Joe told him.

“Right,” Barry said. “I’m there right now.”

And he was. He’d sped over in the microseconds it took Joe to interrupt him.

There was nothing special about the alley. He remembered the puddle—now dried up—in a divot of pavement not far from where the body had been found. That, combined with the dampness on MacDonald's leg, had convinced him that someone had dragged MacDonald in from a particular direction.

But what if that snap judgment was wrong? What if he was going too fast?

"Slow down, Allen," he muttered to himself, and he took a turn around the alley, eyes narrowed, searching for . . .

Well, he didn't know what for.

"Anything?" Joe asked.

Barry blinked. He grinned. He told Joe to wait a moment, then got down on his hands and knees. Not far from the divot, a large Dumpster lurked against the exterior brick wall of the grocery store. He got down on his hands and knees. The Dumpster was on wheels, and from this vantage point, he could see very, very light tracks in the filth of the alley floor. The Dumpster had been pushed into a different position, and recently, too—the wheels still glimmered with wet grime.

Barry got down lower, lying on his stomach, not caring that his clothes were getting dirty. In the light from his cell phone, the area under the Dumpster leaped into shadowy relief.

And there he found exactly what he was looking for.

"Joe," he said, scrambling to his feet, "get down here—*fast*!"

Joe crouched down, one hand pressed against the Dumpster, trying to look underneath without getting any alley grunge on his suit.

"You have to really flatten yourself," Barry told him, pacing the alleyway, biting his thumbnail.

"Man, this is a six-hundred-dollar suit," Joe complained, straightening up. "I'm not scuzzing it up. I'll take your word for it—there's a sewer grate under there."

"It looks like one of the old ones," Barry told him, "from before the big infrastructure remodel back in the eighties."

Joe giggled deep in his throat. "And now you're also an expert on Central City's sewer system?"

"Well . . ." Barry blushed. "I know some things about some things, OK? Anyway, they put in new, more efficient grates around the city, but in a lot of situations, they left the old ones in place, too, so if we had a big flood, they would have additional capacity."

"I can't believe you know these things."

"Joe, come on!" Barry pushed at the Dumpster, but it wouldn't budge. "See this? Whoever moved it is really strong. And he pushed it aside, hauled MacDonald up from the sewers, and left him here. Someone dragged both of these guys down into the sewers, performed meatball surgery on them for their organs, and then tossed them aside. And before they died from complications due to the removal, they picked up a huge amount of *T. gondii* because they're down there in the sewage."

Joe tapped his pen against his notebook, thinking. "You think this is related to Mr. Presto Changeo with the wand?"

"Hocus Pocus? Doubt it. This isn't his style. He's a vain glory hound chasing the adrenaline high of a standing ovation. This other one . . . I don't even know where to start with it."

"Great." Joe heaved out a sigh and threw his hands into the air. "Just great. Two of these bozos running around at the same time."

"You need to check records," Barry said very seriously. "Go back six months. Maybe even a year. See if any other bodies with removed organs showed up. Unsolved cases. The M.E. said the surgery wasn't slapdash—the victims might have died of something else, so the surgery was ignored."

"I'll get on it." Joe turned to leave, then turned back. "What are *you* gonna do?"

"Me?" Barry asked with wide-eyed innocence. "Nothing at all. Go home. Watch TV."

As soon as Joe was gone, Barry made sure no one was watching him. He ran several circuits of the alleyway, building up enough momentum, before flinging himself at the Dumpster.

A loud *CLONG!* reverberated in the alley and in his skull, but it was worth it: The Dumpster skidded several feet, screeching along the pavement. Barry marveled at the strength of whoever had moved it originally to conceal the grate. Definitely a meta. A strong one.

Not his favorite kind.

With the grate now exposed, he knelt down and examined it. The lug nuts that locked it down had been removed. Yeah, someone was definitely using the sewers.

He hauled up the grate. It was cast iron and heavy, but with some effort and a fair amount of grunting, Barry was able to wrestle it from its grooves and slide it to one side, giving him access to the sewer below. In the light of his cell phone, the sewer plunged down into fetid darkness. Grimy rungs disappeared into the abyss. Spots along the rungs had been wiped almost clean by someone climbing.

He took pictures of the clean spots and what appeared to be partial imprints from shoes. Just in case. Not really enough to investigate, but it might be helpful later.

"Well, Allen, what else were you gonna do today?" he asked himself, thinking of the apartment, the sofa, the TV.

Hocus Pocus.

Might as well do something useful, if disgusting.

With a sigh and a deep breath, he climbed down the ladder. The sky shrank to a disk overhead, and then, as he descended farther, a dot above him. He thought of the mysterious card he'd drawn at Madame Xanadu's. But that had been a black dot on a white field, not this shrinking beacon of fresh air and light against the murk of the sewer.

The lower he went, the stronger the stench of effluvia and waste grew. He gagged, then took a moment to pull his

T-shirt up over his mouth and nose. Breathing through the fabric helped a little bit.

Just as Barry was wondering how deep the sewer went, his left foot, questing for the next rung, splashed into something viscous and in sludgy motion. Gross. He'd just stepped in sewage. And these were his favorite sneakers—a gift from Iris.

Oh well. Life with superpowers means getting dirty sometimes.

Barry held up his phone to peer into the murk. The tunnel ran from his left to his right, a slow-moving braid of mucky water trickling around and past him. Which way to go, upstream or downstream?

At superspeed, he could check both pretty quickly, but he didn't relish the idea of kicking up a backwash of gross sewage.

Then he spotted something off to his right, downstream. Creeping closer, walking like someone who's spent too long on horseback, in order to straddle the sewage, he came upon a chunk of concrete missing from the wall. It had crumbled here and collapsed into the sewage, sticking up like an island, the size of a small toaster, maybe.

The chunk of concrete wasn't interesting at all. But what lay *next* to it, shielded from the slow current of effluvia, was *very* interesting.

A shoe.

To be specific: a brown tasseled loafer, worn and threadbare. Left foot. Size 10½, EEE.

Barry hadn't conducted any tests, but he was positive: This was Mitchell MacDonald's missing shoe.

It couldn't have fallen down the sewer grate—the gaps between slats are too narrow. He had to have been down here. And since there was no sewage or filth on his body, someone carried him through here to dispose of the body up in the alleyway. But his shoe caught on the concrete and fell off . . .

Barry continued downstream, shadows leaping and jittering around him from the fragile light of his cell phone. Some part of him thought to call the gang at STAR Labs, just in case.

You don't need backup, he told himself. *You're the Flash! You're just getting nervous because it's creepy down here. Looks like a weird first-person shooter with the brightness level out of whack.*

He kept moving.

The tunnel tightened a bit as he proceeded; small pipes overhead merged into large pipes, reducing the head space. Crouching and ducking, he made his way deeper into the sewer system. So far, there were no other clues. He'd hoped for something else. Maybe something that had fallen out of MacDonald's pocket. A clue that he was on the right path.

Above the trickle of running sewage, he heard something else. Something between a gasp and a snort. It was vaguely porcine, piglike, he thought, and it was coming from right ahead.

Moving slowly, so as not to make any noise, Barry continued down the tunnel. It narrowed further, such that his shoulder brushed against the sides as he moved. He grimaced in revulsion as something grossly dun-colored rubbed off on his shirt. He frowned and futilely tried to wipe it off. Now his hand was disgusting. He wiped it on his jeans. All he accomplished was making them dirty, too.

Another noise caught his attention. A rustling. Up ahead. He aimed his light in that direction and—

—something—

Something moved there. At first he thought it was a shadow cast by his moving light, but then he caught a glimpse of what had to be arms and legs, though they seemed attenuated to an extreme. Maybe it was the angle, the lighting, the shadows. It was a person—painfully thin and tall but crunched into an unnatural position, contorted to move through the tunnels.

A flash of wan, jaundiced yellow went by in the murk, lit momentarily as it passed before his cell phone. Barry heard a hiss of anger, of derision, and then the person vanished before his eyes.

Barry blinked in shock. Where had he—she—it—gone?

A moment later, he had his answer: There was an intersecting tunnel up ahead.

But when Barry got there, he saw that the offshoot tunnel was a much, much tighter squeeze than the one in which he stood. Barry couldn't imagine how he could fit in it. A crushing sense of claustrophobia gripped him at the mere thought of it.

Peering down the tunnel, he saw nothing but a gradation spiraling into darkness. Whoever had run in front of him had had no trouble fitting into the tunnel and had moved through it incredibly quickly. Not Flash-fast, but really speedy for such a dark, tight spot.

What in the world am I dealing with here?

He had no more time for the question. His cell phone dinged its text message tone:

Get back to STAR!

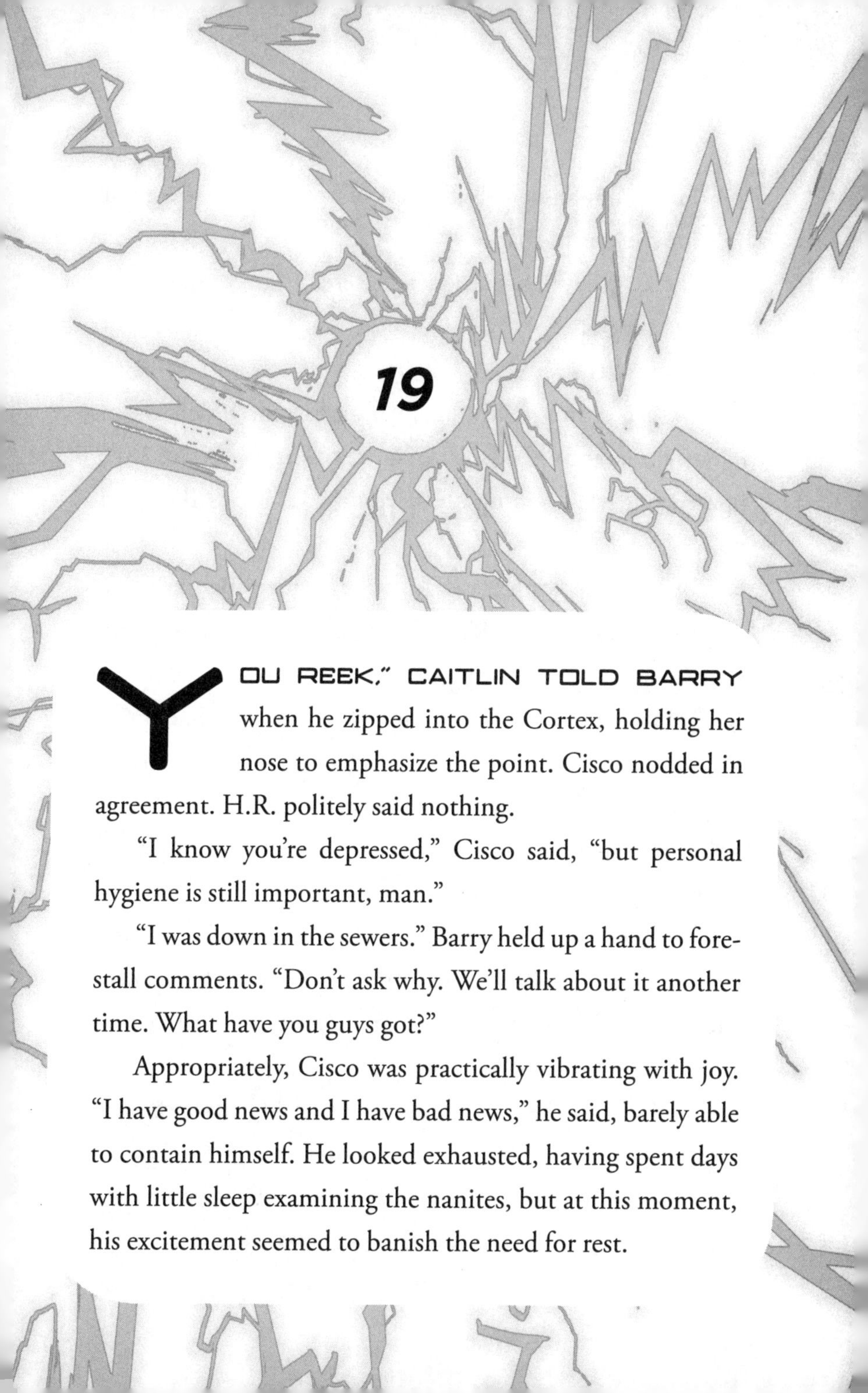

19

"YOU REEK," CAITLIN TOLD BARRY when he zipped into the Cortex, holding her nose to emphasize the point. Cisco nodded in agreement. H.R. politely said nothing.

"I know you're depressed," Cisco said, "but personal hygiene is still important, man."

"I was down in the sewers." Barry held up a hand to fore-stall comments. "Don't ask why. We'll talk about it another time. What have you guys got?"

Appropriately, Cisco was practically vibrating with joy. "I have good news and I have bad news," he said, barely able to contain himself. He looked exhausted, having spent days with little sleep examining the nanites, but at this moment, his excitement seemed to banish the need for rest.

"Given how psyched you look, I'm assuming the good news outweighs the bad?"

Cisco's grin flickered, then faltered. "They're actually one and the same."

"I don't get it."

Cisco gestured to the main monitor, on which was a blown-up image of one of the nanites in Barry's brain. "I've figured out what's going on in your head. That's the good news."

"What's the bad news?" A chill ran down Barry's spine and then back up. He didn't like the notion of *bad news* and *your brain* being in close proximity.

"Let me get to it," Cisco said. "The nanites are designed to peter out after a certain period of time. They have a built-in life span. It's probably a security measure on Pocus's part, so that if he does some kind of weird whammy on something, it doesn't linger too long."

That made sense; it explained why Caitlin and Cisco and everyone else who had applauded Pocus eventually regained their senses. It also explained why the trees had stopped on their own at the park, for example.

"Why am I the lucky one? I'm assuming that's the bad news."

"It's, uh, transitional news. It turns out that when the nanites interact with the Speed Force buzzing through your system, their life span stays the same, but their life *cycle* accelerates. So they . . ."

Barry groaned. He got it. "Usually, they die before they can reproduce. But in *my* body, they reproduce faster than they die."

"Yeah, pretty much." Cisco sighed. "You probably have generations of nanites in your brain."

"Good thing we've been keeping Wally away from him," Barry muttered.

"Good thing, indeed!" H.R. chimed in.

"You'll get your turn in a minute," Cisco said darkly, then turned back to the monitor. "So, that's the good news—we know the basics of why these things are still in your head. The bad news is . . . I still don't know how to get them out."

"Cisco! Come on!" Barry complained. "You're the tech guy! This is what you do!"

Cisco threw his hands up in the air, his face twisted into total frustration. "Tell me something I don't know, fleet-feet! It's not like we can just open up your head and pluck them out one at a time with a pair of tweezers. These things are a billion times more complicated than anything I've ever seen before. I figured out this much just by constant observation, watching the recording of your scans over and over, looking for patterns. I can't even get inside one to see how it ticks."

“Why not?” It was unfair of Barry to expect so much of his friend, he knew, but he was beyond frustrated—he was increasingly desperate. He had to get these things out of his head before Pocus could use him for something truly evil.

Cisco looked around the room as though an answer was written somewhere on the walls. Finally, he said, “It’s like . . . Imagine if someone asked you to hack a computer. Only there’s no USB port. And no keyboard. And no monitor. And there are no cables going in or out. There’s nowhere to start, you know? You just have this thing sitting there and you can’t get into it at all.”

“It’s like trying to unlock a door when there’s no lock,” H.R. offered.

“Very Zen of you,” Cisco said, and flung himself into a chair.

“So we have nothing.”

“That’s not fair,” Caitlin told Barry. “We have more than we had before. We need more time.”

“I’m running out of time,” Barry told them. “CCPD is hunting me, and Pocus’s slowly taking over the city. And we can’t stop him.”

“This is where *I* come in!” said H.R., rat-a-tatting a rhythm on the desk before him. “For *I* have the solution to at least one of your problems.”

"Are you going to talk the nanites out of my head?" Barry asked.

"You should actually listen to him," Cisco said with considerable effort. "He has a good idea."

Barry sighed. "I'm sorry. Go ahead, H.R."

H.R. stood, beaming. He clacked the drumsticks together, then jammed them into his back pocket and clapped once. "I told you before that you have a public relations problem. I'm going to fix it. Today." He checked his watch. "In about thirty-seven minutes, to be exact."

Barry opened his mouth. Cisco shushed him. "Listen."

"You have the people of Central City against you, the cops chasing you. This is a considerable problem. If you could move about more freely, you might be able to confront Hocus Pocus a bit more forcefully. So we need to get the city back on your side and the cops off your back."

"Agreed. How do we do that?"

H.R. shrugged. "You just explain your side of the story."

Barry waited. He knew more would come.

H.R. did not disappoint. "You need to get a huge number of people talking about you and what happened to you. Richard Dawkins—" He paused. "Do you guys have a Richard Dawkins on Earth 1?"

"We do," Cisco said wearily. "Please, speed up."

“Anyway,” H.R. went on cheerfully, “Dawkins was the first person to define a *meme*. He called it an idea that spreads through the community in an ‘unplanned and effortless way.’”

“How does this help me?”

“We need to make your explanation a meme so that it will spread throughout the city like a cold virus in January,” H.R. said, getting more excited. “Cisco! Show him the . . . the . . . the thing!”

Cisco tapped some keys, and the main monitor switched to a view of Julius Stadium, where the Central City Diamonds played. (They’d been the Central City Combines until the Flash started arresting people. Then they changed their name.)

“What does the stadium have to do with convincing people I’m not a bad guy?” Barry asked.

“In”—H.R. checked his watch again—“thirty-one minutes, the local batball team will start its game against—”

“Baseball,” Caitlin told him.

“What?”

“Baseball. Not *batball*.”

“Really?” H.R. seemed incredibly put off by this. “Are you sure? *Batball* makes so much more—”

“Guys! Can we please focus?”

H.R. drew in a deep breath, smiled, and said, "Sure. Here's what we're going to do . . ."

By the time H.R. finished explaining, Barry had twelve minutes to get to the stadium and put the plan into action. That gave him just enough time to take a quick shower and wash the stench of the sewers off before donning his Flash costume and racing to the ballpark.

The plan was simple and, Barry had to admit, sensible. They needed a way to explain his side of the story to the people of Central City without interference. There would be a crowd of fifty thousand at Julius Stadium. Barry would go there, and Cisco would hack into the A/V system. Barry would explain what was happening to him to fifty thousand observers on the stadium's jumbotron.

"Those people," H.R. explained giddily, "whether they believe you or not—and many will—will tweet and message and post and snap about what you said. Through the magic of memes and the glorious Internet, your side of the story will be instantly signal-boosted by fifty thousand people. In no time at all, most of Central City will know what you've said."

"I still think we should just broadcast from here," Cisco grumbled.

“People need to see *him*,” H.R. replied. “They need to know he’s willing to come to them in person, in the flesh. It makes this more than just another video broadcast to the world—it becomes an *event*.”

“H.R.’s right,” Barry said. “It needs to be in person. They need to see me and trust me again.”

It was a solid plan. Barry spent the ten seconds it took for him to get to the stadium rehearsing what he would say. He wanted to keep it simple and short so that it would make an impression.

And he also didn’t want to delay the game. Who likes the jerk who does *that*?

He circled the stadium and ran past security at top speed. Once inside, he navigated the complicated series of ramps and stairways until he emerged on the field.

“Cisco, talk to me.”

In his ear, Cisco said, “OK, I’m patched in. Find the nearest cameraman and start yakking.”

Barry scanned the field quickly. “The nearest camera-man is a woman, you sexist.”

“Mea culpa.”

He ran to the camera operator, who nearly dropped her rig at the surprise of seeing the Flash materialize before her. “Hi, there!” he said. “Sorry to scare you. I just need to borrow you for a sec, OK?”

Mute with shock, she nodded and kept her camera aimed at him.

"Central City!" the Flash said, trying not to flinch as his voice suddenly rang out and echoed throughout the stadium. The crowd went insane—a cacophony of overlapping cheers and boos, depending on how people felt about the Flash right then, whether they believed the news or not. Behind him, reflected in the camera lens, was his own image, blown up over a hundred times on the jumbotron.

"I won't take much of your time," he said, vibrating his voice. "I'm a Diamonds fan, too." That got him some cheers.

"I know you've seen some pretty disturbing stories about me lately. And I want to explain. You see—"

"HALT!" cried a too-familiar voice that sent shivers down the Flash's back.

Barry turned. Hovering a few feet above the field, Hocus Pocus lowered himself to the ground with a grand flourish.

No! Not now!

"THERE IS NOTHING TO EXPLAIN!" Pocus boomed. He didn't need to hack the A/V system to make his voice heard. It shook the stadium. "YOUR HERO IS A HERO NO LONGER. NOW, THANKS TO HOCUS POCUS, YOU SEE HIS TRUE NATURE! HE IS A VILLAIN, THROUGH AND THROUGH!"

"Like *you*!" Barry snarled at Pocus. Thanks to Cisco's hack, everyone in the stadium could hear it.

Pocus's lip curled in annoyance. He flicked his wand in the direction of the jumbotron, and it exploded into a massive fireball shot through with lightning bolts. Shards of glass and bits of metal rained down on the crowd seated below it. The air filled with screams and gasps.

The Flash adjusted his stance, ready to race up the wall beyond the dirt warning track. He would use a combination of arm-spinning wind blasts and Flash-made tornadoes to divert the debris from the innocents below.

"Not so fast," Pocus said, tsking. Against his will, Barry found himself frozen again, helpless, only able to watch as the debris rained down . . .

. . . and suddenly turned into flower petals, showering the crowd with blossoms.

A surprised and genuine round of applause erupted from the crowd at Julius Stadium. They started chanting Hocus Pocus's name.

Barry looked at the magician. He seemed to be moved. For the first time, people were applauding him without his control.

This is all he wanted.

"Now I understand," Pocus whispered. Tears glittered in his eyes as he approached Barry, still motionless. "They love you like this, don't they? Or, they did."

"See, Pocus? You don't have to *force* people. If you do good, they'll naturally . . ."

Pocus wiped the tears from his eyes and leaned in close, his voice a snarl. "There can be no competition for their affection, do you hear me? None! I won't let you take it from me!"

"But—"

"Kill them," Pocus ordered. "Kill every single person in the stands. And when I am the one to end your murder spree, this city will worship me *forever*."

No, Barry thought. *No!*

He couldn't do it. He *wouldn't* do it!

He was a hero. Heroes didn't kill. But beyond that, he was just a good person! You didn't need superpowers to know that killing was wrong, and he just couldn't . . .

But as soon as Pocus said *Kill them*, Barry knew he would have no choice, no matter how stomach-turning and horrific the notion. The nanites in his brain made him incapable of resisting Pocus's commands, even one so pernicious and evil as this one. Barry was about to wipe out fifty thousand people, and nothing could stop him.

Except . . .

The Flash didn't just move fast—he could also *think* fast.

Good thing.

In the nanoseconds after Pocus gave his command, as Barry felt his limbs loosen and freedom of movement return, a thought popped into his head at superspeed.

Not so fast.

That's what Pocus had said when he was about to rescue people from the exploding jumbotron.

Not so fast.

And that made him remember—again, in the fractions of a second between the command and the instant he would take off to claim his first victim—his conversation with Madame Xanadu.

You seek greater speed, she had said. *Always running. Always looking for the quickest path to the horizon. And perhaps now is the time to forsake that.*

He hadn't understood. *And do what?* he'd asked. *Stop trying to be so fast? How does that help? What does that solve?*

She'd exhorted him: *Go further. Dig deeper.*

And he, perplexed, had said, *You want me to try to . . . be slow?*

The Flash looked into the crowd. Fifty thousand people. He had to start somewhere.

He picked a woman in the last, highest row at the farthest point of the stadium from where he stood. And he took his first step toward her.

And then he took his second step toward her.

He moved very, very slowly. It took him almost ten seconds to walk those two steps.

"What are you doing?" Hocus Pocus bit into each word like it was overripe fruit, his teeth clenched, his breath hissing in outrage.

"I'm doing what you told me to do," the Flash replied. "I'm going to go kill everyone here. I'm starting with her." He pointed to his chosen victim. He shrugged. "It might take a while."

Pocus's eyebrows shot up, and his expression contorted into sheer fury. "What are you doing?" he ranted. "You're faster than that!"

"I'm going to do exactly what you told me to do," Barry said with easygoing reasonableness. "I'm just getting a slow start, I guess."

Pocus stared, discombobulated, unable to move or speak for several more seconds as the Flash very slowly and very casually ambled another few steps toward his target.

"Go faster!" Pocus screamed.

Despite himself, Barry grinned. *You didn't say* how much *faster*. At the rate he was going, the people in the stadium would die of old age before he got to them.

He walked a tiny bit faster, enjoying the look of sheer, uncontrollable rage on Hocus Pocus's face. The man's mustache points were quivering. There was a chance, of course, that Pocus would wise up and order Barry to move as fast as he could. But he was relying on his experience with Pocus so far—the man had such power that he didn't seem to understand strategic thinking. Pocus probably didn't think he needed to, given his abilities. Barry was betting that the Flash's apparent denial of an outright order would infuse Pocus with so much ire that the magician wouldn't be able to think straight.

Sure enough—and to Barry's relief—Pocus fell into a rant of unintelligible monosyllables, almost like a toddler's temper tantrum. Barry allowed himself a silent chuckle as he inched farther and farther across the field. It would take him the rest of the day to get to his first "victim."

Better yet, Barry noticed that people were beginning to stream out of the stadium through the exits. Someone somewhere had called an evacuation, and Barry was grateful for it. If he could keep stalling Pocus, they might end up facing an empty stadium, with no victims to be found.

But just then, Pocus shouted, "You think you're so smart? You think you're smarter than me?"

Smarter than I am, Barry silently corrected.

"Turn around! Now!"

When Barry turned, he was facing not just Pocus, but also the camera operator, who was standing only a few feet away, aiming the camera right at him.

"Tell him who's watching," Pocus ordered her.

"Everyone watching the smaller screens here," she said automatically. Barry glanced around. The jumbotron had become flowers, but there were about a dozen smaller screens mounted on the balustrades around the park. "And everyone watching the game on the national feed." She paused. "Millions."

"Excellent!" Pocus chortled. "Flash! Take off your mask! *Right now!*"

And Barry did.

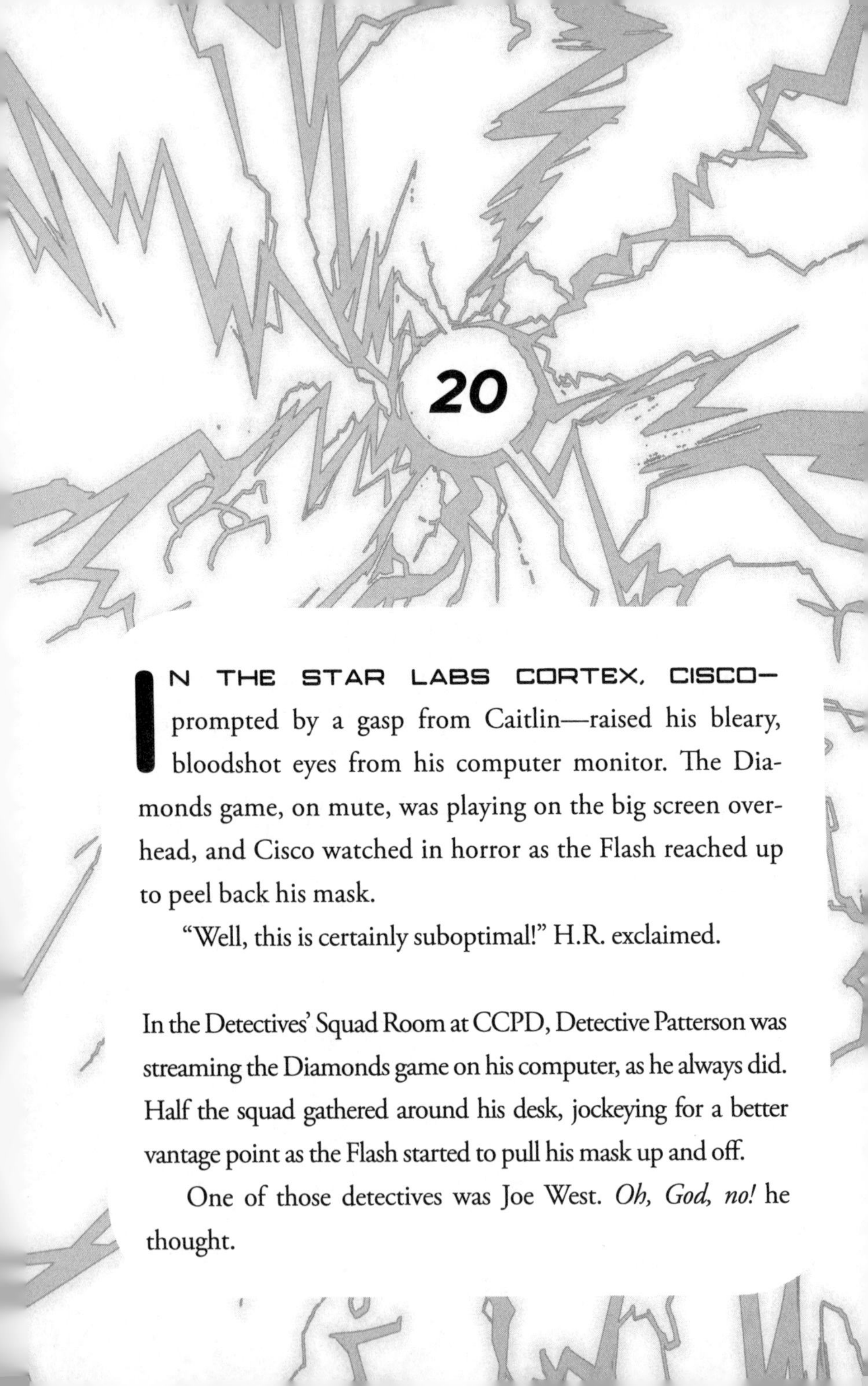

20

IN THE STAR LABS CORTEX, CISCO—prompted by a gasp from Caitlin—raised his bleary, bloodshot eyes from his computer monitor. The Diamonds game, on mute, was playing on the big screen overhead, and Cisco watched in horror as the Flash reached up to peel back his mask.

"Well, this is certainly suboptimal!" H.R. exclaimed.

In the Detectives' Squad Room at CCPD, Detective Patterson was streaming the Diamonds game on his computer, as he always did. Half the squad gathered around his desk, jockeying for a better vantage point as the Flash started to pull his mask up and off.

One of those detectives was Joe West. *Oh, God, no!* he thought.

The newsroom at the *Central City Picture News* had multiple monitors arrayed along the walls of the main writers' bullpen. One of them—Iris thought of it as the Linda Park Memorial TV—was always tuned to the local sports team. At the moment, it was playing the Diamonds game, and Iris couldn't care less. She was up against a deadline and trying her best to channel her boyfriend's speed as she typed away.

But then Scott Evans, the editor-in-chief of the *Picture News*, strolled into the bullpen and said, "Oh my. Look at *that*."

Iris looked up just in time to see the Flash, in an extreme close-up, stripping off his mask. Her heart stopped.

No, she thought. *No, no, no, no.*

Between classes at the university, Wally noticed a group of students clustered together on the quad. Curious, he approached them, noticing that they were all gathered around one particular student with a cell phone.

They were watching a live feed from Julius Stadium.

And there was Barry, about to remove his mask. On video broadcast over the air and across the Internet. To millions of people all over the world.

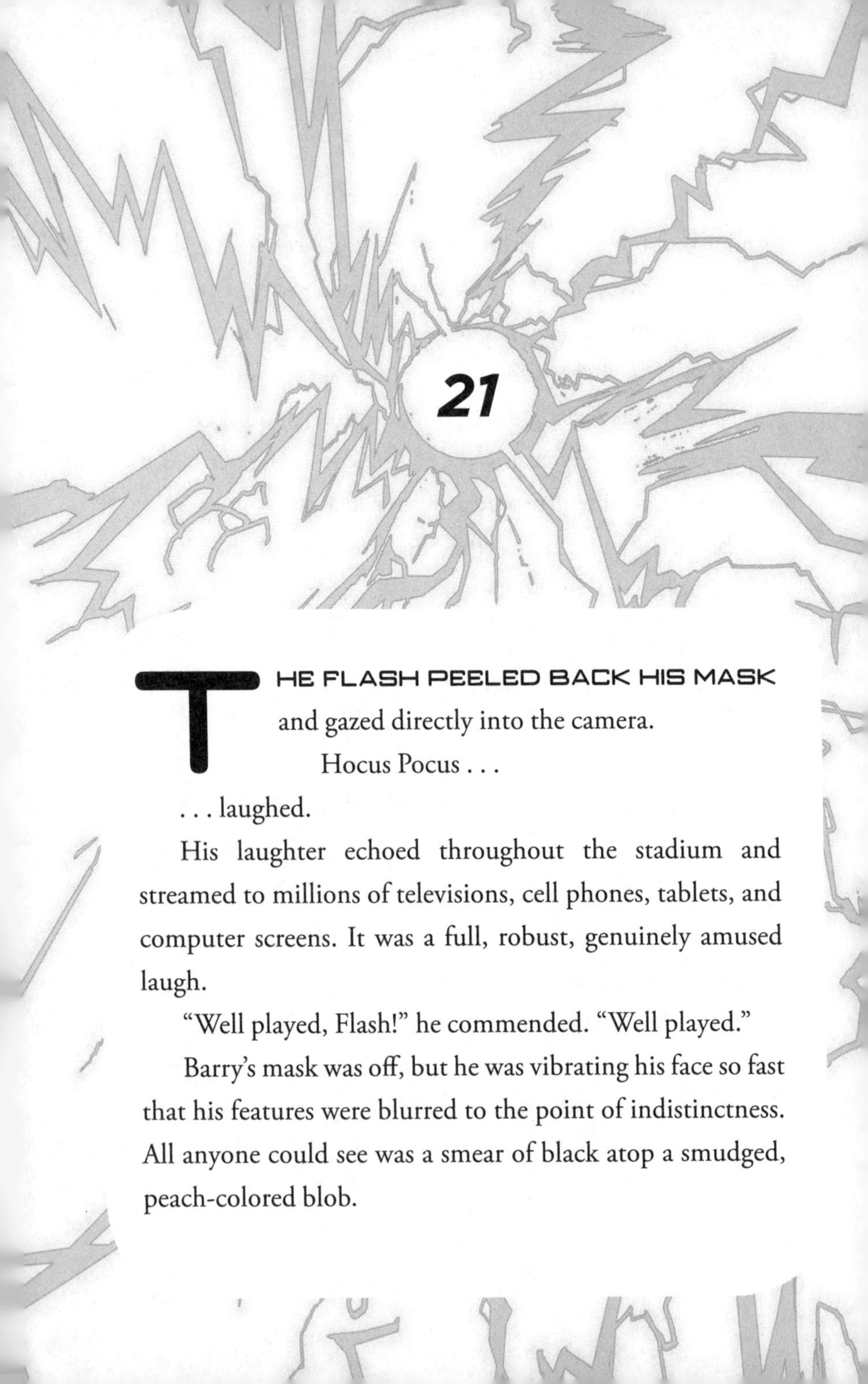

21

THE FLASH PEELED BACK HIS MASK and gazed directly into the camera.

Hocus Pocus . . .

. . . laughed.

His laughter echoed throughout the stadium and streamed to millions of televisions, cell phones, tablets, and computer screens. It was a full, robust, genuinely amused laugh.

"Well played, Flash!" he commended. "Well played."

Barry's mask was off, but he was vibrating his face so fast that his features were blurred to the point of indistinctness. All anyone could see was a smear of black atop a smudged, peach-colored blob.

After all, Pocus had ordered him to stand still and remove his mask. He hadn't said anything about not vibrating his face.

"Mask off, Hocus Pocus," Barry said in the vibrating bass he used as the Flash. "What's next? The rest of the costume? Shouldn't we try to keep this PG?"

Pocus chuckled and shook his head. "Truthfully, I don't care if people know what you look like under that ridiculous mask. It's quite pointless. Go ahead—put it back on."

Barry did so, quickly and gratefully.

Pocus sighed and looked around, his gaze traveling up and around the stadium. There were pockets of empty seats and streams of people at the exits. The evacuation was proceeding well.

"The moment has passed," the magician said, his voice laden with overdramatic regret. "Timing is *everything*, you know, and this is just the opening act. We wouldn't want to spoil the surprise . . ." He gestured theatrically, and sparkles filled the air between them. "Tonight, I will summon you. We will meet. And I shall visit upon you your final humiliation and ultimate destruction in combat before a worshipful public." He leaned in close. "And then, Flash, this city and everyone in it will bow to *me* as its true hero!"

"Doubt it," Barry said with a bravado he did not feel.

Pocus chortled, twirled his wand, and conjured a choking cloud of fire and smoke. He hovered above the smoke, then shot off into the sky, vanishing over the horizon.

Barry felt movement return to his limbs. Before he could run off, the camera operator stopped him.

"Hey, Flash?" she said, her voice still shaking from the ordeal. "I don't believe all the stuff they're saying about you. About how you're a villain now."

He smiled at her. "Thanks. That means a lot. It's sort of a complicated situation."

She hefted her camera. "Want to tell a few million people about it?"

"Barry!" Caitlin yelled in his earpiece. "Get back to STAR Labs! We've got something!"

"Maybe another time," Barry told the camerawoman. "I've got to run."

And so he ran.

In the Cortex, Cisco sat exhausted at his desk. Caitlin was pacing madly, and H.R. sat backward on a chair, leaning forward urgently. Barry took one look at Cisco's lidded eyes and downcast expression and said, "Oh man, it's bad news, isn't it?"

"It's actually great news," Cisco said with a yawn. "I'm just out of gas, amigo."

"He's barely slept since this all started," Caitlin said.

"At this point, the caffeine is just keeping my eyes open. Barely." Cisco struggled to spin his chair around so that he could type at his keyboard. "I ate half a bag of those ridiculous peanut butter coffee beans of H.R.'s and barely got a buzz."

"Hey!" H.R. complained. "Those were *mine*."

Cisco made a half-hearted effort to wave him off, then gave up and yawned again. "So here's what I've figured out . . ." An image came up on the screen, and Cisco yawned a third time. "Caitlin, take over. I'm taking a nap." He put his head down on his folded arms on the desk.

Caitlin shrugged apologetically. "He's really tired."

"I get it." Barry patted Cisco on the shoulder. "Walk me through what he figured out."

She pointed to the screen, which showed, once again, the image of the nanites from Barry's thalamus. "The nanites are in there because Pocus put them in there. We theorize—"

"*I* theorize," Cisco grunted groggily.

"*Cisco* theorizes," Caitlin said with an eye roll, "that his wand stores or manufactures the nanites somehow. That part is still way beyond us, at least until we get our hands on the wand. Anyway, he uses the wand to project the nanites in whichever direction and at whichever target."

"In this case, me," Barry said.

“Right. We can’t just open up your head and scoop out a sample of the nanites, but we *were* able to isolate a couple from one of the trees in the park. And even though they’re too sealed up and secure for us to get into them and see how they work, we were able to observe them, both from your scans and from the ones we found. And what we realized—”

“What *I* realized,” Cisco said, pushing himself to his feet. “If you’re not going to tell the story right, I’ll just have to rally and do it myself.” He yawned once more, as though for effect. “These things are incredibly sophisticated,” he went on, gesturing to the nanites on the screen, “but in one way they’re very simple. They have two states: on and off.”

“A binary system,” Barry said. It was the basis of most computer science—down at the bit level, a computer’s function was either on (represented by the number 1) or off (represented by the number 0). It seemed too crude and simple to make something as complicated as a computer work, but if you had thousands of “switches” and set each one to 1 or 0 depending on what you needed, anything was possible. To a human being, a string like 01010101001111010111 010101010101000000011111110101010101010101010 11111 looked like gibberish, but to a computer, it was an instruction. An order. A command.

Like the commands Hocus Pocus was sending to Barry.

Barry scratched his head, partly working through Cisco's theory, but mostly because the thought of nanites in his brain still made his head feel itchy. "So the nanites are either on or off. Got it. And they keep replicating before they can die. So how do we turn them off for good?"

"That's the tough part," Cisco admitted. "Except for the part where it's *not* the tough part, because, even sleep-deprived, I'm still an absolute genius." He paused, as if waiting for something to happen. When nothing did, he pointed to H.R. "That's your cue, for God's sake!"

H.R. wheeled over a cart with a black cloth draped over it. "We will discuss my remuneration for the purloined coffee beans at a later date," he said in a very calm, measured voice.

Cisco blew it off. "Whatever. Look, Barry, I can't do anything about the nanites in your brain. They're way too sophisticated, which, by the way, I will deny having said if you ever repeat it."

"I sense a *but* coming up," Barry told him.

"Like JLo, my friend," Cisco teased. "Ta-da!" He whipped the black cloth off the cart, revealing something that looked like a skullcap made out of shimmering metallic spaghetti.

"It's an inverse transmitting neuralgic transformer!" Cisco crowed.

There was silence for a moment.

"Uh, what do you call it?" H.R. ventured.

Another moment of silence as Cisco fidgeted.

"Well," he said at last, "I call it an, uh, inverse transmitting neuralgic transformer." He stared at his toes, abashed. "Sorry. I let you guys down. Man, I am *so* tired."

"What does it *do*?" Barry asked.

Cisco perked up. "I'm glad you asked, young man!"

"I'm older than you."

Cisco plowed on. "This lovely bit of kit can take in the ambient controlling radiation and convert its signal, flipping the requisite bits and bytes in the nanites' source code."

"It turns them off!" Barry reached for it.

Cisco slapped his hand away. "Not so fast, fleet-feet! It doesn't hack the nanites all by itself. But what it *does* do is convert a signal that Hocus Pocus sends them. In other words . . ."

"In other words," Barry said slowly, "if we get him to try his wand trick on me again, this time it'll wipe out the nanites."

"Exactamundo."

Caitlin raised her hand. "Sounds great, guys, but . . . why would Pocus zap Barry again? He's got him under control already. There's no need for him to establish control again."

Cisco opened his mouth to speak, then closed it.

He opened it again. Paused. Thought. Shook his head. “Nope. Still got nothing to say.”

Barry grinned. “You don’t need to. I’ve got it figured out.” He picked up the gadget Cisco hadn’t bothered nicknaming. “We’re gonna need Wally.”

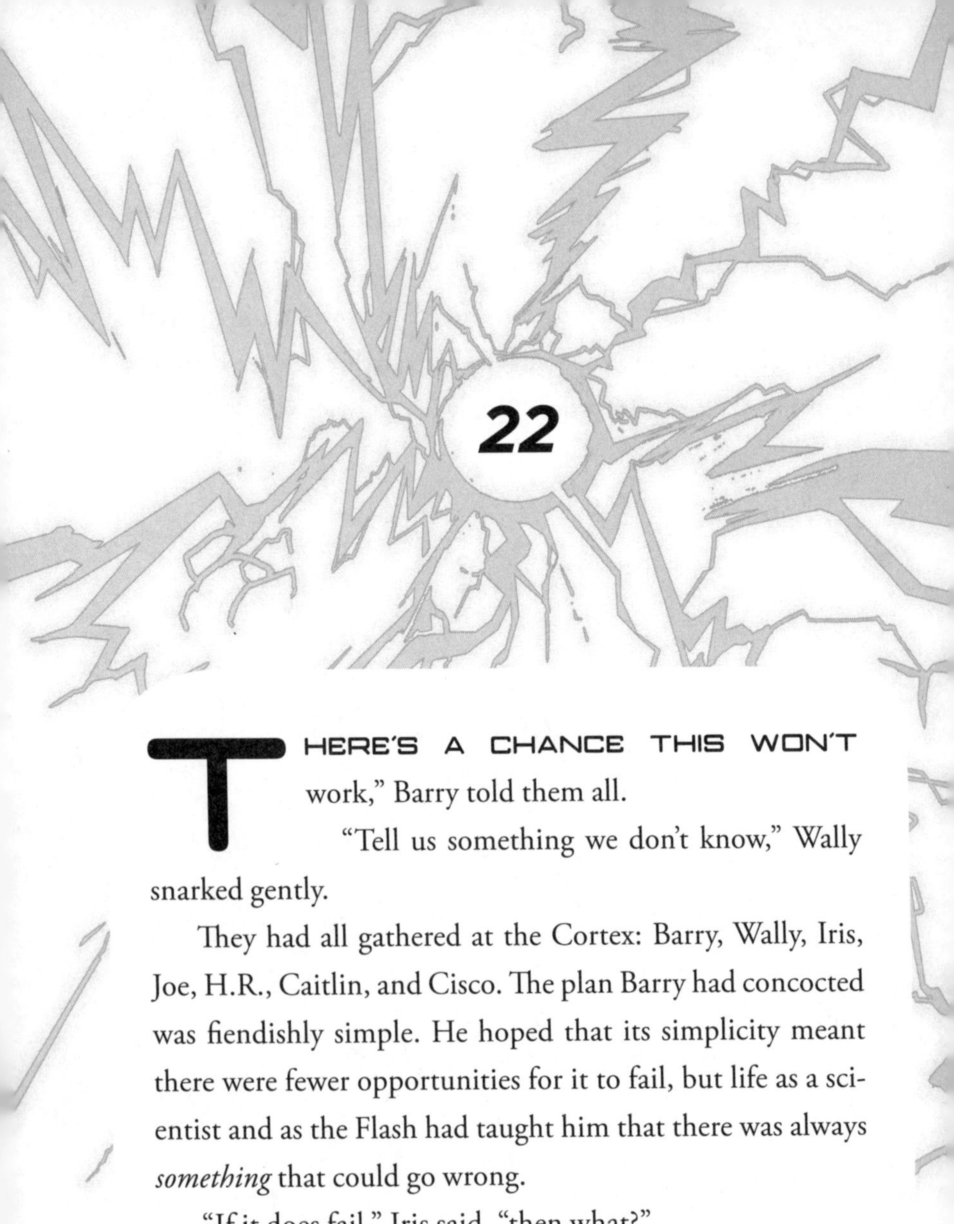

22

"THERE'S A CHANCE THIS WON'T work," Barry told them all.

"Tell us something we don't know," Wally snarked gently.

They had all gathered at the Cortex: Barry, Wally, Iris, Joe, H.R., Caitlin, and Cisco. The plan Barry had concocted was fiendishly simple. He hoped that its simplicity meant there were fewer opportunities for it to fail, but life as a scientist and as the Flash had taught him that there was always *something* that could go wrong.

"If it does fail," Iris said, "then what?"

Barry drew in a deep breath. "I guess it depends on exactly *how* it fails. Best-case scenario, I'll still be under Pocus's control."

"I hate that that's the best-case scenario," Caitlin said.

"Think how I feel," Barry told her. "Worst-case scenario is . . ." He hesitated. "Worst-case scenario, Pocus keeps his control on me *and* gets Kid Flash in the bargain."

"Two speedsters at his beck and call," Joe said, and shivered. "He'd be unstoppable."

"That's why I'm counting on my two favorite groups to stop the unstoppable," Barry said. He pointed to Cisco and Joe. "You both need to be ready. If Pocus maintains control of me or—God forbid—gets Wally, too, I need the combined might of STAR Labs and CCPD to come down on us. Hard."

"You mean on *him*, don't you?" Caitlin ventured.

"Eventually, yeah. But first order of business is to take away his living weapon . . . or weapons." Barry glanced over at Wally, who nodded without hesitation.

"Kneecap us," Wally said. "Whatever it takes. You can't let him use us against innocent people. Robbing jewelry stores is one thing, but what he told Barry to do at the ballpark . . ." Wally shivered. "Don't let him do that. You can't put us above thousands of innocents."

Iris folded her arms over her chest. "I don't like this talk. What if the only way to stop you guys is permanently? You can't expect us to do that."

Barry nodded slowly, then looked at each of them in turn, finishing with Iris. "At my top speed," he said, "I could kill a hundred people a second. So fast I'd be on to the next hundred before the first hundred bodies hit the ground." He jerked his head in Wally's direction. "Double that. So, yeah, Iris—if you have to kill us, that's what you have to do. Otherwise, we could wipe out the city in minutes, if that's what he orders us to do."

Iris turned around and looked as though she would walk out. Joe put an arm around her.

"We'll find another way," he said solemnly. "We won't let you hurt anyone. Trust me."

"I do." Barry realized tears had gathered in his eyes. He was facing the very real prospect that the people who loved and cared for him the most might—in just a short time—have to make the choice to end his life for the greater good. "I'm trusting all of you with my life, Wally's life, and the lives of everyone in Central City."

"We won't let you down," Caitlin said.

Iris turned back to him. There were tears in her eyes, too. "We won't let you down," she whispered.

The others murmured their agreement. What had begun as a rally now had the atmosphere of a vigil. No one wanted to think about what could go wrong.

Cisco went off to make final adjustments to his gadget. The others split off and milled about. Barry turned to Wally and slapped him on the shoulder. "You ready for this?"

Wally bobbed his head. "Yep. Definitely."

"This whole plan relies on you," he reminded him.

"Don't worry. I'm fast enough."

Barry thought of Madame Xanadu. "It's not about speed this time. It's about patience and timing. You have to stand still. That's what I need you for."

Wally nodded. "I got it. I'm your man."

"I know you are. We have to be ready to move at any second. Pocus said tonight, but not exactly when. He could summon me at any time."

Iris approached them both. "Wally, can I have a moment with Barry?"

"Sure, sis." Wally wandered over to where Joe and Caitlin were chatting.

Barry gazed down into Iris's eyes. They were warm and welcoming and moist with tears. "Don't cry," he said, wiping a tear away with his thumb.

"If you get to cry, I get to cry," she told him.

He chuckled and wiped his own eyes. "Yeah, I guess that's fair."

"Are you sure about this plan?"

"I'm sure it's the only plan we've got."

"That's not the same thing, but you're right, so I'll give you a pass on that. Just promise me you'll be careful, OK?"

He folded his arms around her and murmured against her forehead, "I will. I promise."

"And don't let anything happen to Wally."

He said nothing. After all, the whole plan relied on something at least *seeming* to happen to Wally.

"There's one possibility you maybe haven't considered," Iris said. "Another plan."

"I'm all ears." He leaned in as if telling her a secret. "'Cause, honestly? The plan we've got kinda sucks. If you have a better one . . ."

"You're trying to make me laugh so I won't worry, but it's not going to work. Seriously, have you considered just . . . running away?"

"Iris . . ."

She put a hand over his mouth. "No, hear me out. For all you know, his control over you weakens with distance. You've never been more than a few city blocks away from him. Run to Tibet or Japan or Australia. Just to see. Can't you do that?"

Such was the pleading in her voice and the desperation in her eyes that Barry almost did exactly that. It would have taken him a minute, maybe, to run to Japan. And that long only because running across the unpredictable and tempestuous ocean was slower-going than solid land.

"I can't do that," he told her gently. "If I thought it might work, I'd try. Maybe. But nothing indicates that distance affects the nanites. And besides: I can't just keep running away from him. I have to confront him and beat him if I ever want to help the people of this city again. Or get my job back." He tilted her chin up and kissed her softly. "Or have any kind of life again."

"I hate it when you're right," she said, hugging him.

"Yeah. Me, too."

The sun was just starting to go down. Cisco had finished his preparations. Barry and Wally sat across from each other at a table, waiting. For two speedsters, sitting and doing nothing was the worst torture imaginable.

They managed to endure.

Outside, the sky bled red and purple and orange. Inside, the Cortex hummed and glowed with artificial light. Joe had returned to CCPD, and Iris had gone to the *Picture News* office. H.R.'s air drumming had become so annoying that Caitlin stole his drumsticks and was sitting on them. H.R. sulked in a corner.

Cisco had found stronger coffee and a second wind. He was pacing like mad.

"Tom Petty was right," he blurted out into the silence. "The waiting is the hardest—"

“Guys!” Barry yelped. “Guys, it’s happ—”

He was gone.

An instant later, so was Wally.

Cisco and Caitlin flew into action immediately. With the trackers built into both Flashes’ suits, Cisco and Caitlin could tell where the speedsters were going and follow them on the screens in the Cortex.

“Barry’s headed to the pier!” Cisco yelled into his microphone.

“You don’t have to shout,” Wally’s voice came back. “You’re, like, literally *in* my ear.”

“Sorry!” Cisco screamed. “It’s the caffeine! It’s kicking in!”

“He’s almost there,” Caitlin told Wally, pushing Cisco aside. “You have to—”

“I know what I have to do,” Wally said grimly. “No offense, but stop distracting me. I’ve got this.”

Caitlin dropped into a chair next to Cisco. Together, they looked up at the big screen, where the Flash and Kid Flash icons were converging on the Central City Pier.

“Now what?” Caitlin whispered.

Cisco said nothing.

“Now nothing.” H.R. had crept up behind them. “Now we just . . . wait.”

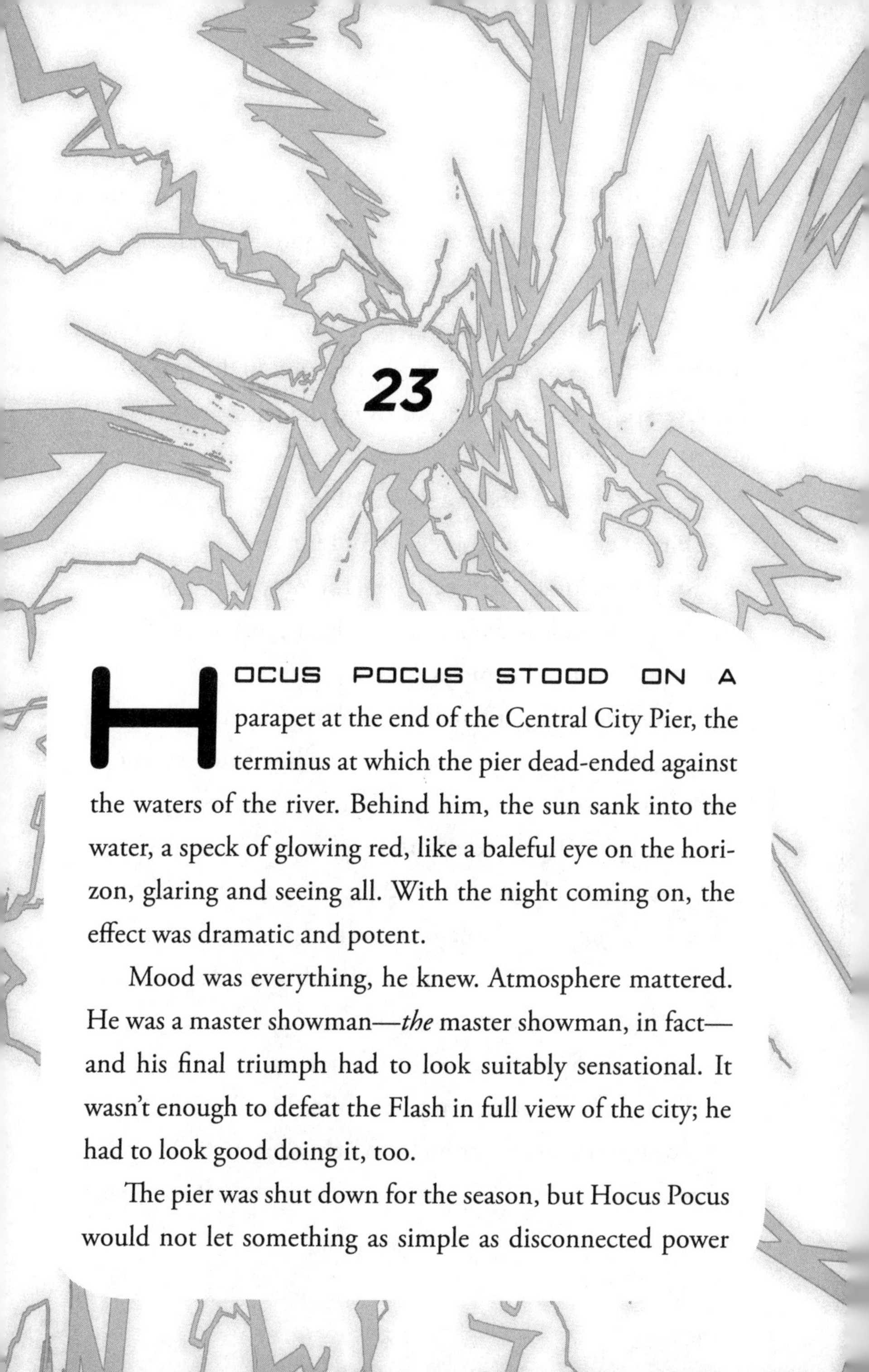

23

HOCUS POCUS STOOD ON A parapet at the end of the Central City Pier, the terminus at which the pier dead-ended against the waters of the river. Behind him, the sun sank into the water, a speck of glowing red, like a baleful eye on the horizon, glaring and seeing all. With the night coming on, the effect was dramatic and potent.

Mood was everything, he knew. Atmosphere mattered. He was a master showman—*the* master showman, in fact—and his final triumph had to look suitably sensational. It wasn't enough to defeat the Flash in full view of the city; he had to look good doing it, too.

The pier was shut down for the season, but Hocus Pocus would not let something as simple as disconnected power cords and mothballed gadgetry stand in his way. This was an event! This was history in the making! It should be a festival, an *occasion*, and so it would be.

With the nanotechnology at his disposal, it was a simple matter to bring power and light and motion to the pier. The carousel spun, its wooden steeds rising and falling in rhythm to the calliope music. The boardwalk sang with the sound of games from the arcades, the shouts of joy from the old Tilt-A-Whirl, the rambunctious clatter of bumper cars.

And everything was free! Free! The only cost would be watching the end of the Flash and the ascension of Hocus Pocus to the exalted name of Abra Kadabra.

Thousands had gathered, a crowd massing up and down the pier, lining up along its edges, spilling into the alleyways. They wore glow-in-the-dark light sticks around their necks and glowing bracelets on their wrists. It was a party!

There were TV crews with their cameras aimed at him, and, more important, everyone else in the crowd was pointing a cell phone in his direction. His ultimate defeat of the Flash would be live-streamed to the world.

Truly, the applause would be deafening.

Pocus's lips twitched into a smile. Finally. Finally, he would enjoy the acclamation he so richly deserved. An entire city, subject to his whims, crying out his name, cheering his every action.

And perhaps, someday, when he tired of Central City, he would move on to a different city. He'd heard good things about Star City, which had a plethora of masked do-gooders he could control. And then another. And another. Someday, indeed, the whole *world* would know his name. Know it and scream it in joy at the top of its lungs! All he ever wanted. Crushing the dreams of his own master and taking his place . . .

A gasp from the crowd. Pocus looked up. There, upriver, a blur of scarlet and crackling yellow zipped across the river, hooked a sharp left-hand turn, and raced down the pier toward him.

"STOP!" Pocus commanded.

The blur resolved into the figure of the Flash, standing ten feet from Pocus. The crowd started booing.

Pocus allowed the booing to continue for a few more seconds, drinking in its delectability. As much as he enjoyed the Flash's humiliation, though, he felt that a proper hero and savior should project a certain magnanimity, and so he raised both hands and bade the good people of Central City to cease their jeering.

Behind him, over the water, fireworks exploded into the night sky. The gathered crowd oohed and aahed as dreadlocks of light spilled out of the sky and melded with their watery reflections.

He regarded the Flash with a cruel leer. It was too easy, he thought. Too easy to win this way. And yet he would take the comfortable victory. He took pleasure in the approbation of the crowd, not in the challenge of combat.

"PEOPLE OF CENTRAL CITY!" Pocus said, knowing his words would carry through the phones and the cameras to every corner of the city. "IT IS, TRULY, SO SAD WHEN A HERO FALLS! THE FLASH WAS ONCE YOUR SAVIOR, YOUR VERY OWN HOMEGROWN HERO. YET ALL FLESH EVENTUALLY ROTS. NOTHING GOOD LASTS.

"FORTUNATELY FOR YOU, I AM HERE! HOCUS—" He broke off and smiled to himself. "I AM HERE: ABRA KADABRA, YOUR NEW HERO!" The name sounded good and right to him. He liked the sound of it on his lips. It belonged to him. "I AM YOUR FAITHFUL AND POWERFUL BENEFACTOR. AND I WILL RESCUE YOU FROM THE CORRUPT, CORRODED REMAINS OF YOUR OLD ONE."

He looked down on the Flash. "Are you ready?" he asked rhetorically, knowing the Flash couldn't answer.

And then, to his shock, the Flash *moved*.

It was just a single step, but that was enough. One red-booted foot came up, hovered for an instant, then moved forward and planted itself on the pier. A step. One step.

"Impossible . . ." Pocus whispered.

The Flash took another step, just as slow, just as deliberate.

"I ordered you to stop!" Pocus howled. "Stop moving! Stop moving *right now*!"

But the Flash took one more step toward him. Then another.

"Stop it!" Pocus ranted, flushing purple with rage. "Stop it! Stop it! Stop moving! I command you!"

One more step, almost infinitely slow, but it was forward movement, and that—was—*impossible!*

With a strangled cry of outrage, Pocus pointed his wand at the Flash. "I *command* you!" he yelled, and fired a burst at his foe.

And then . . .

Well, then things happened *really* fast.

Suddenly, in a vermilion blur, there were *two* Flashes. One of them peeled off from the other, dodging to the left as the blast from Pocus's wand closed in.

The second Flash stood completely still, and the zap from the wand hit him full-on. At that moment, the second Flash started to move.

Pocus realized in an instant what had happened. "Oh no!" he whispered in horror. "Oh *no*!"

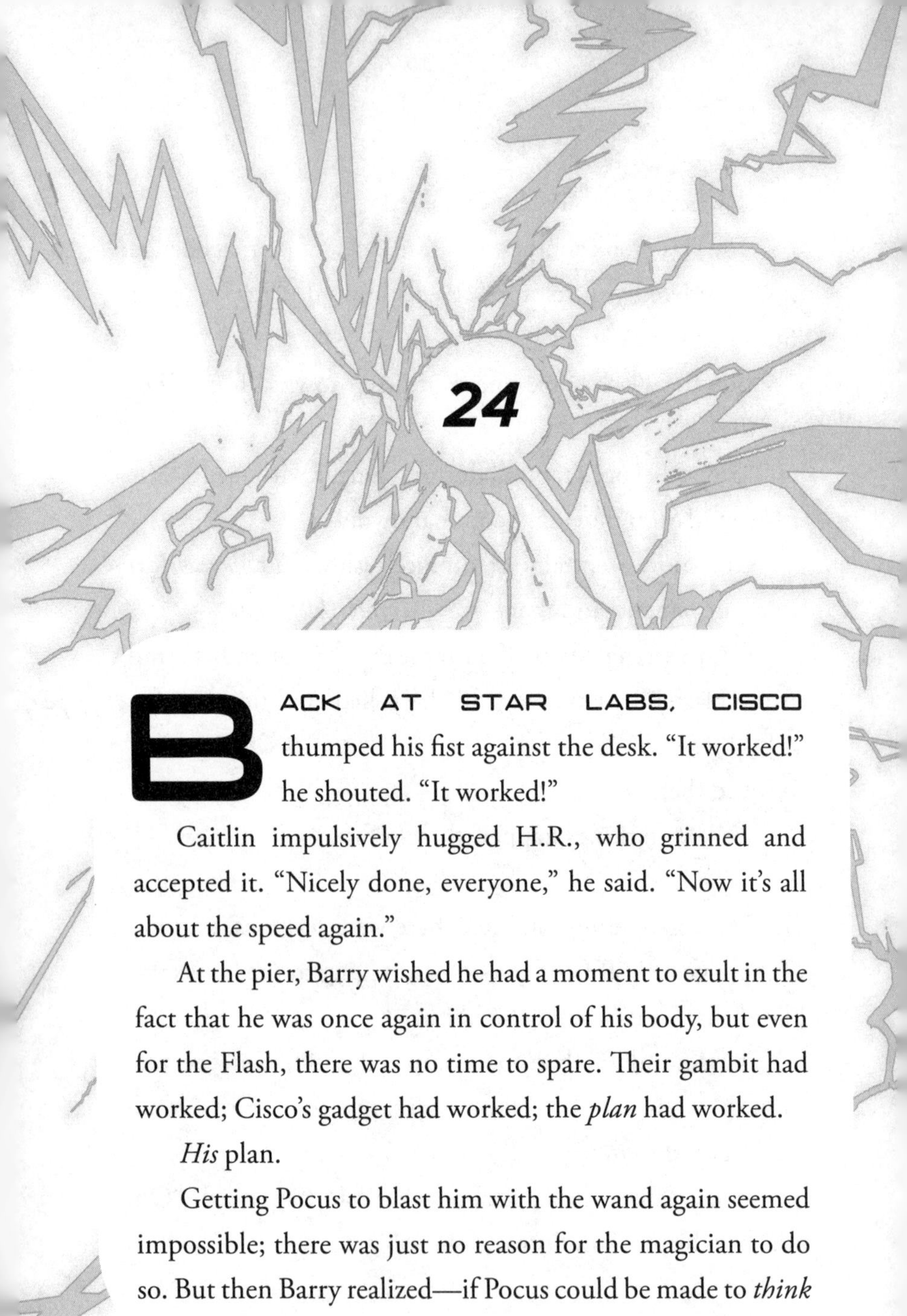

24

BACK AT STAR LABS, CISCO thumped his fist against the desk. “It worked!” he shouted. “It worked!”

Caitlin impulsively hugged H.R., who grinned and accepted it. “Nicely done, everyone,” he said. “Now it’s all about the speed again.”

At the pier, Barry wished he had a moment to exult in the fact that he was once again in control of his body, but even for the Flash, there was no time to spare. Their gambit had worked; Cisco’s gadget had worked; the *plan* had worked.

His plan.

Getting Pocus to blast him with the wand again seemed impossible; there was just no reason for the magician to do so. But then Barry realized—if Pocus could be made to *think* that the Flash had somehow thrown off his control, then maybe the magician would try to zap him again to reestablish dominance.

So he had Wally dress up in a fake Flash costume and blur his face. In that outfit, he looked just like the Flash, especially to those who didn't know Barry or Wally personally. Then Wally followed Barry to the pier and phased, keeping pace with him as he ran. They were so fast that no one would notice.

When Pocus ordered Barry to stop, Wally did, too, staying phased and just slightly in front of Barry. And of course, Wally could move whenever he wanted.

When Pocus saw the person he thought was the Flash moving without permission, he freaked out. He panicked. And he did exactly what Barry hoped he would do: He fired off another blast of nanites designed to enslave the Flash once more.

That was the most dangerous part of the plan. If Wally jumped aside too soon, Pocus would realize he'd been fooled and hold off on the blast. If Wally jumped too late, he'd be hit by the nanites, and Pocus would have two speedster puppets to control.

Fortunately, Wally jumped at just the right time. The blast missed him and hit Barry, where it was captured and altered by Cisco's unnamed gadget, which had been installed in the cowl of Barry's Flash costume. The nanites in Barry's thalamus instantly switched off, and he regained control of himself.

Barry grinned at the horrified expression on the magician's face. "Presto changeo! Hey, Hocus Pocus! How'd you like *that* magic trick?"

Pocus's answer was a snarl and a complicated motion with his wand. For about half the crowd, gravity stopped working.

Uh-oh, Barry thought.

After dodging Pocus's blast, Wally had run at superspeed into the crowd and then started to make his way around to Pocus's flank. He figured he and Barry could catch the magician between them, giving the guy nowhere to run.

But suddenly he was in the air, along with a few hundred other people, flailing his arms. They were already over the tree line. If they kept soaring up at this rate, they would be in the upper atmosphere in no time. Wally was pretty sure he could vibrate enough to maintain his body heat, but everyone else would freeze to death.

Well, if they didn't suffocate first.

Cheerful thoughts.

"Kid Flash!" It was Barry, on his earpiece. "You OK?"

"Oh, sure, just ducky." They were talking to each other at superspeed, so fast that only they could understand each other. The whole conversation would take perhaps a second. "How do I get down from here?"

"You don't."

"That's comforting." Wally's casual tone belied the thrill of panic that made his heart play leapfrog. "I guess I'll see you on the dark side of the moon."

"The nanites he's using to reverse gravity will wear off at some point," Barry reminded him. "Your job is to keep everyone from drifting off and make sure they land safely when the time comes."

With a heroic effort, Wally managed to contort himself and twist in midair to look around. The air was thick with panicking innocents—bodies thrashing and shaking. And rising. Hundreds of them.

"Got any suggestions on that?" he asked, rotating so that he could look down on the pier. The Flash was about to launch himself at Hocus Pocus.

"About to be busy," Barry replied. "You'll figure it out. Think hydrocarbon!"

"*What?*" Wally asked, but Barry had signed off already, ready to fight Hocus Pocus.

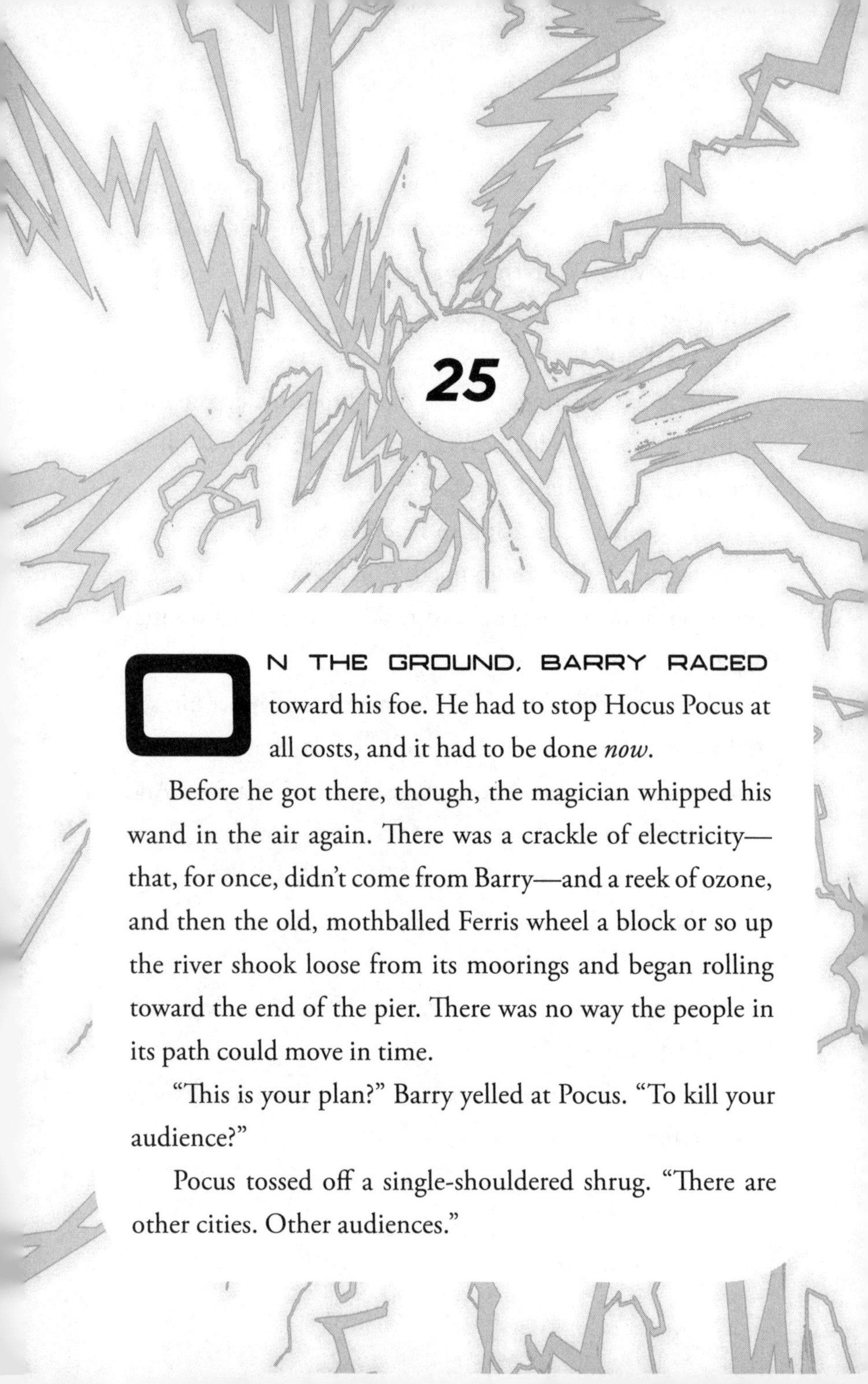

25

ON THE GROUND, BARRY RACED toward his foe. He had to stop Hocus Pocus at all costs, and it had to be done *now*.

Before he got there, though, the magician whipped his wand in the air again. There was a crackle of electricity—that, for once, didn't come from Barry—and a reek of ozone, and then the old, mothballed Ferris wheel a block or so up the river shook loose from its moorings and began rolling toward the end of the pier. There was no way the people in its path could move in time.

"This is your plan?" Barry yelled at Pocus. "To kill your audience?"

Pocus tossed off a single-shouldered shrug. "There are other cities. Other audiences."

If he'd had a moment to pause and let the horror of that philosophy sink in, Barry would have taken it. But he would need every microsecond if he was to save everyone from that Ferris wheel.

He took off. The wheel was turning clockwise. Barry made some quick calculations in his head, estimating angular velocity and speed of rotation around an axis, and then he remembered that the nanites were in control, not physics, so he chucked the formulas out the window. The wheel was weaving a drunken path down the boardwalk, crushing anything before it. For now that meant planters and park benches and the occasional trash can, but pretty soon it would mean people.

Nope. Not on my watch.

He considered a few different ideas: He could rip up part of the boardwalk and let the increased friction slow down the wheel. But that might not be fast enough. The wheel might plow on through anyway or fall over on someone. And besides—with Pocus controlling it, the wheel might just keep going.

He contemplated the river. Could he run fast enough and with enough precision to whip up a waterspout that would knock the wheel off course? It was theoretically possible—and had the added advantage of looking very cool—but he didn't think it would work in practice. Getting the spout to "jump" from the river to the pier with enough force would be difficult, if not impossible.

So he got to the Ferris wheel and, without thinking it through, ran up its side counterclockwise. Once he was at the wheel's apex, he slowed down just enough so that his velocity matched that of the wheel, running in the same direction.

This wasn't a question of complicated math. It was actually pretty simple: The wheel was moving at X speed *forward,* and Barry was running on it like a treadmill at X speed as well. He was running forward, but his feet were moving the wheel in the opposite direction—like a logroller. Running forward pushed the wheel backward, which meant he canceled out all of its forward momentum.

In other words, the Ferris wheel stopped dead in its tracks. It teetered there, like an egg standing on its wider end.

Barry permitted himself a brief grin and moment of self-congratulation. He was in control again. Saving people again.

He started running faster, and the wheel began rolling back toward its original location. He looked up, checking for Wally, and smiled at what he saw.

Hydrocarbon, Wally knew, was a compound of hydrogen and carbon. He knew it well from his days as a street racer, because it was a primary component of oil and gasoline. He didn't think Barry wanted him to rev up an engine, though.

The other thing he knew about hydrocarbon: It formed a chain, the atoms of hydrogen and carbon interlinked like this:

$$
\begin{array}{cccccccccccccccccc}
 & & H & & H & & H & & H & & H & & H & & H & & H & \\
 & & | & & | & & | & & | & & | & & | & & | & & | & \\
H & - & C & - & C & - & C & - & C & - & C & - & C & - & C & - & C & - H \\
 & & | & & | & & | & & | & & | & & | & & | & & | & \\
 & & H & & H & & H & & H & & H & & H & & H & & H &
\end{array}
$$

Or, more graphically, like this:

That's what Barry was getting at: a chain. A human chain.

Wally couldn't walk or run while floating upward, but he could move laterally by kicking his legs fast enough to create friction that resulted in propulsion. It was almost like swimming in the air, only not nearly as graceful. He sort of looked like a toddler trying to walk for the first time, kicking and lashing out with all his limbs, but it worked—he was able to get to the person closest to him and grab her hand.

The woman looked at him with sheer terror in her eyes. “My son!” she managed to say through lips stretched wide in a rictus of horror.

“I’ve got him,” Kid Flash assured her. He reached up and grabbed the kid’s ankle, pulling him down until the mother could grab it, too. “Hold on tight, OK?”

“We’re gonna die!” she said.

“Not on my watch,” he promised her.

The wind roared just then, as though to mock him. Wally gritted his teeth against the buffeting gusts. They were more than a hundred feet up, way above the tree line. The air was already colder, or maybe that was just his imagination. Either way, he wasn’t about to let this woman or her son or any of the others sailing up to the stratosphere die.

He kicked some more and stretched out to his utmost, barely snagging the hand of a man in a business suit who was screaming in a high, trembling voice barely audible over the wind. Wally tugged the man, spinning him around. Without gravity, moving people was both easier and harder at the same time. No one weighed anything, but they still had mass and area, so it wasn’t like slinging around feathers; it took strength and muscle and work. There were wind resistance and friction to consider, too.

Barry probably had all the formulas memorized in his cache of handy-dandy Flash Facts, but Wally would just have to go on gut instinct.

He'd always been pretty good at gut instinct. His gut had kept him alive in situations where he probably should have died.

With a combination of kicking at superspeed and windmilling his arms, he propelled himself through the air like some sort of spasmodic kite caught in a windstorm. It was difficult, so it took him almost a full minute, moving at his best speed, to get to all of the hundreds of people floating above the pier and get them to grab one another's hands, elbows, ankles, feet, and shoulders in order to form a human chain. With everyone's light sticks and bracelets glowing, it looked like a brand-new constellation lighting up the sky.

He was exhausted, but his job wasn't over yet. Below, he could see that Barry had managed to stop the Ferris wheel, and then—in a feat so mind-boggling that even Wally was blown away—run it backward along its path like the world's biggest hamster wheel, until it settled back into the grooves of its original framework.

If he can do that, I can do this!

Wally had saved a big, strong-looking guy for last. He positioned the guy toward the center of the big human loop he'd created, then had a grandmother-looking type grab the big guy's ankles. He spared a half second to smile at her reassuringly. "You can do this," he told her.

"I raised five kids and ten grandkids," she snapped. "Worry about yourself."

Wally was so shocked, he didn't even laugh. He drifted up (or fell downward, depending on how you look at it) until he hovered just over the group, then told the big guy to grab his ankles.

"And whatever you do," he said, "don't let go! Otherwise, everyone's gonna keep falling up until they hit the ionosphere, and then things get radioactive and ugly."

The big guy gulped and clamped his hands around Wally's ankles like giant lobster claws.

Kid Flash was exhausted from his aerial maneuvers, but he knew that was only the first part of his task. Now he had to keep everyone from floating off into space.

He raised his arms above his head and started pinwheeling as fast as he could. Twin tornadoes whipped into existence, pointed upward.

Wally gritted his teeth. Sweat gathered on his brow and dripped along his cheeks. As long as he could keep the air moving above them, the people chained up to each other would stay in a sort of stasis, not rising, not falling.

If he stopped, they would all fly up into the upper atmosphere and be obliterated.

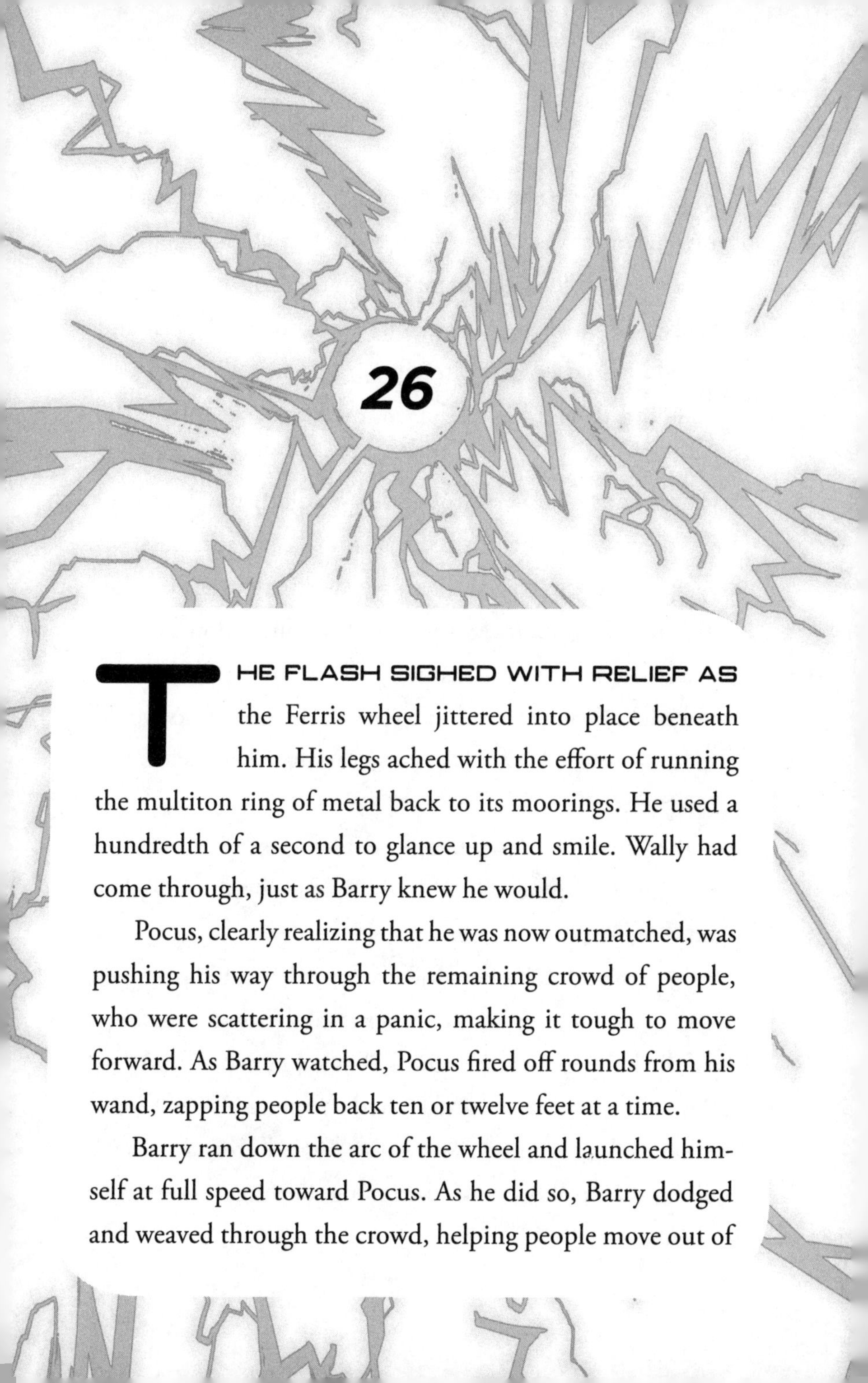

26

THE FLASH SIGHED WITH RELIEF AS the Ferris wheel jittered into place beneath him. His legs ached with the effort of running the multiton ring of metal back to its moorings. He used a hundredth of a second to glance up and smile. Wally had come through, just as Barry knew he would.

Pocus, clearly realizing that he was now outmatched, was pushing his way through the remaining crowd of people, who were scattering in a panic, making it tough to move forward. As Barry watched, Pocus fired off rounds from his wand, zapping people back ten or twelve feet at a time.

Barry ran down the arc of the wheel and launched himself at full speed toward Pocus. As he did so, Barry dodged and weaved through the crowd, helping people move out of each other's way as he went. A mother, jostled, dropped her baby. Her face was frozen in absolute fear as Barry ran by. He scooped up the baby before it could hit the ground, put it back in Mom's arms, then gently straightened her out and pointed her in the safest direction.

He did this and helped a hundred other people in the seconds it took him to get to Hocus Pocus. The magician was trying to shove his way through a particularly tough knot of bystanders. When he realized that the Flash was headed his way, Hocus Pocus waved his wand in a circle over his head. A storm of flaming rocks appeared and rained down on the crowd. The Flash's first instinct was to pull the old whirlwind trick, racing around in circles so that the rocks would end up suspended in midair until everyone down below had managed to get away.

But there were too many people running about in a panic for him to be able to build up the speed he needed. And those rocks were falling fast.

He cast about, looking for anything that could help, and his gaze fell on the Gardner River itself. Without missing a beat, he hopped over the railing that kept people from toppling off the boardwalk and started churning his legs. Soon, he'd kicked up a massive wave that rippled up and over the railing, then collided with the falling, burning rocks, extinguishing them.

People got wet, and a few had bumps on their heads, but no one was seriously injured. They seemed pretty appreciative, too—a nice round of applause spontaneously erupted, and Barry knew that it was genuine.

The acclamation was nice—especially after the last few days he'd had—but he didn't pause to bask in it. Glancing around, he finally located Hocus Pocus, catching sight of the villain's cape just as he disappeared through a door into . . .

Ugh. The House of Mirrors. Barry *hated* the House of Mirrors. Always had. He'd gotten lost in one as a kid, after insisting to his parents that he could go through it alone. And then he'd . . .

Stop thinking about the past, Allen. Get moving!

He raced to the House of Mirrors, paging STAR Labs as he did so. "Guys, he's headed into the House of Mirrors. I could use some help here."

Cisco's voice crackled back over the suit's connection. "What am I supposed to do, hack a mirror?"

"Can you get the blueprints to the maze from the city?"

"For a carnival house of mirrors? You overestimate the Central City Zoning Commission, my friend. I guess I could go wake up Scudder . . ."

Sam Scudder. The Mirror Master. A metahuman who could travel through reflective surfaces and even trap other people inside them. He'd popped up a couple of months after Zoom was defeated and had proved particularly difficult to stop. He was currently trapped in a special cell at Iron Heights Prison. Barry didn't want him ever to get out.

"No time. I'll handle it on my own."

He raced into the House of Mirrors—and promptly bashed his nose on a clear glass wall right in front of him.

Yeah, he *hated* the House of Mirrors.

With a sigh, he raced off in a different direction. His own lightning and speed-blur assaulted his eyes from three different angles, and before he even knew what was happening, he'd plowed headlong into a mirror. The Flash's reflection stared back at him dolefully.

"You and me both, buddy," he muttered, and put out a hand to his left to be sure it was just empty space before running off . . .

. . . and slamming into another wall a second later. Somewhere in the building, a laugh echoed. He could see Hocus Pocus just a few feet away, but that was just a reflection, he realized.

He spun around. The magician was behind him, too. And to his left. Barry groaned and snarled at the smirking villain, who now dodged to one side, causing his mirror-images to move to *their* left, a disorienting feint that left the Flash a little dizzy.

"I'm right here, Flash!" Hocus Pocus taunted. "Reach out!"

Barry reached out . . . and touched clear glass. The House of Mirrors was more than just mirrors—there were also clear panes of glass to make it even harder to navigate the maze. He wasn't sure which way to go, but he had to do it fast.

After running pell-mell into another wall, he started to rethink the "do it fast" scheme.

Always looking for the quickest path to the horizon, Madame Xanadu had told him. *And perhaps now is the time to forsake that.* Her advice had worked quite well before, at the baseball stadium.

He took a deep breath. Being in here was giving him a case of claustrophobia, but worse than that, it was dredging up all those memories of being trapped in a House of Mirrors as a kid. Surrounded by images of himself, with no sense of direction, he'd felt like he would never get out . . .

But wait.

He *did* get out. Obviously.

And suddenly he remembered *how*.

Just like now, he'd panicked, but then forced himself to calm down and take a deep breath. And he looked down . . .

(As he did now.)

And saw at the base of a mirror, where it was attached to the floor, a small, nearly invisible arrow, drawn in light chalk, pointing to the right.

There was one here, too. This one was in pencil, not in chalk, but it was there nonetheless. As a kid, he'd noticed the arrows, which served as a guide through the maze. His father had later explained to him that they were there for the people who worked at the carnival and maintained the equipment, so that they could quickly and easily access parts of the maze.

"It wasn't for you to use, son, but you made it work for you," Henry Allen had said.

Barry realized that for the first time since his father's death, he was able to think of him without crying.

"Well, that's progress," he told himself, then followed the arrows through the maze. Ahead of him, he heard Pocus making *his* way through and resisted the urge to break into a full-tilt run.

He emerged from the maze back onto the boardwalk, just a few steps behind Hocus Pocus, who glanced over his shoulder, saw the Flash, and ran in a panic toward the safety of the crowd.

Nope. Not today.

The Flash sped up, phased through a few people, and found himself standing right in front of Hocus Pocus.

Barry Allen was a thinking man, a rationalist, a scientist. A man who believed people could be explained to and reasoned with. In general, he did not enjoy violence; he preferred to convince people of the wrongness of their actions.

In the case of Hocus Pocus, though, he really, *really* enjoyed socking him in the jaw and knocking him out cold.

Above, the nanites wore out, and everyone falling up fell down, plunging more than a hundred feet from the sky.

But Kid Flash, smartly, had steered them all over the river. Now, with the last of his flagging energy, he spun his arms wildly. The resulting cushion of air slowed the fall, and everyone dropped gently into the water. The Flash ran out onto the water and started hauling people onto dry land, starting with the children and the elderly. Kid Flash jumped right in and helped, too, even though he was clearly drained.

By the time they were done, CCPD and ambulances had arrived. The pier was in chaos: Some were running away, some were sticking around to take selfies and other pictures, and some were just standing there, shell-shocked.

A group of Anti-Metahuman Task Force officers encircled the Flash and Kid Flash, fingers stroking the trigger guards of their STAR Labs–issued anti-speedster rifles.

Captain Singh himself was on the scene. He cautiously approached the two speedsters, who were leaning on each other and trying to catch their breath after their exertions.

"Flash?" Singh said. "Are you back?"

The Flash grinned and nodded, almost forgetting to vibrate his face and voice. "You bet."

Singh sighed with heavy relief and signaled the AMTF to stand down. "Good. I don't want to throw any more men at you."

"I don't want to have to throw them back, Captain."

Singh grunted and nodded toward the unconscious Hocus Pocus. "What about this one?"

The Flash and Kid Flash exchanged a look. "Well, I suppose *technically* you should arrest him and put him in jail," the Flash said.

Singh pursed his lips as though considering it. "I bet you have something a little more secure in mind."

Flash shrugged.

"Crazy thing," Singh said. "Crazy thing: You guys are so fast. I could swear, one minute I was talking to you, and then I blinked and you were gone."

Singh went ahead and blinked. In the time it took for his eyes to open again, Flash and Kid Flash had grabbed Hocus Pocus and sped off into the night.

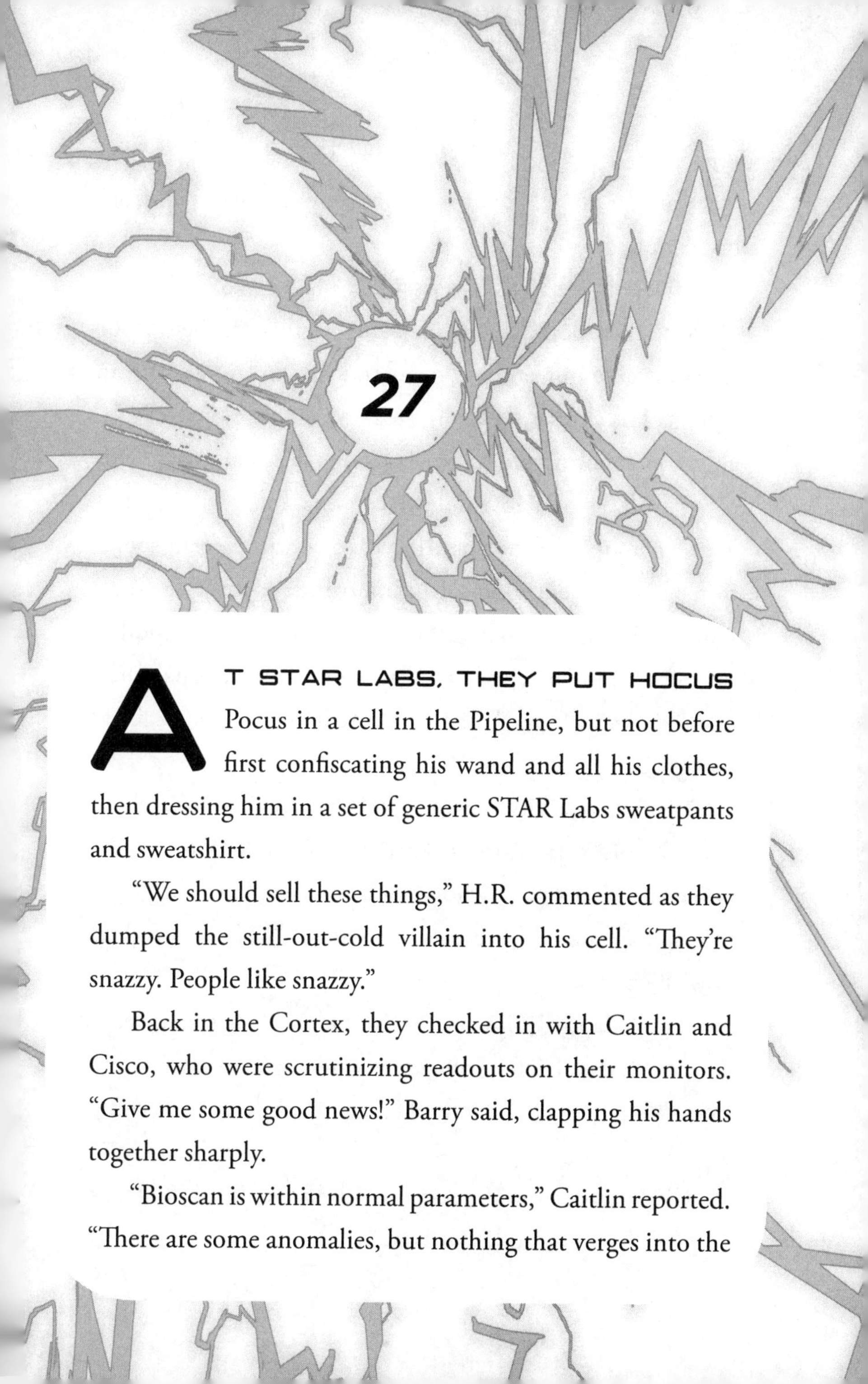

27

AT STAR LABS, THEY PUT HOCUS Pocus in a cell in the Pipeline, but not before first confiscating his wand and all his clothes, then dressing him in a set of generic STAR Labs sweatpants and sweatshirt.

"We should sell these things," H.R. commented as they dumped the still-out-cold villain into his cell. "They're snazzy. People like snazzy."

Back in the Cortex, they checked in with Caitlin and Cisco, who were scrutinizing readouts on their monitors. "Give me some good news!" Barry said, clapping his hands together sharply.

"Bioscan is within normal parameters," Caitlin reported. "There are some anomalies, but nothing that verges into the metahuman range. He doesn't have powers. It was all from his gizmo."

"You're up, Cisco," Barry said.

Cisco nodded quickly. "Let me get this out before the latest caffeine infusion wears off and I pass out. Wand is in storage. His clothes have some tech woven into them. Probably how he projected his voice like he did. Bad news: This tech is still beyond anything we can imagine, and we're not gonna get any closer to figuring it out until I've had something like sixteen hours of uninterrupted shut-eye. Good news: Without all that tech, which is now safely hidden away from him, he's just a regular dude." Cisco paused, then nodded admiringly. "With a particularly righteous facial hair game, I must admit."

"Really?" Caitlin pouted. "I think it's a bit much."

"The old turn-of-the-twentieth-century look has a certain charm. He's got a whole silent movie villain vibe going there." He rubbed his eyes and yawned. "May I go to bed now? Please?"

Barry clapped him on the shoulder. "Get some sleep, Cisco. Hocus Pocus will keep while we all recuperate from the past week." He looked at his phone. "Is it really Sunday?"

Cisco headed out the door, shouting over his shoulder as he went, "All day, buddy! All day!"

Barry looked at Caitlin and H.R. "Thanks for your help, guys. Really. This one was . . ." He trailed off, lacking words to explain it. He was finally back in control of his own body for the first time in almost a week, and it felt phenomenal.

He also felt incredibly tired. He hadn't been powering through without sleep like Cisco had been, but he'd performed more impossible feats of superspeedery in the past few days than he'd attempted in the previous two months. He was beat.

But Barry's problems weren't over. He still had to figure out where Pocus had come from, and why. There was also the matter of whoever was lurking in the sewers, killing people.

And there was Darrel Frye and Captain Singh and the hearing that would determine his fate at CCPD just a few days from now.

He ran home to Iris, who was curled up, dozing, under a blanket on the sofa. The TV showed video of the Flash and Kid Flash saving thousands of lives at the Central City Pier, including a dizzyingly tilted shot of Barry running the Ferris wheel back into place, and very grainy, shaky video of what looked to be a chain of human beings hovering a hundred feet over the river. Barry grinned. He lived in a weird, exotic, baffling world. But it was also incredibly cool. No denying that.

He sidled up next to Iris and slipped his arms around her. She murmured something in her sleep. It took him a moment to realize what she said:

Welcome back.

Not just to the home they shared, he knew. Welcome back to himself. Welcome back to control. Welcome back to sanity. He tightened his hold on her slightly, feeling the weight of her, the realness of her. Iris anchored him to this world; she had ever since they were kids. He could run so fast that even gravity had to bow and let him pass, and he knew deep down that without Iris to keep him sane and grounded, he would just run so fast that he'd disappear over the endless horizon.

Without her, he would've gone back in time. And who knows what would have happened? Things had been bad, yes, but his meddling might have made them worse.

Things had been bad. And he'd given them a chance to get better. Thanks to her.

He kissed her forehead, and she snuggled into him. He had a lot of work ahead of him, he knew, and his job was still on the line, but for now, he just wanted to stop moving so fast. He wanted to take Madame Xanadu's advice and just *slow down* and enjoy this moment for however long it lasted.

He fell asleep thinking that.

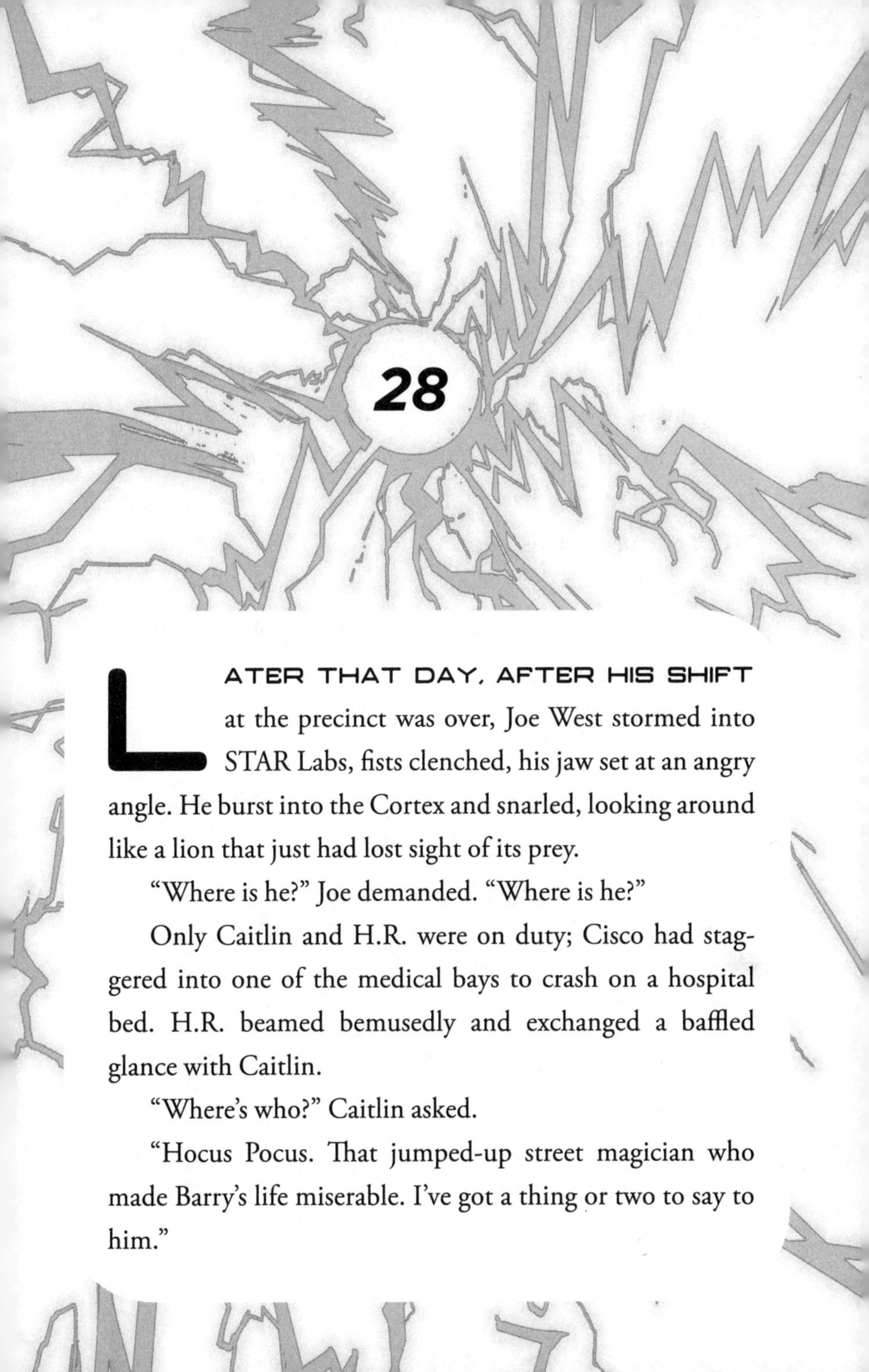

28

LATER THAT DAY, AFTER HIS SHIFT at the precinct was over, Joe West stormed into STAR Labs, fists clenched, his jaw set at an angry angle. He burst into the Cortex and snarled, looking around like a lion that just had lost sight of its prey.

"Where is he?" Joe demanded. "Where is he?"

Only Caitlin and H.R. were on duty; Cisco had staggered into one of the medical bays to crash on a hospital bed. H.R. beamed bemusedly and exchanged a baffled glance with Caitlin.

"Where's who?" Caitlin asked.

"Hocus Pocus. That jumped-up street magician who made Barry's life miserable. I've got a thing or two to say to him."

Caitlin came up out of her chair and approached Joe, holding out her hands in a calming gesture. "He's in the Pipeline. He can't hurt anyone."

"He doesn't need to hurt anyone," Joe seethed. He shook off Caitlin's hands. "He's already done his damage. And now I'm gonna give him a piece of my mind."

Before either of them could speak, Joe spun around and stomped down the hall, rolling up his sleeves as he went. "Turn one of my kids into a damn *puppet*!" he muttered as he went.

Caitlin looked at H.R., who raised his eyebrows. "Well, that seems counterproductive."

"You think he'll . . . hurt Pocus?"

"Hurt? Possibly. Kill?" H.R. drummed a quick beat. "Definitely. But Pocus is safely within the Pipeline. Even Joe can't penetrate our security measures."

The two exchanged a skeptical look.

"Come on!" Caitlin ran down the hall. H.R. tossed his drumsticks over his shoulder and dashed after her.

They caught up to Joe in the Pipeline, where he stood perfectly still, blocking their view of Pocus's cell. His hands, no longer fists, were loose at his sides, shaking slightly.

"Joe!" Caitlin called, running to him. "Joe!" she said again when he didn't answer.

For a moment, she was terrified that Pocus had commandeered Joe's mind the same way he'd taken over Barry's, but then she reminded herself that the magician had none of his tech, none of his weapons. Pocus was perfectly normal and harmless.

She came up behind Joe and tapped him on the shoulder.

H.R. came up beside her. "Joe, let's go have a chat and a cup of coffee before we beat the heck out of this guy, OK? Partly to take a moment to think it through, but mostly because it's been something close to thirty minutes since my last cup of coffee, and I'm feeling off."

"Did you hear H.R., Joe?" Caitlin asked. "Let's try—"

"Uh . . ." Joe said, his voice trembling just the slightest.

Something deep in Caitlin sounded an alarm. Joe was almost never at a loss for words. She pushed past him and understood immediately why he hadn't been moving.

He was in shock.

So was she.

The Pipeline cell for Hocus Pocus was empty.

He was gone.

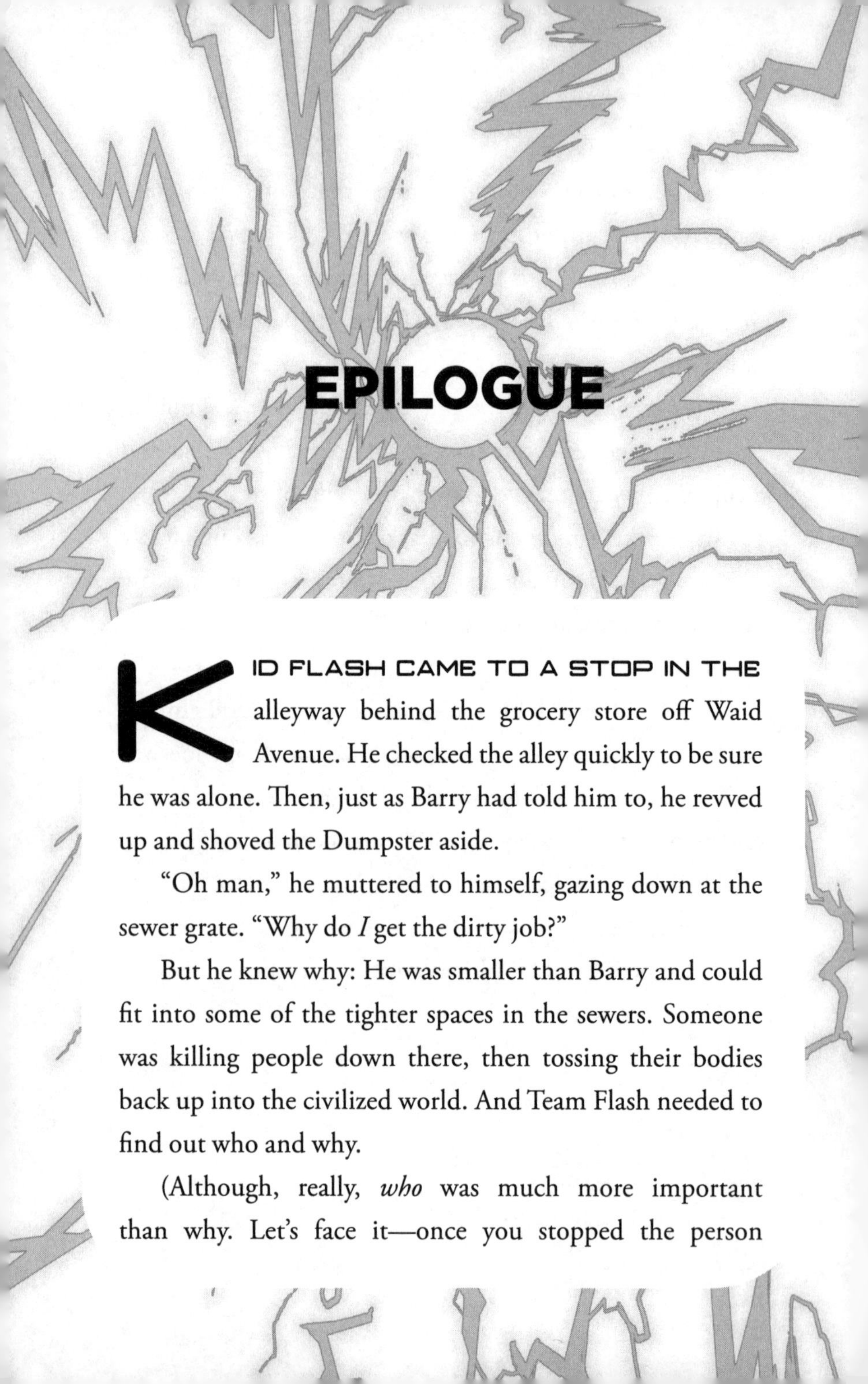

EPILOGUE

KID FLASH CAME TO A STOP IN THE alleyway behind the grocery store off Waid Avenue. He checked the alley quickly to be sure he was alone. Then, just as Barry had told him to, he revved up and shoved the Dumpster aside.

"Oh man," he muttered to himself, gazing down at the sewer grate. "Why do *I* get the dirty job?"

But he knew why: He was smaller than Barry and could fit into some of the tighter spaces in the sewers. Someone was killing people down there, then tossing their bodies back up into the civilized world. And Team Flash needed to find out who and why.

(Although, really, *who* was much more important than why. Let's face it—once you stopped the person responsible, their reasons didn't matter all that much anymore.)

"You did a good job against Hocus Pocus," Barry had told him. "No, scratch that—you did a *great* job." He'd slapped Wally on the shoulder and pulled him in for a hug that Wally thought was super-nerdy but also way cool at the same time.

He'd proven himself to his hero, to the Flash. And now he was being given his first solo mission.

"You're not to engage anyone," Barry had warned him. "You're just doing recon, got it? Go in, look around, get out safe. You see someone, you get out of there at top speed. Understand?"

And Wally, nearly vibrating through the floor with excitement, had said, "Of course! Of course!" and then kept saying it a bunch more times because he couldn't stop himself.

Cisco had threatened to shoot Wally with a vibe that would have him shaking in his boots for a week if he dragged the Kid Flash costume through the sewer, so Wally was wearing a skintight surfer's wet suit that he'd bought with the STAR Labs credit card. It would keep him dry and had the added advantage of no projections or folds that could catch on something down there.

"This is what heroes do," he told himself doubtfully, and climbed down the ladder into the muck. "This is what heroes do."

At the bottom, something slick on the last rung tripped him up, and he landed on his butt in the sewage. He sat there for a second, grateful for the protection of the wet suit but also trying not to pass out from the stench.

"This is what heroes do?" he asked no one in particular. The smell down here was *awful.* Even breathing through his mouth, it somehow managed to work its way into his nostrils and assault his olfactory nerve. Wally didn't think he would ever stop smelling that grotesque reek.

He picked himself up and trudged downstream, just as Barry had told him. Unlike Barry, he'd come prepared with a powerful flashlight, so it was easy to spot the offshoot tunnel where the mysterious *whatever* had vanished.

Wally sized up the tunnel. It would be tight, but, yeah, he thought he would fit. Too bad. He was hoping he wouldn't have to shimmy down a lightless tube sweating garbage. *I'm going to start eating more doughnuts*, he decided. *Lots and lots of doughnuts. They'll never be able to fit me in a sewer tunnel again.*

First he mounted the flashlight on his head with the strap he'd brought. Then, with a heavy sigh and much regret, he hoisted himself into the tunnel. His shoulders just barely cleared the edges, and he had to use his elbows to pull himself along. It was slow going. He didn't want to go at superspeed, because who knew *what* could be in front of him?

Claustrophobia assailed him, and he closed his eyes to remind himself that he was Kid Flash, he was a metahuman, he had superspeed. He could vibrate his molecules and phase right out of here if he needed to.

It took him a good ten minutes to get to the end of the tunnel. By the time he got there, he was sweating, breathing hard, covered in sludge, and wishing he'd been born without a sense of smell. (That was a thing, Barry had told him once: anosmia. Flash Fact!)

He was tired but also impressed by whoever had gone down this tunnel in front of Barry. It had taken Kid Flash ten minutes; the person Barry had seen had done it in seconds. Impressive.

The tunnel ended by opening on the wall of a chamber. Wally leaned out and tilted his head this way and that, playing his light over the room. It was smallish, maybe ten feet to a side and eight feet high. Tough to tell exactly how tall it was because the floor was covered in murky black water that moved and eddied under the influence of unseen, mystery currents. It could be a shallow pool of water or deep.

He didn't want to find out. He hoped he wouldn't have to find out. It was starting to feel like a horror movie or a creepy first-person shooter in here, just like Barry had warned him.

Peering down, aiming his light beam at the water to ascertain its depth, he saw something that made his blood run cold: two thick eyebolts attached to the concrete wall, each one connected to heavy chains that hung down into the water.

Wally shivered involuntarily.

This is what heroes do, he thought as he wriggled out of the tunnel and dropped six feet into the water. It was shallow, thank goodness. Only a couple of inches.

He sloshed over to the chains, then hauled them from their dry ends until they came up out of the muck. As he feared, there were stout manacles there.

Someone had been held captive down here. Down *here*.

He looked around. Another, larger tunnel led in from the north, spilling a thin drool of sewage. Some trash floated on the water, but no other clues.

He crouched down by the eyebolts, and there he saw something that sent another shiver through him. For there, in the hard concrete of the wall, someone had scratched out a word, its letters jagged and ill-formed but perfectly readable in the brightness of his flashlight:

EARTHWORM

TO BE CONTINUED . . .

ACKNOWLEDGMENTS

By all rights, this should include a listing of everyone who's ever written the Flash. But we don't have that kind of time or space, so . . .

Mark Waid, Mike Baron, and William Messner-Loebs revitalized the character in the '80s and beyond, but Cary Bates was the writer who defined Barry Allen when I first discovered him as a kid; and his extended run (pun not intended) on the comic is a whirlwind of soapy drama, slick cop action, and madcap superheroism. I couldn't even contemplate writing Barry Allen without the example of these gentlemen. And that, friends, is a Flash Fact!

Many thanks to the folks at Warner Bros. and the CW, including Greg Berlanti, Andrew Kreisberg, Todd Helbing, Sarah Schechter, Carl Ogawa, Lindsay Kiesel, Janice Aguilar-Herrero, Catherine Shin, Thomas Zellers, Kristen Chin, Amy Weingartner, and Josh Anderson.

And I am eternally grateful to the hardworking crew at Abrams—including but not limited to Andrew Smith, Orlando Dos Reis, Maggie Lehrman, Melanie Chang, Chad Beckerman, Evangelos Vasilakis, Alison Gervais, Maya Bradford, and Liz Fithian—for inviting me on board this wild ride and making it even wilder. Also, a shout-out to copy editor Richard Slovak, who kept me honest.

Plus: How about that gorgeous cover??? A round of applause, please, for illustrator César Moreno. I have nothing else to say but, "Wow."

Last but not least: My undying gratitude and devotion to my wife, Morgan Baden. There was a moment when I thought that deadlines and the birth of our son would force me to back out of this project. "If you don't write this book," she said, "I'll kill you." Now *that* is a supportive wife!

ABOUT THE AUTHOR

BARRY LYGA is the author of the *New York Times* bestselling I Hunt Killers series and many other critically acclaimed middle-grade and young adult novels. A self-proclaimed Flash fanatic, Barry lives and podcasts near New York City with his family. Find him online at barrylyga.com.

READ ON FOR A

SUPE

SNEAK PEEK OF

RGIRL™

AGE OF ATLANTIS

BY JO WHITTEMORE

My name is Kara Zor-El. When I was a child, my planet, Krypton, was dying. I was sent to Earth to protect my cousin, but my pod got knocked off course, and by the time I got here, my cousin had already grown up and become Superman. I hid who I really was until one day when an accident forced me to reveal myself to the world.

To most people, I'm Kara Danvers, a reporter at CatCo Worldwide Media. But in secret, I work with my adoptive sister, Alex, for the Department of Extra-Normal Operations to protect my city from alien life and anyone else that means to cause it harm. I am . . . Supergirl!

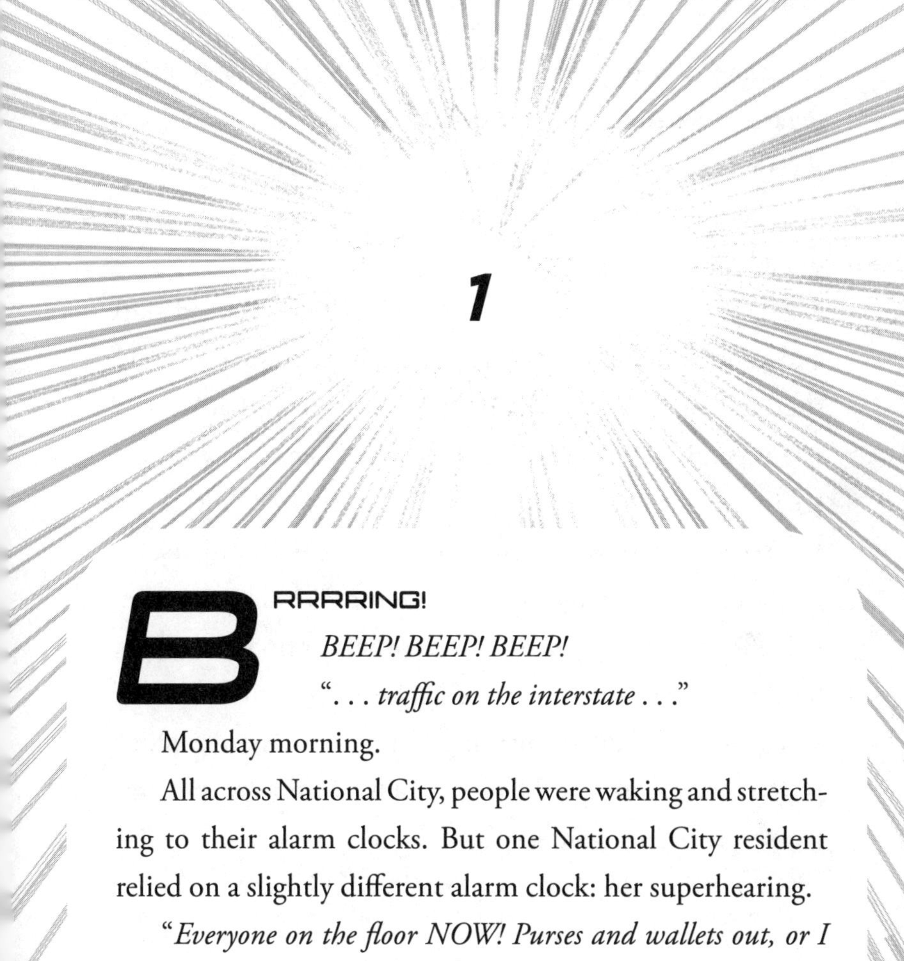

1

BRRRRING!

BEEP! BEEP! BEEP!

"*. . . traffic on the interstate . . .*"

Monday morning.

All across National City, people were waking and stretching to their alarm clocks. But one National City resident relied on a slightly different alarm clock: her superhearing.

"*Everyone on the floor NOW! Purses and wallets out, or I start shooting!*"

Kara Danvers opened her eyes and sat up in bed.

Bank robbers.

And they couldn't even wait until after she'd had her morning coffee.

She tilted her head and listened for other sounds to help her locate the robbery. Squawking parrots and barking dogs placed it near a pet store, and she could hear carousel music from Pineda Park. That narrowed the crime down to one location.

"National City Bank and Trust," Kara said, hopping out of bed.

In ten seconds, she was smoothing down her red skirt and cape as her alter ego, Supergirl. In ten more seconds, she'd touched down on the sidewalk outside the bank.

Supergirl narrowed her eyes and used her X-ray vision to see through the stone facade into . . . an empty lobby.

Yet she could hear weeping and frightened whispers.

Scanning the building's interior more closely, she spotted a floor-to-ceiling vault in the corner. Its door was open, blocking her view of its contents, and the entire structure was made of lead—something her X-ray vision couldn't penetrate. But Supergirl had no doubt the thieves and hostages were hiding inside.

Pedestrians hurried past the bank, absorbed in their busy lives and oblivious to the panic Supergirl could hear through the walls. There was no reason to spread chaos to the street, so she strolled up to the bank's entrance and tried the front door. Several passersby slowed their pace, giving her curious looks.

"I need a loan for a new spaceship," she said with a smile.

The passersby regarded her with wide eyes, and inwardly,

Supergirl regretted the joke. She could already see the *National City Tribune* headline: *Supergirl Broke! Next Stop: The Soup-er Kitchen?*

With a sigh, she tugged at the door handle, but felt no give.

Locked from the inside, she thought.

Supergirl twisted the handle until the metal groaned and the lock popped out of place. The door swung open and she stepped inside, relocking the door behind her.

On feather-light feet, the Girl of Steel crept around wallets and purses that had been strewn across the floor, counting them as she did so. At least fifteen hostages.

Voices echoed off the far wall, coming from inside the vault.

"I already told you, I can't open the deposit boxes!" said a woman's shaking voice. "The locks are fingerprint-activated, so only the box holders can open them."

A man snorted. "That's a lie. There has to be an override."

"Yeah," said another man. "Otherwise," he added in a menacing voice, "what happens when someone loses their fingers?"

Someone whimpered, and a child started to cry.

That was more than enough. Supergirl had to end this—but the vault was likely too cramped for her to risk charging in. She needed to flush the robbers *and* the hostages out of hiding.

Supergirl glanced up and saw fire sprinklers dotting the lobby ceiling. Surely, the vault had sprinklers, too.

She found a mirror among the discarded purses and flew across the room, landing softly behind the open vault door. Holding the mirror at eye level, Supergirl tilted it until she could see inside the vault. There were sixteen hostages, two thuggish robbers, and . . . a sprinkler.

Aiming the mirror at the sprinkler, Supergirl fixed her gaze on the reflective surface. A second later, neon-blue beams of thermal energy shot from her eyes and struck the mirror. The mirror, in turn, bounced the heated beams at the sprinkler inside the vault.

Hissing and sputtering, the sprinkler unleashed a miniature rain shower. With surprised shouts, the hostages fled the vault, the robbers following close behind. None of them noticed Supergirl as she did a quick head count—but they all noticed when the three-ton vault door slammed shut and she leaned against it.

"The weather in here sure is unpredictable, isn't it?" she asked.

At the sight of Supergirl, the hostages' expressions went from downtrodden to uplifted. They whispered her name in excited voices and hugged one another.

Her appearance had the opposite effect on the robbers.

"It's Supergirl! Run!" cried the first robber.

"Superwho?" asked the second, glancing at his partner. Or, rather, at the place where his partner had been standing.

Robber 1 had dropped a bag of money and taken his own advice, dashing toward one of the exits. Supergirl considered chasing him, but she couldn't leave the hostages. Plus, Robber 2 would likely rat out his partner for a reduced prison sentence.

"You must be new in town," Supergirl told Robber 2 with a smile. "Why don't we talk at the police station?"

Supergirl took a step toward him, and the robber pointed a lump in his jacket pocket at her. "Stand back! I've got a gun and I'll shoot everyone in here!"

Several of the hostages screamed.

Supergirl squinted at the robber's jacket, her X-ray vision passing through the flimsy nylon to see a clenched—but empty—hand in his pocket.

"You don't have a gun. You have a *fist*," she corrected, closing the distance between them. "And guess what? So do I."

The robber's eyes widened as Supergirl's arm reeled back.

"You might want to close 'em for this," she said.

Then she knocked him across the room.

The hostages cheered, and Supergirl gave them a smile and a wave before zipping out the bank doors. She wished she could've stayed until the police arrived, but she was already late to meet her sister, Alex.

Supergirl flew across town and dipped low over the roof of Noonan's restaurant, scooping up a change of clothes she'd stowed there. One of the downsides to her superhero outfit? No pockets.

She landed behind Noonan's and, making sure she was alone, quickly pulled on the clothes she wore as Kara Danvers. As she stepped into a pair of red flats, she smiled, wondering what her coworkers would think if she showed up in red Supergirl boots instead. Since Kara dressed conservatively to hide her true identity, she'd no doubt be the talk of the office.

From the left pocket of her slacks, Kara pulled her lead-lined eyeglasses, and from the right pocket her cell phone, which flashed with a message from Alex.

My coffee's getting cold, and I don't have heat vision.

Kara chuckled and picked up her red boots. With a flick of the wrist, she tossed them onto Noonan's roof and then hurried to the entrance of the restaurant. She skidded to a stop just inside, spotting a familiar freckle-faced, auburn-haired woman in line.

Alex's coffee wasn't getting cold. She hadn't even ordered yet!

"It's not nice to lie to family," Kara said, bumping her sister.

Alex shot Kara a wry smile and put an arm around her. "I figured pity was the quickest way to get you here." She held up a finger. "By the way, if you're this late when your boss needs you, no wonder he's grouchy."

Alex was talking about Snapper Carr, Kara's boss at CatCo Worldwide Media, where Kara worked as a reporter. At least . . . when she could get her stories printed. Her boss still didn't treat her like a full-fledged member of the team. Last week, she'd let the mayor cancel an interview, and Snapper had called Kara "Glasses McPushover."

At least it was a change from "Ponytail."

Kara's recent work problems were the reason she'd asked Alex to meet at Noonan's that morning, and as Alex commented on her tardiness, Kara rolled her eyes.

"It's not like I'm late because I overslept," said Kara. "I was stopping a holdup at the bank."

The guy in front of them glanced back at her.

"In a video game I was playing," Kara added with a nervous laugh.

He faced forward again, and Alex pinched her sister's arm.

"Your inside voice needs an inside voice!" Alex whispered.

Alex was right, of course, but maintaining a secret identity was hard work. Kara hated always having guarded conversations—never knowing who was listening or watching. She loved being a superhero, though sometimes she wished it didn't make her such an oddity.

The guy in front of them finished placing his order, and Alex and Kara stepped up to the counter. A shaggy-haired college kid with a name tag that read MARCUS greeted them.

"Hi!" said Kara. "Can I get a spiced pumpkin with extra foam and just a little bit of sprinkles on top, please?"

"You got it." Marcus poised a pen over Kara's cup. "What's your name, pretty lady?"

Alex rolled her eyes and Kara ducked her head and snickered, tucking her hair behind her ear.

"Who, me?"

Alex put a hand on her sister's shoulder. "Her name's Kara."

"Nice name!" said Marcus. "Carla." He wrote as he spoke.

Kara cleared her throat. "Actually, it's Kara. With a K and no L."

"Whoops! My bad." Marcus crossed out what he'd written and scribbled the new name. "Better?"

The cup now read . . . Carka.

Alex turned her head and stifled a laugh while Kara forced a smile.

"Close enough," she said. "Can I also get some doughnuts to go?"

Marcus passed the cup to the barista and grabbed a pastry box, loading it with Kara's favorite flavors. Which was pretty much everything except maple logs.

"You know what? Throw a maple log in there, too," she said as Marcus started to close the pastry box. At a raised eyebrow from Alex, she explained, "For Snapper."

"Trying a little bribery?" Alex asked with a smirk.

"It's a Monday for everyone," Kara reminded her sister. "And maybe the sugar will make him sweeter."

Alex snorted. "Kara, no amount of food is going to make Snapper a nice person."

Kara sighed. "If you have any better ideas, I'm all ears."

"You need to speak his language," Alex told her.

"I do! Every time Snapper's mean to me, I'm just as mean back."

Alex leaned against the counter, arms crossed. "All right, I'll bite. What's a typical Kara Danvers insult?"

Kara inclined her head. "Just last week, he told me my grammar sucked, and I told *him* that"—Kara adjusted her glasses—"that he'd missed a button on his shirt." She swiped at some spilled sugar on the counter. "So . . . he was probably pret-ty embarrassed."

Alex laughed and hugged her younger sister. "Sweetie, being mean just isn't you. And that's not what I meant by 'speak his language.' People like Snapper want big. Bold." She shrugged. "They want attention."

"Big. Bold." Kara repeated to herself, nodding. "I can do that!"

But ten minutes later, as Kara rode the CatCo elevator to the twentieth floor, no big *or* bold ideas had come to her. She'd have to wing it when she reached Snapper's desk. The elevator doors opened, and she took a deep breath before she stepped out.

Snapper, a scowling Latino man with a fringe of dark hair, was reviewing a layout with an equally annoyed-looking black man—one of Kara's closest friends, James Olsen. At one time, James had been a photographer at the *Daily Planet*, where Kara's cousin Clark Kent worked, but Clark had then sent James to National City to watch over Kara.

James was one of the few people who knew Clark Kent was Superman and Kara Danvers, Supergirl. Now James was the acting CEO at CatCo, which meant butting heads with section leaders so much he was constantly rubbing his shaved scalp in frustration . . . or pain.

Snapper and James spoke a few words to each other, and then Snapper picked up the layout and carried it back to his desk. Kara hurried forward, but before she could speak, Snapper cupped his hands around his mouth and shouted across the newsroom floor.

"Investigative journos at my desk!"

Kara pointed to herself and smiled. "Is there a prize for being the first one here?"

Snapper scowled at her. "Danvers, this meeting isn't for you."

Kara's smile dipped a little. "Uh . . . you wanted to see the investigative journalists, and I'm one of them."

"You are?!" Snapper's eyes widened in mock surprise. "Great! I'll take that interview with Mayor Lowell." He held out his hand, palm up.

It took immense willpower for Kara not to grab Snapper's wrist and flip him over her shoulder.

"He canceled, remember?" She spoke in as even a voice as she could muster. "I don't have the interview."

Snapper pointed to the elevator. "Then don't come back until you do."

"You're not serious."

Snapper's finger didn't waver. "Hit the pavement, Danvers. I want that interview."

Kara chanced a glimpse at James in case he might be able to step in, but he was focused on a cluster of television screens in his office. Clenching her fists by her side, Kara turned on her heel and stalked back toward the elevator, pushing the down button so hard the panel sunk into the wall. With a guilty glance around, she tucked her hands behind her back.

Now, instead of thinking, *Big. Bold*, Kara thought, *Totally. Doomed*, all the way down.